CONSTELLATION PRIZE

PATRICK THOMAS

PADWOLF
PUBLISHING

PADWOLF PUBLISHING INC.
WWW.PADWOLF.COM
www.facebook.com/Padwolf

WWW.PATTHOMAS.NET
WWW.MURPHYS-LORE.COM
WWW.THESTARTENDERS.ORG
www.facebook.com/PatrickThomasAuthor

CONSTELLATION PRIZE
Tales of the Startenders
© 2015 Patrick Thomas

Furlough was originally published in an abridged version in Barbarians
At The Jumpgate edited by Bruce Gehweiler

Book edited by Dr. Howard Margolin

Cover Art by Patrick Thomas and Roy Maurtisen

Cover Design by Roy Maurtisen

Startenders, Bulfinche's Pub, barships, Murphy's Lore, and all related
characters are © & TM Patrick Thomas

10-digit ISBN 1-890096-62-8, 13 digit ISBN 978-1-890096-62-5
Printed in the USA
Second Printing

For Kathleen- Aunt and godmother

And thanks to John French for suggesting the Constellation Prize

Contents

SOMETIME IN THE NOT TOO DISTANT FUTURE…

The Startender Oath

I am a Startender which means
*   —I will act with honor and do what's right*
*   —I will not break my word or give it lightly, for my*
promise binds all Startenders
*   —I will put principle above gain*
*   —I will protect life, shelter others from harm and*
defend those who are unable to defend themselves
*   —I will not kill unless all other options have been*
exhausted and then only in the protection of life
*   —I will take care of my own and as many others as*
possible
*   —I will be loyal to my own and to these principles*

OUT OF THE BAG

I wouldn't make a good spy. Blending into whatever world is around me is simply not one of my stronger skill sets. Plus I have trouble not making wisecracks, which is a bad thing for a spy to do despite what decades of British spy movies would have you believe.

I'm not much of a cat person either, which made this mission even more interesting since I was partnered up with Bast. I've known the Egyptian cat goddess since before New York City was destroyed, back in the days where I was still a bartender instead of the head honcho of the barship *Fools' Glory*.

Bast and I are Startenders these days. She's not assigned to a barship, but is head of covert operations, making her the Startenders' head spy and chief of information.

Old gods tend to lose power when they're no longer worshipped. Those that haven't ended up in oblivion have usually managed to adapt. Ages ago, Bast set up her own spy network. Not just on Earth, but out in the universe and other worlds. Seemed a natural progression for a goddess of secrets.

An entrance to her multi-world information network was on Traven, basically one planet-sized city. Easy to hide among the masses I guess. The Startenders maintain a bar on Traven. We won it off some killer robots in a quasi-death match. Relatively speaking, the Watering Hole was in a decent neighborhood. Where Bast was taking me made the South Bronx of my childhood seem like Disneyland.

Unlike the majority of Startenders, I'm only human. We were banned from bringing the barship to Cynosure, the spy network's nerve center. They tend to be more than a tad security conscious and I guess were concerned about letting a ship full of tricksters inside their headquarters.

I followed Bast up to what seemed like an abandoned building. Out stepped a welcoming committee of six blag, members of a very large, exceptionally strong alien race that looked like the offspring of Smurfs and hippos.

"Give us everything down to your clothes and maybe we'll let you live," the largest of the group said in Goblin Prime.

"From my companion Murphy, that would be a thrilling offer, but from the likes of you, it's rather distasteful. Go and leave us," Bast said, acting like she was doing the blag a favor by acknowledging its existence. However, there was a subtle change in her posture and her claws popped out. And the claws on a human sized cat goddess are the size of daggers.

"I'm so glad you made this fun, so we're going to start with you and make him watch," the big one said.

"Excellent. Do you provide popcorn or should I have brought my own snacks?" I said in broken Prime. The six of them stared in my direction like I was insane. Not the first to do it and provided they didn't kill me, they wouldn't be the last. "Now out of curiosity were you planning on ever walking again? And why would you pick the most dangerous woman in the galaxy to start a fight with?"

I was exaggerating, but when faced with death and dismemberment, I find it's better to go big than go home in a body bag.

The blag shared some sideways glances as a small black cat stepped out protectively in front of Bast. None of the blag noticed the cat at first, at least until it reared up on its haunches and hissed. Each of the blag had a fist larger than the cat, but the lot took a step back. The cat took another step forward and gave out a yell like somebody had not only stepped on its tail, but ran it through a shredder.

The six attackers ran away so fast they all but tripped over each other like they were so many mice.

The cat-woman smiled and the black cat leapt up into her arms. Bast pulled him close and scratched his head.

"Thank you, Radek," she said.

It sounded like the cat answered with a purr, but Startender badges mystically translated languages so we can hear them. Sadly they don't do so much for the speaking side of the conversation.

Turns out what the cat actually said was, "My pleasure, Progenitor. It is my job to guard the portal and I would be the one tasked with cleaning up their corpses after you were done with them. We've had previous encounters."

I decided not to point out that Bast was now a Startender and we had rules against killing, except as a last resort.

"Radek, this is my friend John Murphy."

Radek purred, which translated as "charmed." The black cat turned back towards Bast. "Gazer is waiting for you inside."

Bast extended her arms and the cat leapt down to the ground. There was a door that opened outward and it had a handle instead of a knob. Bast motioned for me to do the gentlemanly thing and open it for her, so I did. A blinding light greeted us.

She took my arm in hers and whispered, "Close your eyes and I'll guide you through. Don't make any sudden moves that might trigger the automatic defenses."

I wasn't thrilled with the idea of weapons firing at me so I did as she said. The light was so bright that closing my eyelids only dimmed the brilliance, but did not get rid of it. We walked down a corridor that felt like it was less stable than a wooden ship on rough seas. Likely meant it was a portal to another world. I lost my footing twice, but Bast stopped me from falling.

When we stopped, so did the light. I opened my eyes slowly. It took a while for the afterglow to fade. We were inside a couch potato's dream. Every wall in the auditorium sized room was filled with screens. Some had images, while others had information. Inside were hundreds of cats and cat people trying to work and not look busy simultaneously.

"Murphy, these are my scions."

I'd met some of her children before and knew that many of them were several generations removed from her. And that in English they had chosen an unfortunate sounding name to call themselves.

Bast was a sex and fertility goddess back in the day and she tended to give birth in litters. Hundreds were her actual children and she had a great many more scions out and about in the universe.

"This is impressive. When did they go out into space?"

"Those that chose to leave the Earth did so centuries ago. Not that they had much choice."

"Why is that?" I said.

Bast gave a soft smile. "Turns out Ra was allergic to them. But his loss is the Startenders' gain."

"Welcome back, Progenitor," said Gazer who was in his cat-man form. "Good to see you again, Murphy."

"You too, Gazer. Coming up in the worlds I see." Last time we'd seen each other, he'd been in charge of just Earth's intelligence gathering.

"As you would say, not too shabby. Although I think I may be getting an ulcer. Mother, I'll do this for a few more years and then I want back out into the field."

"Provided we can find a worthy successor, we can discuss it, but I trust you didn't call us here to discuss your career options."

"No, I didn't. As you know, not all the bastarts…"

Bast raised an eyebrow at the mention of her people's name and looked at me, daring me to make a comment.

I took the dare. "I guess you weren't married to their fathers? Who were apparently all bakers?"

Bast rolled her eyes and looked back at Gazer like I hadn't said a word.

"Not all bastarts are part of the family business. While encouraged, working for Cynosure is not mandatory. We keep careful track of all our estranged relations. It turns out that some of them have decided to try and achieve godhood."

Bast let out a meow that oddly translated as *oy vey*. "Wonderful. Who?"

Gazer held out his hand and a ring projected a holographic screen in front of us. It flashed through pictures and dossiers on a dozen would be divinities. Our badges didn't do a thing for the written language and this appeared to be in some form of hieroglyphics.

"As you can see, they're going with the classics, pairing up to share some of the more traditional aspects – storm, fire, water, fertility, harvest, and the afterworld."

"Aren't they technically demigods already? Don't they have mystic abilities?" I said.

"Most of the bastarts can accomplish minor shape-shifting, are able to discourage being seen and the like. Far short of godhood. These twelve aren't using magic, but technology to impress the natives. This world is technologically about at the level of Earth during the Bronze Age. This scam has been tried before, occasionally even successfully. It would be easier for our kin since – as you pointed out – they already have some traces of divine blood for the worship and belief manna to affect. By your own orders, Mother, we rarely interfere directly. However your new affiliation, the Startenders are another matter. Perhaps they could put an end to this before it starts and becomes an embarrassment. Or worse, a threat."

"How exactly would you like us to put a stop to it?" I said.

"You command a ship of tricksters, which is why I requested you instead of one of the other head honchos. They would likely meet the threat head-on, while you would do more in the undermining department. If you can convince the natives that these bastarts are frauds instead of gods, they will never be able to ascend. Will you help?"

"Are the natives in danger?" I said.

"Murphy, you've met a lot of gods past their prime. You've heard the stories. How many people do you think strive for godhood for benevolent purposes versus selfish? And I know mother has pledged herself to the Startenders, but she has not pledged our organization. Do this for us, and I will propose an alliance where Cynosure will actively work on the Startenders' behalf to find threats for you to attempt to stop as well as head off threats to the organization itself."

Bast looked at me and put her furry hand on my shoulder. Fortunately, the claws were now retracted. "Murphy, please."

I could never turn down a friend asking for help. "Okay. I guess we're going into the god-busting business."

Once back on *Fools' Glory*, I brought my crew up to speed.

"You know the best way to prevent them from harvesting the manna is to divert it for ourselves," Coyote said.

"And how, exactly, is that helping anyone besides you, fleabag?" Bast said. She and the Native American trickster had never gotten along well. In fact, they fought like cats and… well, they bickered a lot, at least before becoming Startenders. Now they strive for civility. They didn't necessarily achieve it, but at least they tried.

Coyote stuck his tongue out.

"From the files Gazer gave us, they've been planning this for decades," Loki said and flipped through the holographic files. Apparently the Norse God read hieroglyphics.

"I don't know, I kind of like Coyote's idea. I've always fancied myself a sex goddess," the she-satyr Savannah said, posing for effect.

"You'd also have to deal with lovelorn issues, not just the fun parts," Riga said.

"Come on, you'd make a great goddess of fire," Savannah said.

"I'm already the daughter of a water dragon and a god of fire," the human appearing Riga said, glancing over at her father Loki. "I'm fine."

"Murphy, we're here," Eric said. The golden melog had a direct interface with the ship so the mechanical lifeform could stand around talking and drive at the same time. "Bast, make sure you thank Gazer for letting us use his portal. It made getting to Rchaic a lot quicker."

One of the assets Cynosure possessed were doors to multiple worlds that led back to their control center. Interestingly enough, many of the worlds out there have some sort of native felinesque form, so the bastarts were able to morph into the native cat forms and blend in. Quite helpful when you ran the largest intelligence network in the universe. Simply put, if there is something you want kept secret, don't say it in front of a black cat.

We were able to blend in on Rchaic too. The outside of the golden barship could change size by shunting mass into a pocket dimension. In dust mode the ship is about the size of a golf ball and fairly easy to hide, even on high-tech worlds. On a planet where swords and plows were considered the pinnacle of technology, it was even easier.

The bar room that served as our control center had large mirrors which could double as view screens. Eric sent out some probes so we could check out the place.

"I like it. Nice, lush vegetation," Foster said. The plant, an elemental in a flower pot, had a personal bias for the more primitive worlds, mainly because there was more greenery and other color plants. Advanced worlds tended to get rid of a lot of their flora in exchange for things like living space for the masses.

"The bastarts are not even bothering to shield their energy signatures. They have their main ship in orbit and have at least twelve sky-cycles deployed on the planet. They seem to be clustered on or near the largest city. This world has four main continents. One empire appears to span two of them. People on the other continents are more spread out, so they are focusing on the heart of the empire."

"Make sense. Convince the empire you're a god and they'll spread the religion for you," Loki said.

"Worked for Big Nose," Coyote said. Turns out goblins were not only real, but aliens. The head of their empire was a god named Gob who had slaughtered the rest of his pantheon and now conquered other worlds in order to gain their natural resources, which included belief and worship from the natives.

"We need a crash course in Rchaic culture and history. Let's go with the usual drill. Loki and Coyote go out among the natives and do your thing." Loki's thing involves the ability to pick up reading and speaking any language as well as absorbing a fantastically large amount of information in a very short time. Coyote tended to go and find the more interesting parts of society and figure out how to work them to our advantage.

"Or you could simply look at the information Cynosure has already gathered," Bast said, squeezing what looked like a coin and tossing it on the bar top. Holograms appeared and gave us the historical run down on the place in English.

Rchaic's empire was a militarized republic called the Dorden Empire. They had an incredibly large standing army. On the plus side, not all of their conquests had been bloody. By joining the Empire, the conquered got roads, sanitation and advances in science and medicine. In exchange, they paid taxes and provided bodies for the military. However, soldiers who did ten local years of service were made voting citizens.

Both Bast and Eric lifted their heads up at the same time.

"Boss, sensors are picking up a huge energy signature," Eric said.

Bast frowned. "The self-proclaimed god and goddess of war are firing the opening salvo by using energy weapons against people with spears and arrows."

"It'll be a massacre," I said. "Eric, get us there now."

Now was not soon enough. Hundreds already lay dead on the battlefield. We enlarged and put *Fools' Glory* between the bastart war god who was firing upon soldiers with a sword that had the output of a starship cannon. It worked and the bastart of war stopped aiming at the people below and fired on us. It didn't do any damage. The hull's alloy was designed to absorb all sorts of energy as well as throw it back.

"Will we be giving this bastard…"

"Bastart," Bast corrected.

The mechanical man stared down the goddess. "I was right the first time, Bast. Shall I give him a taste of his own medicine, Murph?"

"No. That would make it look like an epic battle between gods. We want to make it look like anything but. Eric, morph the ship into a secondary body for you. I need you to take him out in the most embarrassing way possible. Avoid epic. Try for comical."

"Will do, boss."

Eric the ship was a tad taller than the actual Eric and the golden man skipped across the battlefield. This particular bastart of war wasn't getting any brighter because he kept firing. When Eric the ship got close enough, the bastart of war swung his sword. Eric shunted enough mass to his hand to not only block the sword, but break it in half. Next the melog molded the hull around the energy core of the sword as it exploded, absorbing both blast and radiation so neither harmed the battlefield survivors.

Eric slapped him across the face, sat on the ground and pulled the bastart down onto his knee like one would a bad child in days of old. Then he pulled down the bastart's pants and gave him a sound spanking on his furry behind. The soldiers of the Dorden Empire and their opponents roared with laughter.

"Okay Eric, that's enough. Let him up," I said from inside the ship.

The bastart of war stood up and ran away, his pants still not pulled up the entire way. He hopped on a sky-cycle and took off into the distance. Eric the ship did a soft shoe routine, took a bow and floated up toward the clouds.

A second sky-cycle dropped down with the female bastart of war. She was packing an axe with the same offense capacity as the sword. Eric stopped midflight and pointed his two fingers to his eyes, to her eyes, then back and forth. He shot forward faster that than she could react, pulled the axe out of her hand, grounded the cycle and repeated the spanking.

Uproarious laughter flooded both sides of the battlefield when she got up and flew off. Eric grabbed hold of the leaders of both armies and carried them above the forces below.

Loki had already learned the language so we let his voice come out of Eric the ship's mouth.

"There's been enough death here today. Reach an agreement so no more die."

"Or what?" the Dorden leader said.

Eric the ship lifted up the two opposing leaders, morphed harnesses around them and took flight. The generals were traveling faster than any native of Rchaic ever had before, straight toward the rock wall of a nearby mountain. Eric stopped when the men's heads were about a foot away from colliding. Our inertia dampeners managed to slow them down gradually enough to not seriously injure either leader. Eric turned them both so they were facing him.

"I'll think of something."

The leaders agreed to settle the matter without further bloodshed and worked out a treaty.

We also helped them bury the dead. It would have taken much longer, but the particle weapon had reduced most of them to ash.

Next we split up to better deal with the remaining pairs of would-be gods in their aspects of storm, fire, water, fertility, and harvest.

Teams Harvest and Storm had joined forces in one large valley where they had planted genetically enhanced quick-grow grain. The stuff wasn't overly good, but you could grow a crop in about an Earth week, provided you had enough water. It turned the soil practically to sand in the process, draining all the nutrients out of it. It was designed to stop people from starving after a natural disaster destroys an area's crops, not be a sustainable source of food. The bastarts seeded some clouds as well as the fields.

Foster the plant elemental went after those four. He could grow something the size of a redwood in minutes. Winding his roots beneath the field, he gathered the engineered grain and encased it.

The would-be gods gathered a crowd of hundreds to watch their magic, going to great lengths to explain what they were doing. The stormers announced themselves as the king and the queen of the gods, then posed dramatically. The fake stormer hit a button, triggering an electric discharge between their two sky-cycles so lightning seemed to flash across the sky. The storm goddess wannabe pushed a button in her palm and rain fell from the seeded clouds overhead.

The harvest god and goddess wannabe posed dramatically with their arms outstretched towards the sky knowing the mutated grain only took a few minutes to poke through the ground after rain and within an hour would be a few inches tall. For a half hour rain fell and not one stalk rose up.

The harvest cat-man decided to up his game, tossed a handful of seeds and shouted at the fields, "Rise, crops, I command you."

Directly in front of them a single flower burst forth from the ground, rose about a foot and then morphed into something that looked like a bright red sunflower. It spurted clouds of pollen towards the harvest fakes, making them cough then fall over.

The farmers were not as amused by the failures as the soldiers had been. They had wasted a day's work in the fields for nothing and simply walked away.

"Stop, I command it or I will strike you down with lightning," yelled the false storm goddess. A few of the natives did stop, but most of them kept walking away from the bastarts, so the wannabe queen hit the button, expecting a lightning strike. Nothing happened. She hit it again and still nothing. When she hit it a third time, tiny roots and branches started to peek out from behind the button and the pair were left to figure out how a plant had destroyed their controllers.

At the capital city's port, the fake sea bastarts had put out a call that had brought all the sailors and fishermen together in the middle of the harbor, gathered with their nets hung. The pair had promised the greatest catch anyone on Rchaic had ever seen, insisting that they bring extra boats to transport all the fish.

The pair had placed special sonic devices to attract the local fish and they had been pinging for days. There were enough fish below the water to fill ten times the boats that were in the harbor.

The sea bastarts hadn't figured on Riga. Dragons normally had powers based on one of the four traditional elements or sometimes a mixture. Thanks to her mother, Riga could comfortably stay underwater for as long as she wanted and she used her shape changing abilities that she got from her father to quintuple her size. Riga swam below the boats, making a spectacle of herself, which kicked in the survival instincts of the fish, especially after she destroyed the sonic bait they'd been attracted to.

Many hours later, the boats and their angry crews sailed away with nothing in their nets to show for it.

The phony fire divinities had set up their show at the base of a dormant volcano, in which they had placed a giant remote-controlled flamethrower which they camouflaged to look like part of the inner volcano.

Loki hid inside. The trickster was able to hear magically and listened to the fiery phonies give their spiel to the natives.

These bastart wannabes were taking a different tact, demanding the sacrifice of animals or they would rain down fire on the nearest village. Sacrificing living beings created more manna than just plain worship. And it wasn't an idle threat. Their flying cycles had barrels of fuel and what's best described as napalm cannons.

The people who lived around the volcano were skeptical. Word had begun to spread of the cat people claiming to be gods, thanks in part to Bast's network of spy cats who were churning out scrolls in the native language and dispersing them throughout the land. There were details of what happened as well of some stuff that hadn't. Never let it be said that propaganda was dead or not extremely helpful in the right hands.

The fire cat-man had preened enough. He took his partner's hand and together they faced the volcano. Their arms had hidden flamethrowers similar to what some magicians use on stage. The pyrotechnics failed to impress the locals who'd seen similar displays from their own fire eaters who spit out booze onto torches.

The cat-woman hit the remote switch, which turned on the volcano flamethrower. Fortunately, Loki had emptied out all the fuel from the volcano and the cycles. Not wanting them to be too disappointed, he let enough flame go off to make a single puff of smoke rise up, much like an old jalopy failing to start.

The bastarts tried hitting the remote again, but this time they didn't even get a puff of smoke. The locals didn't appreciate having been threatened and threw stones, forcing the bastarts to flee on the sky-cycles. They looked even more foolish as they shouted they would rain down fire and instead squirted down water that Loki had refilled their tanks with after empting their version of napalm.

Eric and I took the ship to where the fake death duo had set up shop, at the capital city's largest cemetery. There had been impressive planning in building this metropolis which left hundreds of acres empty to bury their dead with a separate section for fallen soldiers. Or at least markers in memory of them. Many of the fallen soldiers were buried where they died.

There was a state funeral for the local equivalent of a senator happening. Thousands had turned out to pay their respects. This duo managed to get hold of the body beforehand to insert a device into her brainstem which would animate the corpse. It hadn't been designed for the locals, so the movements wouldn't be smooth, but the corpse would still get up and lumber around a bit.

The bastarts waited until a crucial part of the service, and suddenly there was a boom like thunder. Smoke rose all around the front of the service. Out of the mist, the bastarts rose, their bodies covered in the traditional long hooded robes of the Grim Reaper. I was surprised by how many worlds had a variation on that image. I guess my pal John Thanatos didn't vary his wardrobe greatly regardless of the world he might be on.

They were going with pomp, planning on having the corpse tell about what it saw in the after realm of these two fake divinities. Pomp is something our group doesn't mix well with. Humor and mocking we do enjoy, however. While I didn't possess any powers, I did have Eric and *Fools' Glory*.

When the grim bastarts began speaking, I snuck up through the smoke behind them and did an exaggerated pantomime of their every action in day-glow yellow robes.

I made funny faces, then chased a clip-on tail. And as they turned around I would disappear by jumping through a wire thin door to the ship that was perpendicular to the grim bastarts and the crowd. The natives had been intimidated by the initial show of power, but my antics offset that.

The bastarts touched the back of the corpse's neck to activate the puppet device.

In dust mode, Eric and I had already shorted it out. The grim bastarts ordered the corpse to rise up and tell its tale, but it just lay there. The cat-man again demanded it to rise as the cat-woman hit the button several more times in hopes that it cause a jumpstart. I stepped up behind them, both hands behind my back.

"That's not going to do you phonies any good."

"You dare thwart the will of the god and goddess of death?" the cat-man said in the native tongue.

"I dare a lot more than that." I lifted my hands out from behind my back, revealing an old-fashioned cream pie in each which I used to hit both of the bastarts in the face with. Maybe the natives had their own version of the bit, but it didn't matter. It's hard to be afraid of someone who just got pied. Without fear clogging their common sense, the natives wouldn't mistake either of these two for gods of any kind. Each of them pulled a long energy sword out of their robes and moved towards me, but I'd already sidestepped into the door, which Eric slammed shut behind me. It was as if I had teleported away.

The cat-woman wasn't done and lifted the corpse so it faced the crowd. "Tell them of what you've seen in our realm!"

The ventriloquist device was separate from the puppeteer one. The cat-man turned to whisper into a wire microphone on the side of his face, hoping it would still work.

The corpse answered her, just not the way they expected. Its hand shot up and slapped her across the face thanks to our ship being in speck mode in the dead woman's sleeve. We used our speaker systems to blast my voice in the native language. Loki had written my script out phonetically. "I saw many things, but neither of you were there or even mentioned."

Let's just say the rest of the crowd didn't appreciate the sacrilege and the grim bastarts were run off. Literally as it seems some small golden globe had vandalized their sky-cycles.

Few Startenders enjoy their job as much as Savannah. I'd go so far as to say very few people enjoy their lives as much as the she-satyr. The daughter of Pan is gifted with mystic-based pheromones which can do a number on almost anything male and even some females. Species or race typically didn't matter, so long as the target was organic.

The two love bastarts were definitely the most impressive physically of the cat people. They had humanlike anatomy. He was so muscle-bound he must sleep with IV steroids and she had curves that made one think her plastic surgeon was striving for art.

Several alien races had developed subsonic devices that could affect emotions. Most induced fear, but some can do happiness or even lust. The frequencies vary by species, but the would-be love divinities had gotten some local volunteers to help them calibrate the machinery. The subsonics were set to induce the equivalent of what on Earth could be called beer goggles. Everyone in the vicinity was going to look more attractive and none more so than the two cat people who were wearing the gadgets.

The local culture was a matriarchy where the women folk ran things. They had an annual tradition where they would auction off certified male virgins for marriage. I'm not sure exactly how they were able to verify this condition, but a local Virgin Guild did the certifying it. To celebrate they held an orgy and barbeque. When all was done, the women bought themselves a new husband for their harem. Half of the money went to the Virgin Guild, the other half to the groom's family as a dowry. There was a large discrepancy between rich and poor, so some unfortunate families literally lived or died by the amount of dowry they got. We were about to not only break tradition, but shatter it into a million pieces. That didn't mean we ignored what would happened to those poor folks. With the help of Cynosure and Coyote, we'd managed to acquire enough local currency to reimburse the families who were about to lose everything.

The virgin auction, orgy and barbeque took place in large field where a stage had been built, complete with curtain. The virgins' part in the festivities was to stand and watch their future wives sate themselves on sex and food. Maybe the ladies thought it would get the guys revved up for the wedding night.

The love bastarts were in the trenches, getting to know their would-be worshippers quite intimately. The cat folk had promised the rich that their mere presence and godly powers would enable the orgy attendees to have the best sex ever. It was probably true as the subsonics also heightened skin sensation.

Everyone was having a grand old time, except for the virgins. Savannah hated for anyone to feel left out, so she snuck up behind the stage. It was a hot day, so sweat poured off the she-satyr. She used the curtain to wave the mystic libido enhancers towards the fifty men on stage. As one, they turned their heads toward the curtain. She smiled, then opened the curtains further to show them some skin and fur, then motioned for them to join her. Without going into too much detail, the lady with the hooves ensured that none of the fifty were certifiable virgins when she was done. After finishing off the last of the grooms-to-be, she pulled open the curtain. The sight and sounds made the orgy goers stop what they were doing, likely because they realized that they were all in the amateur orgy goer category and were watching a pro.

"All praise the god and goddess of love! I am but their humble servant, doing as they commanded me," Savannah said, bowing to the bastarts.

And then the screaming began. Oh, there'd been screaming before, but it was more of the moaning and panting variety. This new screaming fell into the horrified, *you destroyed my precious possession!* type as the women realized their men were no longer certifiable. The husband-buying tradition was so ingrained that the fury of the attendees was terrible to behold, being scorned and all that. The cat-man took many shots to the groin, a large number of which involved the swinging of large metal objects. The cat-woman had hair and fur torn from her body. As they fled, the natives pelted them with whatever was at hand – stones, food and used animal skin condoms, many of which stuck and leaked out onto their fur.

They left so quickly they had no time to retrieve their own

clothing or their now missing sky-cycles.

The final part of the rogue cat people's plan was for the new pantheon to gather at the capital of the Empire and grant their blessing on the ruling class in exchange for their conversion. Let's just say these would-be divinities were hardly inspiring the natives. If they had arrived stoically, it might have gone better. All their whining and complaining didn't exactly impress the ruling class.

Once they were inside with the native rulers, all the grand chamber's doors suddenly slammed shut, save one. Bast herself walked through it, with me and most of my crew not far behind. That door glided shut slowly behind us. Their feline eyes got wide as the bastarts saw their Progenitor. The sea bastarts looked around for an exit. Personally I thought it odd that cat people who stereotypically hated the water wanted to be lords of the ocean, but I guess it had made sense to them at the time.

The war bastarts became indignant and pulled out weapons. They hid them behind their backs after one look from the cat goddess.

"Bast, you're not welcome here. This is our world now," said the bastart who would be king, in what sounded like ancient Egyptian. Those with Startender badges could understand, but the natives heard gibberish.

"You are my scions and as such must obey my rules. You're welcome to choose your own paths, but setting yourself up as gods and goddesses is forbidden," Bast said.

"We don't care about your rules," the cat-woman of war said. "It won't be long before we're more powerful than you ever were."

Bast laughed and the sound had equal parts meowing and warning mixed in. "Never in a million years. Although you've transgressed, I am noted for my forgiveness. Agree to a ten year service to Cynosure and all will be forgiven."

"Forget about it. You're just worried because I am far more desirable than you ever were," said the cat-woman who wanted to be a love goddess.

"What's that on your fur?" Loki said in ancient Egyptian. He grinned as he added, "At least the patches you still have."

"Loki, do you mind?" Bast whispered in Norse.

Loki apologized with a bow of his head and shut up.

"You think all there is to attraction is mere proportions?" Bast said. "Those are nowhere near as important as style, substance, technique and – most important – heart. Proportions you have an abundance of. The rest you are sorely lacking."

"Shall we see who the natives desire most?" she said.

"Wouldn't be a contest, even when your fur grows back in. Do you all feel the same about my offer?"

Looks were exchanged and the illusion of safety in numbers convinced all the bastarts to say that they did.

"Very well. The means through which you acquired your ship and equipment were all taken from Cynosure, so consider them all forfeit," Bast said.

"You cannot do that…" said the cat-woman who would be queen.

"We already took the ship. Spoils of war, missy. Look it up sometime," Loki said.

"Fine. We don't need them, not with our knowledge of advanced science," the bastart queen said. "It'll take longer, maybe years, but we will still convince these people we are gods and claim our rightful place."

The main door opened and in trotted Coyote, who also, apparently, spoke ancient Egyptian. "I don't think that's going to happen. Bast gave you a chance to get out, but you were dumb enough to turn it down. Allow me to introduce the Dordize, this land's native pantheon. While you were all out playing around and pretending to be gods, I went to visit the real thing and let them know what you're up to."

A large group of men and women who looked much like the natives filed in behind the canine trickster, although they were larger and crackled with mystic energy. Several of them floated. One had wings. The ruling class fell to their knees and began begging forgiveness. "They're none too happy and wish to discuss matters. Unlike you lot, their powers are real. Bast would have protected you from them had you taken her deal. Real dumb-ass move, kitties."

Coyote joined us while the native pantheon surrounded the bastarts.

Bast looked down at Coyote and whispered, "Fleabag, you secured an oath that they will not kill or severely harm them?"

"Of course hairball, sworn on the source of their power." Gods could break their words, but it will cost them power. Sworn on the source of their power or something equally important, a broken oath could turn a god mortal. Few gods want anything bad enough to risk that, especially when there are other avenues available to get what they want.

"They are also aware how upset I would be if they break this oath?" Bast said.

"Yep," Coyote replied. "Played up your rep big time. Wouldn't hurt if you had Cynosure leak a little propaganda locally about you to encourage them."

Bast nodded, then turned and walked out of the chamber, past the kneeling and groveling native ruling class. We followed her.

"Great and merciful Bast, we were foolish to refuse your offer. Please allow us to accept it now," the bastart queen pleaded.

"We will gladly do fifteen years of service, mighty Progenitor," the phony love goddess said.

"We would be beyond blessed to do twenty," the fake war god offered.

Bast ignored their continued pleas as the Dordize gods closed in on the bastarts. The cat goddess slowly closed the doors behind her. Only then did I see her stop a moment to let a single tear fall from her cheek. I held out my hand. She took it and did not let go until we were back on board *Fools' Glory*.

ASK NOT FOR WHOM THE PLANET TOLLS

I've always prided myself and my ability to make people laugh, but this was too easy. Worse, I wasn't enjoying it.

My entire crew was in hysterics as they pointed at me and doubled over laughing.

"It's not that funny," I said.

"It kind of is, Murphy," Savannah said.

Coyote rolled back and forth on the floor of the main bar of *Fools' Glory*. His laughter was mixed with yaps and barks. "It's your own fault Murphy. You should have known better than to bet against me."

My honcho, Loki, was being the kindest of the crew, at least making a token effort to put his hand in front of his face as he chuckled at me. "The fleabag has a point. You really do know better."

"Gold lame is not your color," Riga said.

"Hey boss," Eric said. "Should we start calling you Flash? Or maybe Buck?"

I rolled my eyes and turned to take in my reflection in the barroom mirror. I did look ridiculous. The stakes of my bet with Coyote were simple. If I won, he had to wear a muzzle, a collar with license tags, a leash and a knitted sweater. If he won, I had to dress like someone out of an old spaceman movie serial. I lost, so I was wearing what amounted to a golden shiny space man outfit with black thigh high boots and a skin tight hood which wrapped around my throat and head, but left my face sticking out. There were little cups over my ears and a giant fin on my head. All I needed was a jet pack and a ray blaster and I could've stepped out of something my grandpa might have watched Saturdays when he went to the movies back in the day.

I decided to make the best of it. I stood in front of the bar, put my foot up on a stool and posed heroically with my hands on my hips.

"Murphy, it's not all bad. Those tight shiny pants really make your butt look nice," Savannah said.

"And with that shiny gold color, you and Eric are almost like twins," Riga said.

"I'll see what I can do about making you an honorary melog," Eric said.

"I thought I already was one from back around the time you were born," I said.

Eric shrugged. "I don't remember. I was a baby then. So, where are we off to, boss?"

"You think I'm going to anywhere dressed like this? No way. We can hang here in space until my three days are over." The laughter stopped and the grumbling started. I smiled. "That is, unless Coyote wants to let me out early."

The trickster canine shook his head. "No way. I'm filming all this for prosperity. However what are we going to do when Ming attacks?"

"I don't think we have to worry about a fictional character," I said, sitting down at a table. "Anyone for a game of cards?"

I lifted up the deck and started shuffling. My crew moved to join me. Halfway there, Coyote stopped, fell to the floor and started howling in pain like I've never heard him before.

"Okay fleabag, what your scam this time?" I said.

"Prayers of the dying, begging to be saved," Coyote whispered.

"How many?" Loki said.

"Billions," Coyote said.

"Coyote, this isn't funny. I'm not getting set up for another scam," I said.

"No scam. I'm hearing the prayers of a dying planet," Coyote said.

I looked at Loki.

My honcho shrugged. "I'm not picking up anything, but I'm not as sensitive to it as the fleabag is. He still answers prayers. I stopped that a long time ago."

"Murphy, I give you my word as a Startender that it's not a scam," Coyote said.

That meant it was real. The fleabag would never violate his Startender oath and lie about his word. "Do you have coordinates?"

The canine trickster nodded and walked over to the navigation console in the jukebox.

It was in a section of space that Hermes had mapped on one of his surveys. That meant we could use the transworld drive. But could wasn't the same as should.

"Is it safe enough for us to use the transworld drive?" I said. Anything could be waiting for us on the other end.

Tears streamed down Coyote's furry face as he nodded.

"Eric, get us there as fast as you can," I said.

Coyote started weeping openly. "It won't matter. It's too late."

We tried anyway, but dammit if the fleabag wasn't right on all counts. We emerged outside the orbit of an Earth class planet. It was a little smaller and had only three continents. Up until hours before it had billions of sentient beings.

Now everyone on the planet was dead.

It was mind-numbing. Far too big to get my head around. So big my mind assumed it had to be faked, but it wasn't. We landed in the middle of the largest city on the world. The atmosphere was close to Earth's, but we still used the Startenders badges' life-support as we didn't know what had killed these people. No sense in risking any airborne pathogens. And it was standard protocol. There were corpses everywhere. My stomach wanted to retch, but I managed to hold it back. Not all my crew were so fortunate. Riga was so upset she couldn't hold her human form and was vomiting on the side of the street. A dragon throwing up is not a pretty sight. Loki put his hand on his daughter's scaly back and rubbed it, trying to make her feel better. I could tell from his face that he was feeling ill too. Eric and Savannah were weeping. Coyote hung his head so low it was dragging along the ground.

I was no stranger to death, even slaughter. Loki, I and some others failed to save some Karmans years ago and three hundred and sixty four people died because we couldn't stop it. To this day I can remember each of their names and what it felt like taking care of the dead on that battlefield.

The death here dwarfed that. I needed to focus on something or I would curl up into a little ball and start whimpering. I examined the city. The planet's technology level seem to be akin to late 19th and early 20th century Earth. Lot of steam power, but they had indoor plumbing and good sanitation.

We walked through the streets, corpses were strewn everywhere. Maybe they didn't know what was happening and went quickly. The natives were tall humanoids with bone structure reminiscent of an insect. What looked like ears were set far back on their heads behind two pairs of eyes, each set above the other. They had no protruding nose, but had what appeared to be four nostrils, two where each human ear would have been. Their jaws looked like they would've opened sideways instead of up and down.

"What could have done this?" I said, talking to myself in an effort to get my mind off and around the horror everywhere around me.

Imagine my surprise when I got an answer and not from one of my crew.

"NOT WHAT – WHO." I spun. Standing as still as a grave right behind me was a bony figure in long black robes and a hood. The skull beneath the hood looked like it belonged to one of the natives

"John?" I whispered.

"HELLO, MURPHY," said the Grim Reaper, although I called him John Thanatos. Because of the unique nature of Bulfinche's Pub as a mystic null zone, Death himself had been able to come in disguised as a living man and interact with people in a way that didn't involve his day job as the embodiment of death. John rather enjoyed being one of the gang.

That anonymity wasn't an option for him on Startender Station. Which was likely why I hadn't seen John since New York City was destroyed. We were lucky enough to make sure he wasn't busy that day.

We weren't that lucky today.

Death tends to appear to the dying as they picture him. The Grim Reaper motif is fairly universal, although what he holds varies. I'm guessing the locals had seen him as one of their own, explaining his current appearance.

I started to ask him what he was doing here, but considering the circumstances decided it was a foolish question. "I didn't expect to see you here."

"DEATH IS UNIVERSAL. I HAVE MANY ASPECTS ON EVERY WORLD."

I nodded. I guess I realized that, but hadn't incorporated the thought that the Grim Reaper on Earth is the same Grim Reaper everywhere.

"What do you mean who?" I said. "One person did all this?"

"YOU KNOW I CANNOT TELL YOU THAT," said the Grim Reaper, but he was nodding at the same time. Death had broken the rules once before to help avenge a little girl who was brutally killed by her own mother, but he told us what was happening inside of Bulfinche's Pub which gave him some cover so it didn't come back and bite him in his bony butt. Since the magical null zone that was Bulfinche's was light years away and underwater, we needed another option.

"Murphy, why are you talking to yourself?" Savannah said.

I turned. My crew had come up behind me. They all looked worried – some because they couldn't see what I did and others because they could.

"Reaper," the fleabag said.

"COYOTE." Death then turned to Loki. "TRICKSTER. NICE-LY DONE ESCAPING ME AT RAGNAROK." Death seemed to mean it as a compliment.

Loki bowed his head. "I couldn't have done it without help."

"What are you three talking to?" Riga said.

"I think they are speaking to the embodiment of Death," Eric said in a whisper.

"Then why can they see him and we can't?" Savannah said.

"Fleabag and I are gods and the melog have a special relationship with the universe," Loki said.

"But that doesn't explain why Murphy can see him. He's human. Is he about to die?" Savannah said, stepping protectively next to me.

"No. He and Death are old friends," said a voice from the sky above us. I looked up to see black wings flapping as Moni flew toward the ground. The graveyard angel was carrying Master Hex, the head honcho of *The Accursed*, with her. When they landed, Moni let go of Hex, walked up to death and genuflected down on one knee, then bowed further.

"Greetings Master Thanatos," Moni said.

"HELLO MONI THE LASA."

I inched up alongside Hex. "How did you guys know?"

"Moni felt the presence of an entire planetary grave that was about to be desecrated. You guys?"

"Coyote heard the prayers of the dying," I said. "What's this about a desecration? Did we do something unintended by landing?"

A lasa's magic is tuned into protecting the dead. "Not you. Members of the Cyndicate are fast approaching. And ships from the Goblin Empire are on the way. Both plan to lay claim to this world, then strip it bare."

"Great. The bodies aren't even cold yet," I said.

Moni had risen to her feet. "How did this happen?"

"YOU KNOW I CANNOT ANSWER THAT UNLESS IT PERTAINS TO YOUR DUTIES. THUS FAR, NO ONE HAS DIS-TURBED THE DEAD OF HIVEN."

"But it won't be long before that happens," Moni said.

That's when I heard a very disturbing sound – Death's sigh. "TRUE. ONCE IT STARTS, I WILL BE ABLE TO ANSWER YOU."

Hex bent down and picked up the local equivalent of a brick and tossed it through a window. "It's been disturbed now. Tell her what happened."

"YOU MAY BE A MAGÍ, BUT DO NOT ATTEMPT TO ISSUE ME ORDERS. DO NOT PRESUME WE ARE FRIENDS, EVEN IF WE DID ONCE HAVE A REGULAR CHESS GAME."

"I would never presume that, especially after you went mad and deserted your duties," Hex said.

"THAT DID NOT HAPPEN IN THIS REALITY. AND LET

US NOT FORGET THAT YOU INHABIT THAT BODY ONLY BECAUSE I ALLOWED IT."

The Hex that is a Startender is not the same Hex that hung out at Bulfinche's Pub. That Hex died like he lived, trying to protect others.

Many years back, a group of tricksters – with me among their number – stopped the United States military from nuking Faerie and prevented the dark alternate future of the Mysticaust. The Hex from that apocalyptic timeline sent his spirit back in time to lead the charge to stop that reality from ever occurring. With his timeline wiped from existence, the future Hex had nowhere left to return to. Rather than lay claim to his past self, he willingly left his body, but not before uploading the stories of those who fought against the darkness of the Mysticaust into my old laptop.

When our Hex died, the Hex from the alternate future laid claim to the body and brought the corpse back to life, apparently with the blessings of our Hex and the Grim Reaper. Our friend had gone by Mr. Hex. This one goes by Master Hex. He still had the curse that both of them suffered from, but it was lessened by the peculiarities of his current existence.

While Master Hex might be potentially one of the most powerful people on Earth, Death was a universal force. Hex wasn't in the Grim Reaper's class. Apparently Death went a little crazy in that alternate universe and Hex and I had been among those who stopped him. Let's just say, Master Hex was having difficulties with forgiving and forgetting in this particular instance and there were some issues between them.

This was a pissing contest I needed to stop and then I realized why John had sought me out.

"Wait a second. Thanatos, while it would be very kind of you to stay around to answer Moni's question that's not why you're still here is it? Why would you hang around if everyone was dead? You would have done your job and have no reason to stay. That means someone or many someones are still alive and you're here waiting to claim them, right?"

"JOHN MURPHY, YOU KNOW I CANNOT ANSWER

THAT." That's what Death said, but this time his bony fist was nodding in American Sign Language. John spent enough time in Bulfinche's Pub to know we used sign language to talk to Judah Maccabee, a mute golem. I guess with all these witnesses, he wasn't about to risk a full head nod.

"Okay people, listen up. This just became a rescue mission. We are working under the assumption that there is at least one person left alive on this planet. We are going to find that person and we're going to save them."

"ONE CANNOT CHANGE THE HOUR OF ONE'S DEATH."

"But many people have different points in which they could die." Death himself told me that. Some had no choice, but others did. The person, not Death, got to make the call then. "The survivors…" John's index and middle fingers snapped shut like an alligator's mouth. That was sign for no. "Or survivor…" Another hand nod. Damn. I was hoping for more. "Will have to make that choice."

Death smiled and nodded ever so slightly to me. His way of saying thanks. Most of the time John had no problem doing his job. He just had some issues when what happened was especially heinous. A planet full of corpses definitely qualified.

"We start with this city," I said.

"Why?" Savannah said.

"Because a planet is an awful big place to search, so we have to start somewhere." And because Death himself is here waiting, not somewhere else, so it seems a pretty good guess. But saying that out loud would be selling out my friend, who was breaking rules to help us. And Death answers to an even higher power. "My gut tells me that here's where we'll find any survivors."

Coyote started sniffing. "Too much death for me to smell anything else.

Eric tapped into Fools' Glory's sensors. Hex used his Startender badge to give the same order to his melog, Ally. His ship – *The Accursed* – had returned to orbit so it could stand watch for any ships coming in-system

That done, Hex looked me up and down. "Is there a reason

you're dressed like a baked potato from Mars? Trying to distract your crew and us from the genocide?"

"I thought the outfit odd as well. Have the Startenders started wearing uniforms?" the Grim Reaper said with a smirk

"Murph lost a bet with me," Coyote said

Moni had collapsed into the fetal position onto the ground from trying to search the planet with her abilities. I knelt down and took her hand.

"I can't find anyone. The world is too big," she said.

Lasa became more powerful when they're on a grave. The more graves, the greater their power.

"Moni, relax and start thinking differently. I figure at this moment you're the most powerful lasa there has ever been." Moni tilted her head. She wasn't getting what I was saying. "This entire planet is a grave for billions. You have access to power you've never had before. If there's anyone alive, any survivors, even their presence on this world will be disturbing the planetary grave in some way. Figure out how to filter all of us out and anything alive should stand out like a candle in the darkness.

Moni nodded, closed her eyes and took a deep breath. Slowly she floated off the ground. Her wings weren't even flapping

Moni looked down at me. "I should be able to search out and find any life, but something seems to be blocking me."

"Is it what or whoever did this?" I said.

"No, it's your outfit," she said. "I can't seem to get past it."

I rolled my eyes, but kept my mouth shut. I knew what it was like to have to make a joke in order to function under stress. In fact, it was a good part of the story of my life.

Moni reached down and took me by the hand. I mentally lessened the force that my badge was allowing gravity to have on me and the lasa pulled me up into the sky.

"Follow us," Moni said to the other Startenders. We flew a couple of blocks over and found a local hospital. It didn't seem overrun with patients, so whatever killed everyone must have happened quickly. On the second floor we found a pediatric ward. All the children and their caregivers were dead until we got to the end of the hallway. There was what appeared to be a young alien adolescent. She was unconscious and hooked up to what was probably the local equivalent of an IV. Her chest moved up and down.

She's alive," Moni whispered, smiling. My crew and Hex were right behind us riding on top of Fools' Glory.

"Hex, what's your assessment?" I said. Hex had been a medical doctor back in the day.

Hex went to the bedside and examined the Hiven girl. "Her name is Quan. She's weak, but not dying by any means. Take her up to *The Accursed* and have Az do his golden glow and see if that helps."

Aziel is a guardian angel. Years ago he had been assigned to watch over Bulfinche's Pub. After New York was sunk, he was assigned to the Startenders as our very own guardian angel and serves as Hex's honcho. Guardian angels had an ability to heal. There are some limitations but he was the best shot this little girl had.

"Eric–" I started.

"Got it boss. One transport to *The Accursed* ready and waiting," he said, transforming the hull of the golden ship into a door outside the nearest window. Savannah and Riga carried the bed onto our ship. The door closed and they flew up into the sky.

John Thanatos suddenly appeared in the room. Death seemed pleased.

"THE YOUNG ONE WILL LIVE. MY WORK HERE IS COMPLETE."

"Wait, if you leave you will not be able to answer my questions," Moni said.

"WHILE THAT IS UNFORTUNATE, NOW I HAVE NO REASON TO STAY."

"Actually, you might. We have a fully stocked bar onboard *Fools' Glory*. I know you're allowed to take breaks. Come on board and I'll buy you some drinks."

The Grim Reaper placed a bony hand on my shoulder. He meant it to be a warm, friendly gesture, so I worked hard not to shiver from the cold wave that shot through my body.

"I WOULD LIKE THAT VERY MUCH. I HAVE MISSED MY FAVORITE BAR."

We waited in an awkward silence where Hex tried to stare down the embodiment of death and the Grim Reaper pretended to ignore him until Eric returned with *Fools' Glory*.

Moni elected to stay behind alone to honor the dead as only she could. The rest of us returned to orbit.

I gave Death a quick tour of the ship, then had him sit at the bar and poured him a zombie, one of his favorite drinks. I poured drinks for Hex and my crew, then myself.

As one we raised them. "To the people of Hiven," I said.

"May they rest in peace," Loki said.

"And may their killer or killers pay," added Master Hex.

We all drank.

Savannah was squinting to try to see the Grim Reaper. She saw the glass get raised and the liquid drain and was trying to figure things out when Hex came behind the bar and grabbed hold of my arm.

"Excuse us. Head honcho stuff." Hex pulled me to the far side of the bar.

"Murphy, you can't trust him. He's only one really bad day away from snapping. We have no way of knowing if this is going to be that day," Hex said.

"I've known Thanatos for years. He's really not a bad guy."

"In my world…" Hex said.

"He *is* the Grim Reaper. You think just because we're on the other side of the room that he can't hear us?"

"I'm mystically interfering with anyone else hearing us," Hex said, rubbing at his ear. A side effect of his curse caused him pain anytime he used magic. Right now he likely had an earache from using that spell.

"Fine. I refuse to condemn him for something he might have done in another timeline," I said.

"By that logic, I shouldn't give *you* any of the credit for the things you did in that timeline," Hex said.

"Technically, the me that I am right now never did them so I can't take the credit or the blame for anything the other me did in that timeline."

Hex chuckled. "You did a lot. You've done a lot of good in this one too, so I have no problem giving you credit for both."

"Thanks. Please cut him a break," I said. "As a favor to me."

"I'll think about it. Either way, I'm still keeping an eye on him," Hex said.

"Exactly how would you stop the personification of death from doing anything?" I said.

"I helped stop him once. If need be, I can do it again," Hex said.

SLURP.

Hex and I both jumped at the loud sipping sound behind us. A quick look to the side told me that the Grim Reaper was no longer sitting at the bar. We turned around slowly to see Death standing behind us.

Hex glared at Death. The Grim Reaper actually smiled and wiggled his bony brows. He was messing with Hex.

"SORRY TO INTERRUPT HEAD HONCHO STUFF, BUT I WAS WONDERING IF I CAN GET A REFILL?"

I took the glass from his hand. "Happy to oblige. Let's go back over to the bar and you can tell me what's been going on with you."

Death shrugged. "YOU KNOW ME. SAME OLD SAME OLD…"

"It's a living I guess."

John smiled at the old joke. "I GUESS."

"This must be your worst day on the job," I said.

"SADLY, IT IS NOT, BUT IT WAS FAR FROM A GOOD ONE."

"So what can you do to help us catch whoever did this?" I whispered.

"THESE ARE NOT CIRCUMSTANCES WHERE I AM ABLE TO SHARE WHAT THE RECENTLY DEAD MIGHT KNOW."

"Fine. Forget about what really happened down there. How about we speak hypothetically. How could someone slaughter an entire planet?" I said, refilling the Grim Reaper's glass.

Death sipped on his third zombie. Outside of Bulfinche's Pub, I doubted alcohol had any effect on him. John just liked the chance to socialize. Guy had a lonely job.

"YOU ARE FAMILIAR WITH EARTH'S SERIAL KILLERS." I nodded. "THERE ARE ALSO SERIAL KILLERS THROUGH THE UNIVERSE. SOME SIMPLY WORK ON A MUCH LARGER SCALE, WORKING TOWARD GENOCIDE OR KILLING ON A PLANETARY SCALE."

"So someone murdering an entire planet has been done before?" I said.

"YES."

"Often?"

Death shrugged. "MORE OFTEN THAN IT SHOULD."

"How could it be done? Hypothetically of course."

"NUCLEAR EXPLOSIONS. MAKING A PLANETARY CORE UNSTABLE. SHIFTING AN ORBIT. ASTEROID STRIKE. MASS POISONINGS. PLAGUE."

"So if we were going to try to duplicate what was done on Hiven, it would seem that some sort of mass poisoning would be the most logical route to go. In theory of course."

"I SUPPOSE IT WOULD."

"Okay Startenders, how would someone poison an entire planet?" I said, looking around the bar room. I have to say what I saw was amusing. My crew and Hex had taken up positions on the far side of the room from where Death and I were drinking. All of them, even the gods and the magí, seemed very nervous.

I had always told John he didn't need to have a secret identity to come into Bulfinche's Pub because the patrons would treat him just fine even if they knew who he was. John didn't share my view so kept coming incognito as John Thanatos. Sadly, I finally realized he may have been right. If these people weren't able to see past John's job, very few others could.

"Eric, you checked the atmosphere. You didn't notice any poison, right?" I said.

"Nothing that would be poisonous to anybody on our ship.

I can't be entirely certain what might be poisonous to the natives," Eric said.

"Contact Moni and ask her to see if she can read anything from the dead." The locals for the most part practiced burial customs. To lay a corpse back down to rest on Earth, Moni could part the soil over a grave better that Moses could the Red Sea. We had a bar mirror focused on her and the black winged woman was a wonder to behold. Alone on the surface she was shifting entire land masses the size of cities in order to bury the Hiven dead. She had asked us all to leave so she didn't have to worry about accidentally hurting one of us. We didn't want her hurting herself, so both ships were keeping a careful eye on her. So far, the influx of power she got from the dead seemed to be invigorating her. Moni showed no sign of tiring.

Death spun on his barstool to look at the crew. Coyote, Loki and Eric all looked elsewhere, which queued in Savannah and Riga that something was going on. Hex just tried to stare him down again.

"I'M BEGINNING TO FEEL SELF-CONSCIOUS WITH ALL OF YOU STAYING WAY OVER THERE. DO I SMELL?"

Actually, he had, down on the planet of the dead – he had a putrid rotting odor, but up here not so much.

"Stop picking on them. It's only natural to be nervous in the face of death," I said.

"NOT TRUE. THE SECOND TIME WE MET, YOU LAUGHED IN MY FACE."

"True." I wanted to be able to tell people I looked Death in the eye and laughed in his face. "But that didn't mean I wasn't nervous." In fact I was downright scared. "My desire to see my dearly departed first wife Elsie was stronger than the nervousness." And we had never talked about Terrorbelle's death. On my part it was because I was afraid I would ask him to let me see her, which would be a lot like asking an honest cop to let you walk away after he saw you murder someone just because of your friendship. In your head you know it would violate everything the other person believed in and that they could never really allow it. And even though I know he had to turn me down, I'd resent him for it and it would be the beginning of the end of our friendship and despite it all, I like John. "And to be truthful, on some primal level, I'm always a little bit nervous around you."

The Grim Reaper frowned. "BUT YOU HAVE NEVER SHOWN IT OR TREATED ME DIFFERENT THAN YOU DO ANYONE ELSE."

"Why should I? We both know you have a difficult time socializing. To make you feel bad because I was a little nervous would be rude and wrong. Besides, deep down you're just a nice guy with a lousy job."

"NOT ALWAYS AS LOUSY AS TODAY. AND SOME DAYS NOT LOUSY AT ALL. I BRING RELIEF TO MANY AND HELP REUNITE LOVED ONES, BUT THAT IS THEIR COMFORT, NOT MINE. EVEN AFTER SO MANY AEONS…"

"Aeons?" I said.

"EACH AEON IS A THOUSAND MILLION YEARS."

"Wow. How old are you? Because you barely look half an aeon old."

Death smiled. "OLD ENOUGH TO BOTH NO LONGER CARE AND BE INCREDIBLY SENSITIVE ABOUT IT."

"We can talk about your weight instead. Or maybe politics?"

Death grinned. "OR I COULD CONTINUE."

"Let's go with that," I said.

"DESPITE MY AGE, IT STILL BOTHERS ME WHEN SOMEONE IS TAKEN BEFORE THEY HAVE TO BE. WHEN IT HAPPENS TO AN ENTIRE WORLD…" The Grim Reaper downed the rest of his drink in a single gulp.

I put my hand on Death's shoulder and he sighed and patted my hand with his bony one. The joints in my hand hurt from the cold.

"I would like to figure out who did this, so we could stop it from happening again," I said, holding my hand near the coffee pot to warm it.

"VERY LITTLE WOULD MAKE ME HAPPIER, BUT THE RULES THAT GOVERN ME ARE DIFFICULT TO GET

AROUND."

"Do you know where the killer will strike next?" I said.

"IF I DID, I COULD NOT SAY. *HYPOTHETICALLY* SPEAKING I WOULD IMAGINE THAT THERE ARE THOSE WHO KNOW THIS INFORMATION. AND ONE COULD IN THEORY ASK HOW ANYONE WITHOUT MYSTIC ABILITIES COULD KNOW THIS HAD HAPPENED? AND IF THEY KNOW THAT, WHAT OTHER OF YOUR QUESTIONS MIGHT THEY BE ABLE TO ANSWER?"

I poured John another zombie and tried to figure out what he was trying to tell me without actually saying it when our proximity alarm went off.

"Boss, we have a Cyndicate ship in-system. ETA to Hiven three hours.

I guess I had the answer. But I also had another question. "Does them being in-system qualify as desecration?"

Death sipped his zombie and nodded.

I hit my Startender badge. "Moni, Thanatos is ready for a game of twenty questions. Are you able to ask them?"

"ACTUALLY, TWENTY SEEMS EXCESSIVE…"

"An old game," I said.

"I KNOW."

On the bar mirror, several blocks of the city were floating in the air, as the ground seemed to move like a conveyer belt, sliding the corpses beneath it. When the last body was moved, the blocks, complete with roadway and buildings gently settled back onto the ground.

"I am now," Moni said, in between gasps of air. She hit her badge so a screen showing us appeared in front of her. "Did one person do this?"

Death nodded. "THERE WAS ONE KILLER."

"Were there others who helped him?" Moni said.

"NOT IN THE KILLING, BUT IN THE PREPARATIONS."

"What is the killer's name?"

"I CANNOT SAY."

"How did the killer do this?" Moni said.

"I CANNOT SAY DIRECTLY."

"Moni we may have that one covered. Hypothetically," I said.

Moni nodded. "Is this the first world the killer has slaughtered?"

"IT IS THE FOURTH." Death listed three other worlds.

"Where will the killer strike next?" Moni said.

"I CANNOT SAY DIRECTLY."

"How about hypothetically?" I said.

"HYPOTHETICALLY YOU HAVE BOTH THE ABILITY AND THE OPPORTUNITY TO FIND HIM –" Death looked at the flashing proximity alarm, letting us know where that opportunity was and that the killer was a male, which actually narrowed down the races he could be from somewhat. "– BEFORE HE STRIKES AGAIN."

"Thank you Master Thanatos."

Death nodded and Moni closed her connection and returned to burying the dead of Hiven.

I took out something from behind the bar and held it up to the Grim Reaper.

"WHAT IS THAT?"

"A signal ring we give to Startender Affiliates. It allows them to contact us in case of emergency. If we don't make it to the next targeted world before people start dying, you could signal us and maybe we can do something to save that world."

"THAT WOULD BE A BLATANT DISREGARD OF THE RULES THAT I AM BOUND TO FOLLOW. HOWEVER IF YOU HYPOTHETICALLY WERE ABLE TO PLANT SOME SORT OF TRACKING DEVICE ON ME WITHOUT MY KNOWING ABOUT IT AND I TOOK PHYSICAL FORM ON A WORLD, IT MIGHT SIGNAL YOU WITHOUT MY KNOWING IT EVEN EXISTED."

"Good to know," I said, looking toward Loki and Coyote. They nodded at me and got to work on rigging something up out of one of our probes.

"Now we need to stop the Cyndicate from plundering this world," I said.

My crew and I had come a long way since we first encountered the Cyndicate. We learned a lot. For one thing, even as big as the universe was, it had rules. Rules varied from place to place, but they existed. The key was to figure out which rules which people followed and which ones they didn't. Most of the time rule-following was tied very closely to the rule enforcement.

The Cyndicate didn't do much long-term business on places like Traven. The reason for that was simple. There were few rules there and even fewer that were enforced. Traven had no police force as such, just small bands of security and mercenary forces, so the rules were made by the stronger against the weaker. The largest and strongest force chose the rules.

The Cyndicate didn't like doing business that way. They dealt in the acquisition of power and wealth. Wealth involved some sort of currency. For all intents and purposes, the Cyndicate ignored any rule that didn't serve its purposes and its members were usually powerful enough to skirt most rule enforcement.

The sole exception to this was the Cyndicate Charter. Members of the Cyndicate were basically cutthroat robber barons that tried to project a united front to the universe at large. What united them was the charter.

It outlined what could and couldn't be done when dealing with outsiders and each other. There was plenty of room for loopholes, the finding of which seemed to be their primary pastime.

The charter was their Bible, rulebook and guiding force wrapped up in the one. The members of the Cyndicate guarded what was in the charter fiercely. There was a light version that they released for those in their employ. Those rules were fairly well-known and easy to get hold of. The full version was so fiercely protected that any member who shared the contents with an outsider was subject to severe penalties including but not limited to expulsion and death. Not necessarily in that order. Any Cyndicate member that was expelled would no longer have the protections of the charter or the group and would likely wind up on the deceased list anyway, either from someone they had cheated or robbed or a follow member they crossed.

My crew had defended a planet we named Eden from one

member of the Cyndicate. We tricked and scared him off, then followed with an incursion into his ship in order to wipe the planet's location from the database. While we were on board we managed to acquire a copy of the full and unabridged charter.

Several Startenders have been studying it ever since, coming up with ways we could turn it to our advantage. The team included Loki, Coyote, Sun WuKong, Xen, Paddy and Hermes.

The Cyndicate ship hailed us. It probably seemed like a good idea since *The Accursed* and *Fools' Glory* had moved into an intercept course to place ourselves between the ship and the planet of the dead.

I took the call. "This world and system are hereby claimed by the bond of rule of first present."

The face of the Cyndicate boss appeared on a bar mirror with a very confused look on his face. "Excuse me?"

Cyndicate ships and members of the Cyndicate had some of the best translators I've ever seen. The Startenders all have lation stones which allow us to understand others and them to understand us if they come in contact with it. Whatever the Cyndicate used translated what they heard and what they spoke.

"Did I stutter? We have made our claim by rule and order as proscribed by the charter. You are now trespassing. Or do you ignore the code of the Cyndicate?" I said.

The boss was a race I didn't recognize but was bulbous and multi-tentacled with a sickly yellow skin color. If his body language was similar to that of the Cron, his facial tentacles were moving in the equivalent of a smirk. "You claim to be Cyndicate?"

The charter was very clear that any imposter was subject to immediate death, although that could be preceded by torture depending on an actual Cyndicate member's discretion.

"The right of claims extends to all, as long as it is made first." Which is why it was the first thing I said.

Now the facial tentacles stiffened and extended, my guess as an expression of shock. That information was not common knowledge.

"I do not recognize your claim," the boss said.

I shrugged. "Pity as it was done correctly. For you to refuse recognition is in violation of the Cyndicate charter. I hereby claim my right to your trial by a triad of your peers. We are running recordings using Veritasian verification." It was designed by a group of technologically advanced holy monks (a male term although their race were hermaphrodites) and could not be altered. We know. We've tried, including putting both Xen and Bubba Sue on the job. Any altering of said recordings forever changed them and interestingly enough any copies made, even if they were stored separately. Bubba Sue figured it was some sort of quantum connection where the copy was not an actual copy, but another aspect of the same recording, simply kept in another location. Yes, I know. It makes my head hurt too. The long and the short of it was, it was the only type of recording the Cyndicate and many others accepted as truth.

"Looks like we got him by the short and curlies," whispered Hex.

"I shall send out the request now and await the arrival of your peers," I said.

"Wait. Perhaps we can come to some sort of an arrangement instead," the boss said.

"I'm intrigued. What are you proposing?" I said.

"I'm not comfortable discussing it over an open channel. Whom shall I be negotiating with?"

"You introduce first," I said. Again, in Cyndicate custom, the one who went first loses some prestige in negotiations. Under the circumstances, it had no choice. "I am Alom, chaircreature of the first order of the Cyndicate."

"I'm John Murphy, head honcho of the barship *Fools' Glory* and member of the Startenders." I could see through our video link, Alom motioning with his lower and rear tentacles for one of his crew to find out everything they could about us.

"Well, then, John Murphy of the Startenders, I invite you to parlay on my ship now."

"Then I claim immediate and lasting parlay protection for myself, those with me, all Startenders and our personnel."

This time it was all the tentacles that shot out straight and stiff. "That is too much to grant."

I shrugged again. In theory, it would prevent the chaircreature from working against the safety of those under that protection until such a time as I deemed our business complete. It was within my rights to never deem our business complete, thus gaining full and everlasting immunity. In fact, Alom would be bound in certain instances to actually defend us from harm against other members of the Cyndicate.

"Then I shall call for your trial."

Alom's skin turned from sickly yellow to a blotchy orange. We were only able to find a record of one case in which someone who was tried by a triad of their peers was not voted against and expelled. In that lone case, two of the three were killed before a verdict was reached, so the only surviving member apparently found in the defendant's favor in order to avoid a similar fate. The Cyndicate members do not like each other and their alliances are simple matters of convenience. Any of them would throw each other or their own parents under a passing spaceship if there was something to gain.

Any expelled Cyndicate member automatically lost half of their holdings. That half was divided equally among the other members of the Cyndicate. The other half was open for grabs for those waiting in the wings to become members.

I was at a bit of a dilemma myself. The Startenders code states we cannot kill unless all other options were exhausted and then only in the defense of life. Calling for Alom to be tried by its peers would likely be a death sentence. I was hoping the chaircreature wouldn't call my bluff, leaving it with two choices – grant us the protection or not. Choosing the not option meant it had to kill us before we sent out the call for the triad, which would lead to loss of its wealth and life at the hands of its fellow members.

"Fine. I hereby grant parlay protection for you."

"That is not what I requested."

A tentacle lashed out, knocking one of the crew to the floor. Alom repeated my request verbatim. Of course it was contingent on my going over to its ship.

Alom designated an airlock for me to enter. "I'll be there shortly."

We cut the transmission and the Veritasian recording.

Hex stepped next to me. "The boss is planning a death trap that will appear to be an accident."

"I know."

"It would be incredibly foolish of you to go by yourself," Eric said.

"I agree," Loki said.

"Me too." I could see from the look on Loki's face that he expected me to take him along. Normally, he'd be my first choice, but I had a better idea.

"Thanatos, how would you feel about going over to negotiate with me?"

The Grim Reaper smiled. "IT MIGHT BE INTERESTING."

"Why him? None of the Cyndicate crew will be able to see him unless they were about to die," Hex said.

"THERE ARE SOME EXCEPTIONS – CERTAIN CHILDREN, MYSTIC BEINGS AND FELINES, AMONG OTHERS," the Grim Reaper said.

"Not to mention that the Cyndicate have some of the best mystic sensors ever developed. They may not be up to see that Death is with you, but their sensors might be able to pick up his presence," Loki said.

"That's what I'm counting on."

The Grim Reaper and I headed for an airlock and looked out into the void of space.

"I wasn't aware your Startender badge allowed you to fly," Death said. Now that we were alone, he stopped with the scary death voice and talked to me like he was a regular person. He also shifted his appearance to how I perceived him – John Thanatos, handsome man and stealer of wives by way of death.

"Not yet, but Vulcan, Bubba Sue and the Pink Reaper are

working on it," I said

"Then how do you propose we get to the Cyndicate ship? Run and jump out the airlock and hope you have really good aim? Not that I'd be harmed either way," Death said grinning.

I like to I think I had a positive effect on John's trying to develop a sense of humor. It was still a work in progress.

I hit a button on my watch. An instant later, a motorcycle with a sidecar appeared next to me.

I motioned to the sidecar. Death shrugged and got in.

"Eric, open the airlock," I said.

I revved the engine and we flew out through the vacuum between the ships. The bike provides its own atmosphere, just like a Startender badge. Since I had the badge I didn't need the bike's atmosphere. I was pretty sure the Grim Reaper didn't need it either.

"Not that I don't appreciate your help, but isn't you riding along breaking some of those rules you are always talking about?" I said.

"Some, but lesser rules since I am not dealing with matters of dying. You and Paddy are two of my best friends. For you Murph, I'll deal with any trouble it might cause," John said.

"Thanks," I said and sighed. I was going to point out the elephant on the bike. "You know we've never talked about Terrorbelle. I don't blame you. I'd just need to know that she's okay wherever she's at. Don't worry, I won't go on a quest through the afterlives again."

"Murphy, normally I would tell you within the confines of the rules, but on this particular issue I'm bound by something else. Mosie asked me to promise not to discuss it with you until after he did. And if he had, you wouldn't need to ask me," John said.

"Mosie? He knew who you were?" I said. As far as I knew only Paddy and I knew about his secret identity as John Thanatos for sure, although I think Hermes, the Manhattan Sewing Club (also known as the Fates) and a couple others suspected.

"Mosie was the greatest psychic who ever lived. Or died," the Grim Reaper said.

"He was." And one of my closest friends.

"Mosie could potentially know anything. And he followed

your example when dealing with me. He thought highly of you. A large compliment since he could see you at your worst and best."

"When did he ask you?" I said.

"On my third or fourth visit to Bulfinche's Pub as John Thanatos."

"But I hadn't even met Terrorbelle back then," I said. Which meant he knew I'd marry Terrorbelle before I even knew she existed. Not that it should have surprised me.

Normally it's rather difficult to chat with a dead man, but Mosie had left a number of recordings before he passed away. Each is rigged to play at a set time and place. He left one for us right before we started the evacuation of New York City. And during that message, he told me he was going to return a favor at some point in the future.

I trusted Mosie enough to know there was a good reason for him to ask Death to keep mum about the death of my wife. "Okay. Forget I asked."

Death nodded. "Terrorbelle was wonderful for you and you for her. I mourned your loss. I have always appreciated being invited to your wedding and reception. Even if you did have me dance with the bride."

I chuckled. Terrorbelle was an enthusiastic dancer and very strong. She had a habit of throwing her dancing partners around, myself included. Some of my fondest memories are of the two of us dancing.

"You are my friend. Of course I would invite you. Although I've always been afraid to turn over that hourglass you gave us as a gift," I said.

It was John's turn to chuckle. "I wanted to give you a gift that would make you smile. It's just an hourglass."

"Glad to hear it, because Elsiebelle was flying around our apartment as a kid and knocked it over. The glass cracked and some sand leaked out. I put it back along with any dirt or dust that was on the floor and sealed it back up just in case," I said.

"Elsiebelle is a wonderful girl. There are very few people who invite me to not only their child's christening, but their birthday parties. You even let me hold her as a baby." It was in Bulfinche's Pub so I figured it was safe. "I never get to hold living babies. It was an honor."

"Having you as my friend has been an honor too," I said. I held up the tracking device my crew had rigged up out of a probe. Bubba Sue could have made it small. It was the size of a golden softball. Death looked at it and smiled. There was no way to sneak this onto his person. John pulled open a pocket in his robe.

I pointed into space. "Look, a swarm of cron."

Death obligingly turned his head and let me drop the probe into his pocket.

"Where?" he said.

"My bad. Must have been a trick of the light," I said.

Our conversation stopped as I pulled up outside the Cyndicate ship's designated airlock. I pressed a button on my handlebars.

"Honking the horn? Isn't that somewhat pointless through a vacuum?" Death said.

"Not as much as you'd think. The Pink Reaper rigged up a carrier wave for me. When it hits something metal, it causes it to vibrate and mimic the sound of the horn.

"Kaye Chandler is one who should've fallen to me a long time ago. She is a very smart, resilient woman. I like to think by her choice of name that she's a bit partial to me," Death said.

"Why? Are you considering trading your black robes for pink ones?" I said.

"Only if that's how the dying perceives me." Death looked up to me as we approached to the airlock. "How are you holding up, Murphy? You've always been a sensitive soul. What happened on Hiven has got to be hard on you."

"Some bastard just wiped out an entire planet for kicks. I'm sick to my stomach. I'm upset. I'm angry. I want to kill the SOB that did this."

"Is that not against the Startender oath?"

"Yep."

"So will you try and do it?"

"No. Not unless it's a choice between him and an innocent."

"Good. I've always liked that you aren't a killer."

The Cyndicate airlock opened so we flew and landed. We got off the bike and I pressed a button that sent my flying motorcycle back to *Fools' Glory*. It had anti-shielding technology, but was decades behind current Startender badge technology, but there was no reason to give the Cyndicate any added scans to try and reverse-engineer the tech.

Death held back as I stepped forward. Beams of light shot out from the wall, scanning me. The tried to scan the badge, but the beams dissipated inches away.

The doors opened and a humanoid in the equivalent of a business suit stepped forward with a few dozen armed security forces around him. Their weapons were drawn, but they were careful not to point them at me.

"I am first servant Oslo. Please walk this way to bask in the presence of Master Alom."

I've been waiting for that straight line my entire life. Oslo had legs that were rigged like a grasshopper and he walked like a drunken cowboy that had been in the saddle too long. I fell in behind him, mimicking his gait.

"This is the Master's boardroom," Oslo said, stopping in front of a silver wall. Most people aren't too familiar with metal morphing technology, but my ship's hull was made out of an advanced morphing alloy. Oslo waited, apparently for me to ask where the door was.

Instead I knocked on the wall. "Alom, I haven't got all day."

The wall sported a circular door that opened like an iris. I looked through, but I didn't see anyone obviously lying in wait and stepped inside. A quick look over my shoulder showed me Death was following. Actually he was skipping and trying to make me laugh. I covered my face and turned forward. The boardroom was opulent to the point of being ridiculous. Every surface shone with some valuable metal or jewel. All the seating was near the floor, no higher than a thick mat with the exception of a grand throne on a dais far above my head. It was supposed to impress and intimidate, but I'd seen bigger and better.

I yawned and pointed to a bare surface of the wall. "Looks like you missed a spot. What happened, run out of money?" The yellow bulbous body became angry orange again, but Alom got himself under control and became yellow again.

"Shall I have one of my servants bring you a seat?" the boss said, pointing to a mat.

I mentally adjusted the gravity settings on my badge, leaned back in the air and put my feet up on nothing and just floated in place. Startenders badges can't make someone fly, but they had floating down pat.

"I'm good."

"Head Honcho John Murphy, you are here to negotiate the rights to the planet Hiven. You may share your offer."

"I think it's best if we spoke in private," I said, trying to be diplomatic and spare him embarrassment in front of his underlings.

There was a sound which I assumed was laughter. "So you can try and assassinate me? I think not."

"Just have it noted that by the Cyndicate charter, that I offered to spare you embarrassment and you declined. We both know you have no claim to the planet now by Cyndicate rules and we have the means to enforce our claim. What I'm really here for is to find out exactly how an entire planet came to be slaughtered. Did you have it done simply so you could claim the resources?"

"Head Honcho John Murphy, you overstep your bounds and assumptions about your own protection. We scanned you when you came in. With the exception of that badge bobble, you have no special power or ability. It may provide you with a shield, but we have technology that will penetrate any shield, given enough time. I'm now going to kill you and begin negotiations anew with your second-in-command."

Technically there were gray areas in the charter and my perceived insult could be considered reason for him to try and kill me, but it wasn't going to happen. I had faith in Vulcan's shields and in my often grim friend.

I turned my head towards Death and motioned for him to come by me. He pointed in front of me and I nodded. Death took a position between me and the Cyndicate boss. I had to look over his shoulder to see the lower parts of the throne, but the Grim Reaper was still invisible to everybody else.

"Then your scanner technology must be defective. Does it even bother with mystic or primal universal forces?" Because that's exactly what I had standing in front of me. "Before you do something foolish and offend me, I suggest you scan me again," I said stepping up so my front was just brushing up against Death's back, doing my best to ignore the chill that ran through me at the touch.

More beams shot out from the wall to scan me and literally went through Death to get to me.

Alarms blared to life.

"Master, it is as if Death itself is standing before you," said a technician.

Alom shook its bulbous head side to side and made the laughing noise again. "Nonsense. It is some trick that fooled the sensors. It was a nice try, Head Honcho Murphy. You may have been able to fool the ship sensors, but you will not be able to fool this." It held up a band that was wrapped around a tentacle like a watch. "This is a single greatest scanner in the universe. It can find something as small as an electron or as elusive as a tachyon. It will see whatever false data you are feeding into the system for exactly what it is."

"No, it won't. As I said, I've got places to be and things to stop, so scan me already," I said.

While the wall sensors were single blue beams of light, what came off the band was hundreds of sensor beams.

Alom read the results, then looked at me, shook its band and scanned me again, all the while a white ooze flowed down its body. Probably its race's equivalent of sweat. The chaircreature checked the results again and then floated down on a seat cushion in front of me, then fell to the floor and bowed with its lower tentacles on the floor.

"Head Honcho John Murphy, it is as if the force of Death itself is inside of you. Please, I beg your forgiveness."

"Begging isn't going to be enough." I stepped to the side to walk around the Grim Reaper, looking down at the bulbous alien. "I was kind enough to allow that aspect of me to be scanned. Normally no scanner would be able to pick it up."

"You can hide that?" Alom said.

John Thanatos realized where I was heading and walked back to the far side of the room.

"Of course. Scan me. Use the ship's scanners again." I didn't want to give his sensor another chance at the badges without Death's power running interference.

The beams did their thing.

"He's clean sir," said the tech.

Alom get off the floor, shaking a host of tentacles in my direction. "So it is a trick."

"Are you really trying to make me angry?" I said. The Grim Reaper did his part by walking up to one of the sensors and touching it with a bony finger. The alarms flared back to life.

Alom fell back to the floor. "No, Head Honcho John Murphy. I would never do anything to anger one as powerful as you. Why, with a thought, you could destroy my entire crew. Tell me, are you a form of the Lord Reaper?"

That was another one of Death's names.

"No, Lord Reaper and I just have a very special relationship."

Death was now leaning against the wall with his arms crossed and smiling. "True enough," he said, although I was the only one who could hear him.

"What is it you wish of me?"

"Several things. First and foremost acknowledge our claim to Hiven as first present and incontestable." For a Cyndicate boss to do that would not only block the rest of the Cyndicate, but several other groups that won't want to challenge or anger the Cyndicate. It would even give the Goblin Empire pause.

"Done."

"I want to know how you knew to come here at this time." I may not have known Alom's species, but I knew its type. It was already formulating lies in his mind. "Stop thinking about lying to me for that will make me gravely upset."

The Grim Reaper reached up with his hand to the sensor and put his entire palm over it this time. The alarms got louder, almost sounding like they were about to shatter.

"We had an arrangement with Davin, Slayer of Worlds. At least that's what he is called. It seemed appropriate as he does kill entire planets. After he slays, he has no further use for the world. With all the inhabitants gone, the entire planet becomes salvage. The resources of an entire planet are incredibly valuable. The Slayer of Worlds lets us know when and where he plans to work next. We don't encourage him. I did not hire him."

"Nor did you try to stop him. Do you think me stupid enough to believe that he tells you this information purely out of the goodness of his heart? What do you do for him in return in this arrangement?" I said.

"A few meager things. We supplied some material possessions, a few ships."

"What kind of possessions?"

"Food, medicine, basic necessities."

"What else?" I said.

"Nothing."

"Are you so tired of this plane of existence that you would really lie to me after I warned you not to?" I said, hoping he didn't call my bluff.

"You cannot make me speak any further."

I was weighing my options when John Thanatos walked over. "Murphy, mind if I jump in and lend a tentacle?"

"Nope," I said.

"Nope? What do you mean?" Alom said.

"I mean that isn't good enough and it is time for your consequences to begin. Unless you care to tell the whole truth?" I said.

"The risk is too high. You could still be tricking me somehow," Alom said.

An instant later John transformed into a terrifying version of whatever race Alom was. The alien Death was a giant, easily filling up the space all the way to the ceiling. He did not have normal tentacles. Some were made of fire, there were ones made of barbed metal, others had hungry mouths with moving teeth that looked like they were trying to feed.

Alom and I were the only ones who could see Death.

"Head Honcho John Murphy, save me from the Lord Reaper and I will tell you whatever you need to know."

I casually walked in front of the giant, tentacled Death and held up my hand. The Grim Reaper's form stopped undulating and became still.

"Tell me."

"Everyone, leave the room quickly." All the servants ran out and the three of us were left alone. "To kill an entire planet the Slayer often needs materials to facilitate his work. I would get him those materials."

"So..." I flipped on the Veritasian recording device, making sure Death wasn't in the frame. "... you're saying that you're an accessory to the genocidal murders of four planetary populations?"

"Yes. It was just one continent when it started," Alom said.

"And that makes it better? You are just as guilty of these murders as he is," I said.

"No! I had no limb in them. He never told me what he needed them for. How was I to know?" Alom said.

"What did you think poisons would be used for?"

"Pest control perhaps?"

"You will give me a complete list of everything he's asked you for on every world you've claimed after his handiwork," I said.

"Even the next one?"

"Especially that one." Now my stomach turned into a fireball. We might be able to step in before this Davin the Slayer claimed another world of victims.

The chaircreature waved a tentacle over a pad and with another tentacle produced a list engraved on what looked like platinum that floated in the air in front of me. Luckily it was written in goblin and I could read some basics – a description of the slayer, lists of what was delivered and so on. I couldn't make out everything, but we had plenty of Startenders who were fluent in it.

I turned off the recorder. "One more thing. You work for us now."

"For the Startenders? I'm a Cyndicate boss. I work for no one."

I shrugged and stepped out of the way between him and the tentacled Grim Reaper, who started roaring and moving towards the Cyndicate boss.

Alom collapsed onto the floor with his tentacles weakly waving over him to ward off death. "Fine, but no one can know."

It wouldn't do for us to share that information, but I didn't need to let Alom know that.

I held up the camera. "We now have a Veritasian recording of your confession to participating in four genocides and a continental mass murder. Cross us and I will turn you over to the Koniversal Court." They are not a nice bunch of people. Usually kangaroo courts, but they had the power to enforce verdicts where others didn't. Occasionally they did some good in between massive collateral damage. "And they will turn you over to my good friend here, who believe it or not isn't a big fan of genocide. Right now you're out of the death business. I hear about you having a tentacle in anyone dying and you are done." I reached into the utility belt that was part of my spaceman costume and pulled out what looked like a small gun. It was actually a tissue sampler. I sucked a sample out of the Cyndicate boss. Alom wasn't stupid. The chaircreature knew that with his tissue and his equivalent of DNA there was nowhere in the universe he could hide from us.

"We'll be in touch about what we need you to do for us," I said.

"No. You can't get through my shields. You're trapped here. We're going to renegotiate this if you want to live yourself."

I chuckled.

"I'm no good to you dead," Alom said.

"And you are no good to me not following my orders. Dead, I won't have to worry about you coming after me," I said. "And your shields mean nothing to one such as I. They may as well be a soap bubble for all the trouble I'll have leaving."

I might be telling the truth or I might be bluffing. I honestly wasn't sure yet.

I put the tissue sampler back in the belt pouch and pulled out a metal cylinder. I walked to the wall and pretended like I was examining it when in reality I was putting a sigil on it. One that would let Gani get her magic elevator inside the ship anytime she wanted, shields or no shields. I could even call her for an exit, but that would let the Cyndicate boss know it was there and it would post a guard near it.

I looked at the Grim Reaper. "You need a ride out of here?"

"THERE IS NO PLACE IN THE UNIVERSE THAT IS OFF-LIMITS TO ME." John was back on the clock and the spooky voice was back. "I WILL BE FINE."

"Remember, Alom, you work for us. We'll be in touch as to what exactly that that means," I said.

My gold costume may have looked ridiculous, but allowed me to wear a golden band around my ankle that blended in and resisted the sensors. It was a large drop zone, a piece of *Fools' Glory's* hull that part of the ship could materialize around, shields or no shields. At least that is what I was hoping.

"Exit," I said and the ankle bracelet expanded to a circular hole in the floor which I fell through. It didn't close right away.

I stood inside and watched as the alien-looking Death lifted up the Cyndicate boss towards his maw. "THAT IS MY FRIEND. HARM HIM IN ANY WAY AND THE WORST HORROR YOU CAN IMAGINE WILL SEEM PLEASURABLE COMPARED TO WHAT YOUR AFTERLIFE WILL HOLD."

He dropped Alom who ran off into what I assume was a safe room. Death walked through the glowing field and metal wall. The faintest scream escaped the safe room.

The tentacled Grim Reaper exited the wall the same way he went in, then shifted back into his John Thanatos appearance and waved at me, bowed, then simply disappeared.

I turned to Eric to shut the door and pull the drop zone back inside our ship. Cyndicate bosses were devious and Alom might be to find a way to use the drop zone to invade our ship. It wasn't worth the risk to have an easy second way to get on the ship. We had used it our first time on a Cyndicate ship, but that boss hadn't known it was there.

"We got it," I said.

"Good job, Murphy. Where are we going?" Loki said.

"The planet Gallop."

I had Eric set course for Gallop and went into my office. Each head honcho was able to determine what their office on their ship looked like. Some went all out in decorating, but I kept mine simple – a desk and a few chairs with some photographs. I had one of each of my deceased wives – Terrorbelle and Elsie. I had one of my daughter Elsiebelle and my godchildren John and Pixie. There was a photo of me and the rest of the staff at Bulfinche's Pub back before New York was sunk by a mad sea god. There was a very big picture of me and most of the regulars at one of the parties at Bulfinche's Pub. There's another of me and the rest of the first graduating class of Startenders Academy. The ones of my wives and my daughter are on the desk. The rest are on the walls. Also on the wall was Rainbow's End, a painting Elsie had done of the gang at Bulfinche's Pub before she died. It hung behind the bar until we evacuated. It was a very unusual painting. It wasn't that the painting featured a painted version of itself hanging over the bar at Bulfinche's Pub. Or the fact that it showed two versions of some of the staff and patrons – one as a traditional representation in the painting in the paint and the other as they really appear in the bar. The amazing part is that I was in it. Elsie hadn't painted me in it before she died, but when I started working at Bulfinche's Pub, suddenly there I was. And later after I married Terrorbelle, she appeared in the painting and was wearing a new wedding band. Elsiebelle showed up as soon as she was born and her painting-self grew as she did. Now what was once a sunny street scene outside the window with a rainbow ending outside our door was now a street underwater, with an altered rainbow that that still lead to the door. Oddly, Rebecca was in a different chair these days.

Paddy gifted it to me on moving day. He had bought it from me when I first followed my own rainbow to the bar for more than enough for me to pay off a loan shark I had borrowed money from to pay for Elsie's chemo.

It may have been a better gift than the flying motorcycle, another of Paddy's presents to me.

My desk had a slide-out board with several controls, including a big red button which was an emergency call for help. I thought about hitting it, but that was supposed to be for emergencies that were in progress.

Instead I pressed a blue button that wasn't quite as large. It summoned all the head honchos and higher-ranked Startenders for an immediate videoconference.

Immediate is a relative term and it took over fifteen minutes before everyone was available. We had the technology to make everyone appear as holograms that looked like flesh and blood, but I preferred old-fashioned screen mirror on the wall.

Sir Dagonet of the barship *Excalibur* was the last one to sign in. "All right, Murphy, I'm here. What's going on?"

I brought them up to speed.

"He killed an entire planet?" Rumbles, the head honcho of the barship *Big Top*, said.

"It was his fourth," Hex said from back on board *The Accursed*.

"We have the next planet he's set his murderous sights on – Gallop in the Ordon system. We have a hologram as well some biometric readings of the so-called killer of worlds." Alom had embedded the data in the metal he gave me. "Gallop has three billion inhabitants, which makes this a needle in a planetary haystack that we're looking for. We need all hands on this. I recommend we move all barships not directly involved with immediate protecting of life to Gallop immediately, as well as all available Startenders and Startender Academy cadets," I said.

"Murphy, what about the barships stationed in our system?" Paddy said.

"I know it's against policy, Paddy, but I recommend we leave just two ships in-system and a skeleton crew of Startenders to protect Earth. We know this planet will be wiped out and we have to do everything we can to stop it," I said.

"I assume we don't have the killer's genetics?" Nellie, *Perdu's* head honcho, said.

"If we did, we'd already have him," Hex said

"Does he have any powers?" Hercules said. These days, the legend was in charge of the barship *Argo II*.

"We have no idea," I said.

"How do we know we can trust this intel?" said Buzz, the garba who commanded the barship *Bitter End*. "After all, it was gotten from the Cyndicate boss who helped the slayer. You can trust one of them as far as I could throw them." Buzz topped out a little over two feet tall and as a rule wasn't able to throw anybody.

Hex laughed. "He tried to lie several times. Murphy had him too scared to do anything, but sign up as a lackey of the Startenders," Hex said, explaining in more detail what John Thanatos and I had done.

"You got Death to do all that?" Vulcan said, more than a little surprised.

"That's me boy," Paddy said

Nellie smiled. "That's not that impressive. Had he gotten the Grim Reaper to enlist in the Startenders, now that would be something."

"Actually, he's going to be joining the next Academy class," I said.

Several jaws including Nellie's dropped at that. "Really?" Nellie said.

"No, not really."

"What's your estimated time of arrival at Gallop?" Paddy said.

"Nine AM day after tomorrow, New York time," I said. We had to have a set unit of time no matter we were in the galaxy in the universe. There were some issues involved with traveling between galaxies and how time passed for people on the ships and on Earth, but many of the Startenders have been dealing with quantum geography for a very long time and this was just another aspect of it. The barships compensated to keep our perceived time all lined up.

"Too long. Hermes?" Paddy said.

"I can be there in about an hour." The Greco-Roman god of travelers, thieves and physicians could travel far faster than our barships, but even he had some limitations. "I'll leave as soon as Vulcan has a probe ready."

"What do you mean, Vulcan?" Bubba Sue said. She, Vulcan, Pace, Kaye Chandler, Hermes and others were permanently assigned to Startender Station and were all together in the meeting room. The gremlin handed Hermes what looked like a golden torch with a large ball on the top.

"I'll send back coordinates as soon as I get there," Hermes said and left so fast he seemed to disappear. Barships could travel quickly to places we've been before or at least had coordinates on. It wasn't just the position of the place in three dimensions. There are a host of forces involved including inertia, gravity, and speed of the solar system traveling through space and many others. Without knowing all those, there is a risk of being destroyed in reentry. Or destroying someone or something else. The transworld wasn't exactly as instantaneous as Gani's elevator, but it wasn't too far off.

"Looks like we've got about an hour. What's going on with Hiven?" Hercules said.

"Moni insisted on staying behind. She refused to let any other Startenders stay behind, saying it was a lasa matter. However she did agree for us to bring some help, which is why I suspect Dagonet was late," Hex said.

"I got a hold of Mica and she rounded up another five lasa." Mica was Moni's mother and one of the original lasa goddesses. Most people don't realize that what we think are angels in graveyards were actually originally statues of lasa to help guard over graves. Mica and Dagonet, along with the Pink Reaper, Nemesis and Wisp were part of a group that formed back in the Great Depression called the League of Shadows. The survivors still had a strong bond. "We used Gani's elevator to get them there." Gani was the *Excalibur's* honcho. "The seven of them are hard at work to lay the planet's dead to rest."

"What about the survivor?" Nellie said.

"We also used Gani's elevator to get Quan off *The Accursed* and to Startender Station," Dagonet said.

"Quan's a mess, but she's strong. She's got a fighting chance," Hex said, speaking I'm assuming as both a magí and a shrink. "It helps that she was unconscious and didn't witness the dying."

"Murphy, speaking of messes, exactly what are you wearing?" Dagonet said.

"I don't know, but I love the head fin," Rumbles said.

"And people said my Pink Reaper outfit was out there," Kaye Chandler said with a smirk.

"I'm capturing an image of this to show it to Elsiebelle," Nellie said. My daughter was part of her crew.

"Always good to know I can count on you, Nellie. As for the outfit, I lost a bet with Coyote, but we have more important matters to discuss than my fashion emergency," I said.

"Very true. How did this bastard kill the populations of four planets?" Kaye Chandler said.

"He likes to vary his methods to a certain degree as far as the actual agent of death, but in all cases he introduces something deadly on a planet-wide scale. On Hiven, he did something to the water supply by seeding the clouds. The only reason we have a survivor is because she was hooked up to the local equivalent of an IV," Loki said. He reads and takes in information incredibly fast and is fluent in Goblin and hundreds of other languages.

"His first planet was called Brixton and was probably the most brutal. He introduced a psychogenic hallucinogen to the atmosphere. Within hours, everybody on the planet was trying to kill everyone else. From the Cyndicate records, it seems like families and friends simply tore into each other until they were dead, worse than rabid animals. And even the survivors didn't last long, eventually being driven so berserk that they ripped themselves to pieces. That was the only time he duplicated a method as that's also what he used on the continent he slaughtered by putting it in a number of reservoirs.

"On the second world, Paddon, he released airborne microbes that devoured oxygen and secreted carbon monoxide. That world suffocated to death. On the third world, Theca, people were given cybernetic implants as soon as they were born to interface with each other and the world's technology. Implants had a failsafe against electromagnetic pulses, but the killer figured out a defect. If an EMP hit the implants during a reboot, it could cause a power surge. The bigger the EMP, the bigger the surge. He managed to electrocute that planet's population from the inside of their own bodies," I said.

"For his latest murderous endeavor he developed some sort of slow-acting poison. I've transmitted the details to all of you. Alom didn't know much more than the basics about it. Buzz, will you have Xen research it and see if he can figure out how it works then reverse-engineer a way to neutralize it? My organic chemistry is pretty much limited to the basics," I said. Xen had been a planetary intelligence before transferring his consciousness to the small but cute robot body he occupied. Despite his harmless-looking appearance, he was quite possibly one of the most dangerous beings in the universe. Xen had helped my crew and me out of a jam and became a Startender. The robot didn't know everything, but he knew a lot. "Bast, I'm asking the same of you and the bastart network."

The cat-headed goddess nodded. "Of course, Murphy. I'll get Cynosure on it immediately. In fact, I'm ready to send several of my agents to the planet to help in the search."

"Do they need transportation?" Buzz said, looking at the notes and writing. His translating abilities extended to the written word.

The black-furred feline goddess grinned. "We can handle getting around, but thank you." Ever since we helped Bast out with her renegade descendants, we had the full resources of the bastart network at our disposal. That didn't mean that we were let in on any of their secrets though.

Buzz chuckled. "I redid the molecule's diagram using Earth's periodic table and chemistry standards. Sending it now."

The woman once known as the Pink Reaper cursed as soon as she saw it. "This is bad."

"You mean there is something worse than planetary extinction?" I said.

"This Davin is a chemical genius. If I'm translating this correctly…" Kaye Chandler had many doctorates, more than a few in various branches of chemistry, and was a genius. "… he's figured out a way to make trimethylcadmium."

"And how bad is that?" Paddy asked.

"Dimethylcadmium can go into the blood stream and the cadmium breaks off and gradually creates toxic compounds that usually kill the person. And if they survive, they would almost certainly develop cancer. Luckily, it's not used much because it's volatile. Friction makes it explode. Mixing it with water does the same. Spill some and let it dry out and decompose and it forms dimethyl cadmium peroxide. Friction makes that explode. If what I'm running in my head is accurate, it looks like he figured out a way to use triethyl ether instead of diethyl ether, which minimizes the halide salt."

"Well obviously," I said, not really understanding any of it.

"That would diminish or even get rid of the volatility factor. That means it could be put in food or water and it would bond. It could even be released as a gas and be breathed in," Kaye said.

"The cadmium would build up and kill them," Dagonet said.

Kaye nodded on the screen. "It would break down slowly, causing a gradual release of the cadmium, so they would die slowly and painfully. In humans, cadmium poisoning is a nasty way to go. Eating or drinking it would cause vomiting, nausea, cramps, diarrhea, then it irreversibly destroys the kidney and sucks the minerals out of bones making them soft and fragile. If it's too much, the victim dies. Breathing it in would cause the same symptoms plus flu-like symptoms, such as body aches, chills, weakness, abdominal pain, shortness of breath, and swelling of the nose, pharynx, and larynx. Low phosphate levels in the blood causes weakness, which can lead to a coma. Acidity in the blood causes gout. It increases chloride in the blood too. Assuming a similar carbon-based physiology for the Gallopians, we can extrapolate similar breakdown of their bodies."

"So what do we do for cadmium poisoning?" Nellie said.

"Treat the symptoms and hope the person recovers because

we don't have a cure," Kaye said. "And even if they do make it, it will likely cause cancer down the road."

"Wait. The cadmium breaks apart to bond with something else in the blood?" I said.

"An oversimplification and breaks apart isn't the right term, but basically," Kaye said.

"So can we figure out something else that the cadmium would rather hook up with than the blood? Neutralize it either in the environment or in the body?" I said.

"Cadmium likes organometals, but it's not that simple…" Kaye said.

"But it could be," Xen said, having been brought in on Buzz's screen.

Vulcan nodded. "If we built or found a compound that…"

The trio of them started talking in language that not even the lation stone could translate for me.

We left them to work out the science while the rest of us tried to figure out where best to put our efforts.

After about forty more minutes of planning strategy, our consoles all beeped and the coordinates of the Gallop system appeared.

Hermes had made good time. Every available barship engaged its transworld drive and arrived in the Gallop system soon after.

Gallop was significantly more technologically advanced than Earth. They had a planetary network of machines to make their lives easier. No planetary AI like Xen, but apparently they were working on it. They had devices to control the weather, the air quality and even provide meals. I was impressed with the place. Unlike most worlds we had seen, there was no poverty. Nobody was hungry. That is not to say that they didn't have economic classes, but their lowest echelon lived as well as the middle class on Earth. They had terraformed their own planet as well as used genetically engineered grains and animals so they had a surplus of food which they stored against future emergencies. The natives were partly humanoid, all with different shades of pink skin. They had two arms, but four legs. Their average height was between four and five feet.

The Slayer of Worlds was humanoid with two legs, so he would stand out here. That's assuming he didn't have some sort of illusion tech or magic. We discussed how we should approach matters, particularly whether or not we should make our presence known. The planet had a governmental setup not too much different from Ben City. It was an actual democracy with professional politicians, but the populace voted on the laws. They had no executive branch. If we came forward to the representatives, we were fairly certain it would be announced to the world at large. Not only would it start a panic, but it would alert the so-called Slayer to our presence.

We decided on stealth. All the barships went to dust mode. We spilt up and scanned the atmosphere and the water for signs of the poison with sensors our science and mystic teams rigged up.

Chet Coyle is a mage with the power of illusion and was also a member of the League of Shadows. He was older than the Pink Reaper and not in as good shape. He wasn't a Startender, but he was in the Startender Society, as was his grandson who shared the same name and powers. They were able to make illusion bands by transferring magic to gold or silver bracelets that let Startenders pass as natives. Coyle the younger was able to make one about every twenty minutes. The senior Coyle took about fifteen minutes and was able to make five at a time. A number of Startenders were able to shape-shift and didn't need the illusion bands, including Loki and Coyote. Sun WuKong had split off ten versions of himself to go out and search the world, each of them looking like a native. His original body sat on board *Fools' Glory* in a quiet room, allowing him to meditate and control the bodies. Although he could literally form hundreds, if not thousands, of copies of himself, Sun still only had one mind to control them all with. The more bodies, the less control he had. For fighting purposes the bodies could go on automatic pilot to a certain degree, but for something like this he needed more concentration.

Gallop had contact with other worlds, but mainly for trade

purposes. It had a fleet of ships for planetary defense and another for intersystem trade. All the barships were scanning for any vessels not native. It helped that we had the specs of the ship from Alom, but it had a pretty sophisticated cloaking device. What made it even harder to track was that the cloak had a number of different frequencies that combined to mask the ship. By mixing them, there were hundreds of possible combinations it could be hiding behind. And there could be a way to continuously rotate through the combinations, meaning we'd have to be scanning for the same frequency at the same time it cycled through.

So far we hadn't found it.

Each crew's melog stayed with the barships. Everybody else was searching planetside including the Startender Academy cadets which included Herschel. He was a yumin – a race of humanoid chicken people descended from Manuk Manuk. She's the blue cosmic chicken who laid the egg that hatched the universe by helping trigger the big bang. Yes, sometimes this stuff is hard to get my head around too. Herschel had helped out my crew and I recommended him for the academy. So far he was doing me proud and was at the top of his class. He was leading a team of cadets.

Xen, Vulcan, and Kaye had figured out a compound that could be used to bond with and neutralize the cadmium if we couldn't stop the release. The key ingredient was something called solance. Bast had Cynosure searching the galaxy for several tons of the stuff.

That job finished, Xen had joined us planetside.

Bubba Sue was working to build an interface to allow the robot to tap into the planetary network. In the movies, computers – even those from other worlds –just happen to be compatible with each other, but in real life the interfaces are a bit more challenging. Binary code is only one of hundreds of ways to make operating systems run. Xen had a lot of experience controlling planetary technology networks, something that might be beneficial to helping us stop the toxin. The system would let him monitor water, weather and food distribution systems.

I was searching the capital city with my honcho. Loki had turned into one of the natives and I had one of the Coyles' illusion bands. Eric cut in on the tiny speakers in our ear canals. "Boss, Hermes found the ship." Hermes had been cycling through the different cloaking frequency combos as quick as he could, trying to find the slayer. "Unfortunately, Davin wasn't onboard. Hermes wants to know if you'd mind if he left him a welcome home present."

"What, like exploding flowers?" Loki said.

"We'd have to check to see if Foster –" The Startenders' resident plant elemental. "– could pull it off. But I'm sure Hermes has something better in mind."

"Someone better. He wants to leave Sun WuKong on the ship in case the slayer comes back. Since Sun is currently on *Fools' Glory*, he wanted your permission."

I smiled. Sun WuKong is probably the most powerful and versatile Startender, although Xen is a close second in terms of power. Of course, there were those who felt Xen was holding back and might actually be more powerful than Sun, although even if that were true, as far as I was concerned the Monkey King still rank tops in versatility. Even if this slayer of worlds had powers of his own, it would be unlikely he'd be able to take out Sun WuKong, especially if the Monkey King had the element of surprise. As the Startenders' best shape changer, he could turn into a piece of furniture or a little fly on the wall to lay in wait.

"Granted," I said.

"I'm going to shuttle him over then, so I'll be in orbit if you need me," Eric said.

"No problem. We'll keep up the search down here," I said.

"All we're doing is basically walking around in search grids," Loki said. "There's got to be a better way to track this SOB down. We need to think like him. You helped stop a serial killer in New York by getting inside his head."

That killer had a twisted sense of humor and Jason Cervantes, back when he was on the NYPD instead of chief of police for Startender Station, asked for my help. "You've got a point. He's not killing for money as he's giving the financial benefits to Alom, so we'll have to assume he's killing for kicks. He doesn't seem to like it up close and personal, but I can't imagine him wanting to leave before watching everyone die."

Loki nodded. "We've got Startenders and barships guarding against tampering with food, water and the weather control system. We have to consider the possibility Davin has already delivered the toxin. That means he may just be sitting around waiting for the show to start. Where would he have the best view?"

Gallop actually had a unified planetary government. Believe it or not, that's a relative rarity. Not counting the Goblin Empire, which holds sway over hundreds of worlds, maybe fifteen percent of planets have one central government.

This world used a type of holographic technology which utilized millions of tiny liquid jets and lights to project 3-D images using ionized particles. They looked real unless you tried to touch them – then the fluid dispersed around your hand.

"The planetary entertainment network has both a news channel and a geographic channel." People could flip a switch and have miniature versions of any place on the planet appear in their home. "Maybe he hacked into the broadcast feed command center. Then he'd be able to watch virtually anywhere on the planet."

Then a big gaping hole in our prevention strategy hit me. "Loki, where does the fluid for the holo-projectors come from?"

"I don't know, but I don't think it's from the main water supply, because it's not plain water. They mix in other chemicals, so it can hold electrical charges to form the shapes and light up," Loki said.

I hit my badge. "Bubba Sue, who's watching the fluid supply for the holographic projectors?"

"We've got Kintaro and Main guarding it." Both real old time heroes stationed on the *Argo II*. "Why?" Bubba Sue said.

"I was worried we'd overlooked it as a delivery system for the toxin," I said.

"Don't worry, Murphy. We thought of that too, as well as the sewage and a few other things," Bubba Sue said.

"Who's guarding the sewage?" Loki said.

"A team of cadets," Bubba Sue said. "Herschel's in charge of the team."

"Did he complain?" I said.

"Nope. He's used to taking orders he doesn't like, I guess," Bubba Sue said.

"I'm in. I have control of the planetary computer systems," I heard Xen say over Bubba Sue's badge. "I'm searching now."

There was a large zapping static noise. It was Xen's equivalent of a curse. "We're too late. The toxin has already been introduced through the water, food, and entertainment distribution centers. The Slayer wasn't taking any chances. According to the log, it happened twelve hours before any Startender arrived on the planet."

That last part was a general broadcast to all Startenders.

"I am not going to lose another world," Xen whispered, emotion making his voice crackle. He wasn't referring to the Slayer's other victim worlds, but his own. He had been a planetary AI running most basic things. His people decided to disconnect him and ended up destroying themselves. Xen had been helpless to save them. It's what spurred him to build his robot body and go out exploring the universe.

"Then there's no need to be undercover. Dion and Kamile, go meet with the governing body. Xen, shut down the food, water and entertainment distribution centers. Send out a general broadcast, sound only, telling the people not to eat or drink anything," came Paddy's voice over the badge.

"Paddy, it's too late for that," Hermes said. "I'm here with Xen and Bubba Sue. It's been over a planetary day. The toxin has been introduced to the entire population. By my calculations, people will start dropping within two days. The entire planet will be affected within five local days. I'm still trying to study their physiology to figure out exactly how the cadmium will affect them, but my best guess at the moment is we are looking at planetary extinction in no more than eight Earth days."

"Bast, how are ye coming on finding several tons of solance?" Paddy said.

"It's even rarer than I thought, but we found some on the planet Ogra in the Chant system. Vapellan Prime, one of their city states, has a manufacturing processes that actually creates it as a waste product. Ogra is one of the richest worlds in this part of the universe and applies more controls to wealth than the Cyndicate. They have little use for solance and usually have to pay to have it removed. In its pure form, it's toxic because it bonds to other things besides cadmium in the bloodstream. Once they know we want it, they will likely make us pay dearly for it," Bast said over the comm link.

"Bast, are ye comfortable opening negotiations?" Paddy said.

"Of course, but what are we willing to pay for it?" Bast said.

"To save a planet of three billion? Pretty much anything we have," Paddy said.

"Understood, Paddy. I already have my people searching to see what they might be interested in that we can provide and to wrangle myself an invitation to meet Trade Lord Vapella, the local city state's ruler. It normally takes months, but I plan to be in much sooner," Bast said.

"Bubba Sue, can we adopt the Startender Emergency Broadcast System for Gallop?" I said. "It's possible that somebody, somewhere, may have been too busy working or doing something else, and hasn't been eating food and drinking water from the system," I said.

"No need, Murphy. I can broadcast," Xen said. "Buzz, will you do the honors?"

As a Garba, Buzz has the mystic ability to speak and understand any language. The lation stones he provided allowed Startenders to at least understand others, but others had to make contact with the stone to understand us.

Off to our side, one of the pink natives fell. Loki managed to catch the person before they hit the ground and lowered her down. Loki hit his badge. "It's already starting."

"I think our best bet is to go to the broadcast center," Loki said.

I nodded, as Buzz's voice boomed out of speakers to warn the natives. Xen shut down the fluid hologram projectors, as well as water and food systems.

I called Eric to have *Fools' Glory* take us to the broadcast center.

While our Startenders badges provided us with a breathable

atmosphere, the killer might not have something similar and have to breathe the Gallopian atmosphere. Maybe when we caught this killer, we'd get lucky and he'd have an antidote that we could use or manufacture immediately. Hermes' search of his ship came up empty in that department.

Eric dropped us off a local block away. The broadcast station headquarters had decent security, with scanners and security guards. It wasn't something that would be too difficult to get past, but there was a chance of us getting caught. That chance decreased dramatically if I waited outside.

"Loki, you check out inside. I'll keep an eye out here for anything strange," I said.

Loki nodded. "Might as well make yourself comfortable. It's a big place, and it'll take me a while to recon."

The Norse trickster shape-shifted to a local flying pest that was similar to an insect, but not quite the same. He flew in over the scanners and by the guards.

As I stood there over the next couple of hours, I watched more of the natives drop and listened to reports from my fellow Startenders over my ear nub. No one had found the killer, but Hermes' predictions weren't too far off. People all over the planet were collapsing from cadmium poisoning, but it was worse than we thought. One of the natives fell near me and when I tried to help her, she started screaming and thrashing as if she were having most terrible nightmare imaginable. And she probably was.

I hit my badge. "Kaye, this is Murphy. The victims seem to be progressing to a point where they're having some major fear-induced nightmares. Since you're something of an expert on the subject, I thought maybe you and Hermes could look into it. I've got someone here in front of me."

"I'm game. I'll just wait for the Hermes' ex..." Kaye stopped mid-word, then she and Hermes appeared by my side in time for her to finish it. "...press"

Part of Hermes' skill set as a god of physicians meant he was a living MRI, CAT scan and just about any other medical test rolled into one.

"Good call, Murphy. These people are presenting similarly to victims of my fear gas," the former Pink Reaper said.

Kaye Chandler fought bad guys starting back during the Great Depression, using gadgets and science developed by her and her uncle. She used a lot of weaponized gases, the most useful of which was her fear gas.

"We should be thankful it's not exactly the same effect or these pink people would never stop screaming," Kaye said. One of the strange attributes of her gas is anyone who was doused with it had their terror heightened by viewing the color pink.

Hermes went into details about how the cadmium bonding was inducing the fear by releasing something in her brain, but it was medical speak. I was only getting the gist of about a third of it, but Kaye was understanding it pretty well.

"Do you think your counter agent would work to help these people?" I said.

Kaye didn't answer, but creased her brow.

"My get best guess is the increased metabolic reaction caused by elevated heart rate and blood pressure will shorten their lives significantly. The population will be wiped out in five instead of eight days," Hermes said.

Kaye sighed.

"I've shared a lot of my secrets with the Startenders, but not the details about my fear gas and what makes me immune from the effects myself. Using the gas has helped me stay alive as long as I have. I even figured out how to make it work on mystic-based physiology. If the immunity gas formula became well known, it would negate the effectiveness of my fear gas as a weapon. But I can't cut these people's chance for survival almost in half, either. Hermes, you think you could adapt my gas for their alien physiology?" Kaye said.

"I'd say I have a better shot at it than just about anybody else," Hermes said.

"Then I'll give you and you alone the formula, but you'll have to give me your word as a Startender that you'll never share or use it for any other purpose than helping these people," Kaye said.

Hermes paused, probably running through about a million scenarios in his mind. "With the exception that I reserve the right to use it in defense of people should your fear gas ever fall into the wrong hands, I can do that."

"Get us to the nearest barship and we'll use the lab on board to see what we can come up with," Kaye said.

"Murphy, hold the fort," Hermes said and flew off so fast it looked like they disappeared into thin air.

"Murphy, Davin was using an illusion charm of his own, but it didn't change his smell. I've taken the charm, but he's running away. I'm chasing him outside toward you. I'd appreciate it if you'd slow him down," Loki said over our badges.

"Will do," I said.

"Riga and I are airborne and not too far away. We are heading towards the broadcast center to help," Savannah said over the comm channel.

As part of its security, the building only had one working entrance and exit. I lay down on the ground in front of it and started mimicking the symptoms of the Gallopian I'd been watching over. Someone who looked an awful lot like a human, except his ears were set too far back and his nose was flatter came running out the door, but stopped when he saw me. Looking down, he smiled. "What a beautiful dance of death you do."

"Thanks, Davin," I said, my legs already sweeping his and knocking him to the ground. "I hope you don't mind if I lead."

One of the things the Cyndicate boss provided for Davin was a lation stone, so I figured he'd understand me. I was already up and smashing his face into the local equivalent of pavement. Unfortunately, it was a lot softer than concrete or asphalt. The man known as the Slayer of Worlds pulled a blade out of his sleeve and tried to stab me. I managed to block the blow and move out of range. The Startenders badge had a force field that would block a regular knife, but who knew what kind of blade this guy was wielding.

"You're done," I said.

Loki walked out in his regular form. "More than done."

Riga, with Savannah on her dragon back, dove down from

the sky and landed on the street where he was starting to move. A little fire came out of her mouth and nostrils. "And if you try to run, you'll be well done."

Davin pulled out a small device and let loose a cloud of something at the dragon. Riga incinerated it with a blast of fire from her mouth.

"Dragonstar, you are ruining this for me." It was an understandable case of mistaken identity. Riga's badge was smaller, but worn in the same spot around the neck as a Dragonstar, an organization similar to the Startenders. It was composed entirely of dragons, who by the way are from Earth originally. They just left the planet ages ago. Dragonstars are respected, feared and much better known than Startenders. They have no compunction against killing and their badges do more than ours. Riga was dating one. "I was supposed to have five days to enjoy Gallop's death dance. But I will not forget this. I would find the worlds each of you come from and slay each of them, making sure everyone dies screaming."

The killer reached for something that could've been a belt buckle if there'd been a belt attached. Davin flipped it open and hit a button, then disappeared a flash of light.

Loki and I looked at each other and smiled.

"That went rather well," Loki said.

Savannah jumped off Riga's back. "Well? He got away!"

"But got away to where?" I said.

"Probably to his ship that's cloaked in orbit." Savannah put it together. "Where the Monkey King is waiting for him.

We all shared a dark laugh.

"He had considerable fighting trickery. Davin tried no less than twenty-three ways to kill me in less than three minutes. Only two of them were from him directly. The rest were tech and magic booby traps he built into his own body," Sun WuKong said. "They combined with enough force to throw me across his ship when I broke his arms and his legs. It would have killed someone else, even with a Startender badge. You were lucky he thought Riga was a Dragonstar and ran from you."

"Did he tell you anything useful?" Loki said. The Slayer of Worlds had been brought on board *Fools' Glory* for his interrogation. Right now, there was a team of three interrogating him. Buzz was doing most of the talking, but Hex and Dagonet were in the room. Each of them brought something different to the table. Hex can usually tell if someone is lying and his power will sometimes give him flash visions of the past. No matter what Davin said in any language, Buzz could understand it better than someone with a lation stone. And Dagonet had over a thousand years of practice in reading people.

Our Startender oaths prevented us from leading off with things like torture, but it didn't mean we couldn't advance to it as more people started to die. Didn't mean we would either. Gani was working on a truth spell, but Hex had sensed several layers of magical protection built into his body and umbra, which is the shadow a soul casts. Some of them would've been quite painful to acquire.

"He hasn't given up much of anything except the threat to destroy all our worlds. He even seems to think that I was from a place called Stone Egg, but he didn't know exactly where that was," Sun said. "Unfortunately."

"Do you think it could be where your people vanished to while you were buried under the mountain?" I said.

The Monkey King shrugged. After doing some serious damage to the home of the Chinese pantheon, the Buddha beat him and buried him under a mountain for five hundred years. During that time, his monkey subjects mostly vanished. To this day, he doesn't know what happened to them. It's been rumored that they went to another world, but he has yet to find them. There are other intelligent monkeys on Earth, but most were descended from Hanuman's tribe, not his. And they've mostly left as well for greener jungles. The rest were the results of magic, like Jane the monkey princess. She was originally a lab monkey Sun freed during the Fools' Day episode. Jane spent enough time around the magic in Faerie to become intelligent and ended up joining the Startenders.

"I'm certainly going to be looking into it."

"What about reverse-engineering a cure?" I said.

"We're having problems. Hermes scanned him and had trouble isolating any antidote he might've injected into himself. It's tough to see past his defenses and wards he carved into himself. In fact, it took Hermes almost ten minutes to figure a way to get past all of his defenses to get a sample. As soon as the blood and tissue was taken a few feet away from him, it incinerated itself."

This guy was good. Anyone who gets a hold of someone's genetic material – not everyone in the universe has DNA – can use it for all sorts of good and evil purposes. It can be used to control or kill remotely, which is why most people involved with the mystic are very careful what they do with things like cut hair or nail clippings. And why we took some from Alom.

The only thing that could be remotely considered a plus was the gas that Hermes and the former Pink Reaper whipped up was being distributed. Bubba Sue modified the fluid-based holo-screens to emit gas. It wasn't the most effective system, but it was spread all over the planet, at least indoors. Xen used the weather system to blanket the atmosphere of the entire planet. It used up almost all of our emergency chemical supplies and we still weren't sure it would do any good. We were gambling on the assumption that we'd get the solance to make the anti-toxin. I mean what kind of monster wouldn't help save three billion people?

My badge started blinking blue. That meant someone had pressed their blue button and all head honchos had a meeting to get to.

I went back to my office.

It took five minutes before we were all there. The interrogation team had their honchos standing in for them – Gani for the *Excalibur*, Kyna for the *Bitter End* and Aziel for *The Accursed*.

At the last second Buzz, Hex, and Dagonet joined me in my office. As they pulled up chairs, I asked, "Who's with the prisoner?"

"We decided to give Loki and Sun WuKong a try," Hex said.

"They couldn't have gotten any less than we did," Dagonet said. "Although he lost his cool when we let him know that there was a survivor on Hiven. Hoped it would make him angry enough for Hex to probe past his defenses."

"Sadly, it didn't work. Davin may not be a magí but I've never encountered anyone with his sigil and body-warding skills. And not knowing his species, I'm having trouble reading his body language," Hex said.

"He is among the foulest-speaking individuals I've ever met," Buzz said as the mirrored view screens lit up.

Bast had called the meeting.

"I made some progress on Ogra. Vapellan Prime apparently had a few citywide celebrations and is very low on fermented beverages. I brought some samples to the Trade Lord and she was rather partial to the whiskey. I made a deal for every last ounce Startender Station has. In exchange, Trade Lord Vapella agreed to give us enough solance to save the Gallopians. Paddy, I know that whiskey was earmarked to make back some personal wealth for you after you used your fortune to evacuate New York City…"

"It's only money." Paddy is simultaneously the most generous and cheapest person I've ever met. He'd hunt down somebody who owed him a buck and give his last cent to save a life. I know he was thrilled that he was able to engineer a better way to brew whiskey in space and what he had would bring in fifty million US dollars. Station currency was still finding its value in the world economic system. "Unfortunately, the whiskey's not mine alone. I have a hundred people in the station who helped make it and each of them is slated to share in the profits. Each of them has to agree before it we can use it, because I don't have enough cash to simply buy it from them."

Paddy had once been the richest person on earth, but he used his wealth to fund the Startenders, including our barships and space station, not to mention fund the evacuation of New York, including food, medical supplies, and even housing for the refugees. He still owned a lot, but did not have much actual liquid cash holdings. And he viewed the currency involved in station commerce to not be his, but the station's. "I'm going to talk to them. I'll be back in less than a half-hour. Bast, be prepared to broker the deal."

We had almost eleven thousand people on Startender Station. And what was probably one of the most unique governments ever seen on Earth or above it. The station had been declared a country by the United Nations and was owned entirely by Paddy Moran. There was no unemployment, except for children. There was free education, entertainment and much more. Everyone got a salary and free room and board. And people who worked on certain exportables got profit-sharing and partial ownership of what they made. Paddy had been training a hundred people to brew whiskey. He hadn't told them all his secrets and probably never would. In the few short months they'd been working, each apprentice brewer had learned enough to ensure that they'd make a nice living if they ever left the station to move down to Earth.

Paddy called them altogether in the station where the brewery was set up and explained the situation.

"So what you're telling us is you want to give away everything we've worked for almost a year to make. We have enough here to sell on Earth and make a small fortune," said Walt, one of Paddy's apprentice brewers.

"True. Wholesale value is about fifty million US."

"Which comes to over two hundred grand for each of us."

"If ye didn't reinvest it back in the brewery," Paddy said.

"And you want us to give up the whiskey and the money we'd make for a bunch of aliens that none of us has ever met?" Walt said.

"Yes," said Paddy. "But if we don't do it, three billion people on the planet Gallop are going to die. We can trade the whiskey to get something we need to make medicine that will hopefully save them."

"Hopefully? We have to give up everything and we're not even sure those people are going to live?" Walt said.

"There are few guarantees in life. 'Tis the right thing to do," Paddy said.

"But Paddy, do we even have enough grain left to make any more? And does the whiskey division have the funds to buy more?" said Angie, another apprentice brewer.

"We have a little bit left, enough to make about ten percent of what we would be giving away. While we don't have the money to buy everything we need right away, we can take what we make off that ten percent, reinvest it to make a quarter of what we have now. Twice more and we'll be back where we are now,"

"But that would take almost three years," Walt said.

"It would. But if we don't do it, these people on the planet Gallop will not be alive in three weeks. And for that time, ye will all still live on the station and have all the creature comforts you need. Time is of the essence. An entire planet will be dead in less than five days. I need ye answers now. If you vote to give it away, stand to my left. If you vote to keep it and sell, go to my right. I know all of ye and trust ye will all do the right thing. However, if the vote is not unanimous, we will divide up the supply and hope we can renegotiate. If we can't, then hopefully we will at least be able to save a portion of the planet Gallop's people," Paddy said.

"How do we decide who lives and who dies?" Angie said.

"I don't know, but it is a decision that will have to be made. The first decision to be made is yours," Paddy said.

The first one to move to Paddy's left was Walt. As he walked by Paddy, he put his hands on the old man's shoulder. "Paddy, I appreciate everything you've done for us. You saved us all when New York was destroyed and gave us a new home. I want to be rich even more than the next guy, but not like this. You've taught me more than just how to make good whiskey. You've shown me what it is to be a good man." They were cheers of people agreeing with Walt. Every last brewer's apprentice moved to Paddy's left.

Paddy smiled and nodded at them. "Thank ye all. Ye've made me proud." Paddy hit his badge. "Bast, make the deal."

Not all deals are easy to make.

"That bitch!" Nellie said, smashing the table in front of her on the view screen. She and her crew on the *Perdu* had been the ones chosen to make the whiskey delivery.

"I trust you are not referring to me," Bast said. She was still on board the *Perdu* and sitting at Nellie's side for the latest blue light meeting.

My daughter Elsiebelle had called me on a private communications channel. Things had turned ugly in Vapellan Prime. Trade Lord Vapella took the full delivery, then tried some and declared it unfit for consumption. Then she declared that she wouldn't need to give it back, nor deliver any of the solance to us, then ordered the *Perdu* to leave. Nellie had wanted to steal it, but Bast is one of the Low Startender Council. The cat-headed goddess pulled rank and told her to pull out.

"Of course not, but she didn't have to order me out of the system," Nellie said. "My crew and I could've gotten the solance we need."

"Of that I have no doubt. However, Vapella would know the Startenders took it. This planet holds a lot of influence in this part of the universe. You would effectively have us blackballed by the Ogra Planetary Trade Board and everyone they do business with. That means we would not be welcome on those worlds or near those systems, which encompasses hundreds of planets. And they can afford the best bounty hunters in the galaxy. Some of them would be trouble even for the Startenders. We can try to negotiate again," Bast said.

"No," said Paddy from his view screen. "The woman has shown herself to be untrustworthy. Another negotiation would end the same. We just have to expand upon the current negotiation."

"Dad, send us back. I can get her to give it to us," Nellie said.

Paddy shook his head. "No, my dear. If our next effort doesn't work, you and Hermes will lead the effort to steal it."

"But Paddy…" Bast said.

"Bast, I know how crippling that will be to the Startenders, but in the face of stopping three billion deaths we can deal with being persona non grata. But I don't think it will come to that," Paddy said.

"So if not me, who are you sending?" Nellie said.

"Murphy."

"Murphy!?" Nellie said.

"Murphy, I want you and your crew to leave immediately for Ogra. Ye need to beat this Vapella at her own game. Ye need to do what ye did to that Cyndicate boss. Don't just get what we're owed. Take her down and teach her a lesson that will let others know what happens to anyone who messes with the Startenders," Paddy said.

"We'll do our best. Bast, fill me in on what we need to know," I said.

"Like the Cyndicate, they have a very stringent set of rules that they have to follow and do their best to get around. And like the Cyndicate they don't let outsiders know what all those rules are, although they offer much more protections for both sides. Cynosure has all the rules on file and I'm sending it over to *Fool's Glory* now. I'm having my people working on translating it into English, but it will take a while, probably longer than we have. Loki, are you up for the translating job?" the cat goddess said.

Loki's voice came over the comm.

"I'm already going through it." Loki had the ability to learn another language, both written and spoken, very quickly. It forced Loki to use a little bit of his manna, so it was something he did sparingly. Without manna, gods fade away to oblivion.

"Paddy, I'd like to add Sun WuKong, Foster, and Bubba Sue to my crew for this one," I said.

Paddy nodded and hit his badge. "Bubba Sue and Foster report to *Fools' Glory* immediately." Sun WuKong was already here and Foster had a plant body on each barship. He body-hopped between crews.

A second after Paddy's request, Foster's body moved. "Thanks for including me on this, Murphy."

"Wouldn't have it any other way," I said.

As we waited for the gremlin to arrive, we transferred Hex, Buzz, Dagonet and our prisoner onto *The Accursed*.

Bubba Sue arrived via Gani's magic elevator and did an

entrance she hasn't done much since she married Vulcan. She somersaulted toward me, then leapt up into my arms and kissed me. In the old days it would have been on the lips. Now it was on the cheek.

Eric set course to Ogra without being asked.

"Now that we're all here, we need to figure out a way to get the solance and take down Trade Lord Vapella," I said.

"What if we can only manage to get the solance?" Savannah said.

Coyote chuckled. "Youngster, look around at the trickster talent we have here. Sun WuKong and Loki are almost as good as me. Bubba Sue is not far behind them. And despite his outfit, Murphy is damn good most of the time, especially for being only human. Even the rest of you lot show some promise. There is no excuse for us not to own this bitch before we're done."

"I think I disagree with the fleabag's ranking system," Loki said.

"I know I do," Sun said, grinning.

"We can have it out right now, fleabag," Bubba Sue said.

I held up a single hand. The bickering stopped. "What everyone is trying to say is we are all Startenders. We put egos aside and protect life. We have never had a bigger protection detail than we do right now. And there is nobody in this room who won't do everything possible to save the Gallopians. The only restriction on all of us is to not kill anyone. Right now, I pity Vapella. Let's get started."

FURLOUGH

*C*onsidering I love my job, I was hating this assignment or at least the reason for it. I've done well for someone who started out as a bartender. I helped found the Startenders and have command of the barship *Fools' Glory*. Not an easy job for a human to ride herd on a gaggle of tricksters in space, but I've always managed.

This collection job had me worried, despite my earlier speech. Billions of lives hung in the balance.

I guess in a sense we were very lucky the SOB was sadistic, otherwise the people of Gallop could be dead already instead of doing the dance of death as Davin called it.

We'd received word that the gas Hermes and Kaye whipped up was working, extending our five day deadline to six and a half. Not as good as the eight we thought we'd have at first, but still an improvement.

Today was day three.

Of course we'd come up with a plan, but it had taken some time to implement what we needed so it had a chance of working. It wasn't a particularly nice one and originally I had some qualms about inflicting it on the woman in question, but used *the needs of the many* argument to justify it.

Within seconds of speaking with her, my need for justifications was vaporized by Trade Lord Vapella's attitude.

"As I told your colleges we simply won't pay for inferior merchandise, Captain Murphy." The humanoid woman on the view screen had beige skin and was trying for charming. Charming people pay for their shiploads of whiskey, not pull a con to try to get it for free. If anyone was going to be pulling a con, it'd be us.

"Actually it's Head Honcho. Or sir. Or Murphy the Wonderful." Usually I dispense with titles, but this lady, or lord as she preferred, was ticking me off more with every utterance. "We're not a military organization." The Startenders started out as a bunch of barflies in

Bulfinche's Pub helping those in trouble and now we go out into the stars in flying barships looking for people who needed our help. Which is even more impressive when you realize the rest of Earth hasn't managed to get people past Mars. The Startenders have many powerful resources, but we hadn't been doing this very long and our reputation is in its larval stage. We were still learning our way, but we were very aware that there were forces and worlds out here with power that dwarfed ours. There were at least three military organizations we knew of that could destroy entire solar systems. If we let Vapella get away with stiffing us, not only would three billion people die, but we'd look like easy marks. We'd be constantly having to deal with the interstellar equivalent of someone trying to take our lunch money. By making an example of this trade lord we'd make others think twice about messing with us, especially when lives are on the line. At least that was the plan. "And I can assure you that anything with the Bulfinche's brand on it is far from inferior."

"Compared to Ogra, you and your backwards world are practically barbarians. I wouldn't be surprised to hear you stole your ships from a more advanced culture. You're lucky I even allowed you to do business with me. Why, most of our everyday technology must seem like magic to you."

"No, I've seen magic. It's much more impressive." Although this world had technology much more advanced than Earth, the existence of magic was not widely accepted here. Ogra's tech was very imposing and included orbit based battle platforms that could hold off an armada. A full frontal assault on our part would have been foolhardy.

Vapella continued as if I hadn't spoken. "Let me assure you that my experts, from the greatest civilization in the galaxy, I might add, found your libations wanting."

"So you went off-world then?" I said and got a glare for my trouble. Neither my trouble nor I wanted it and I did my best not to return it.

"No, I did not."

"And who would these experts be?" I asked.

"Why me, of course." Her smile was the best money on

her world could buy, complete with shiny green teeth, but the condescension in it was all natural talent. "Your baleful beverage is barely better than urine."

"So you are an expert on the taste of urine? Interesting. How many glasses a day do you have to drink to get that good? Where do you get the best urine? Do you find much work or do you have to hang around public rest rooms to practice? If it would help you perfect your craft, we'd be happy to trade some for what we need."

"I was being invective."

"You look it, but we've had our shots."

Puns never translated well and I got a blank stare. I knew I was nervous and angry from the amount of wisecracking I was doing.

"Three billion lives on Gallop hang in the balance. We agreed to trade the whiskey for the solance." Hermes was tending to the people as best he could. Assuming we got the solance, it would still take him the better part of a day to mix up the cure. For anyone else it would take a lot longer. Distributing it will take an estimated day and a half and that's figuring in everyone we have available helping. That meant we didn't have much time left to fix the issue with Lord Idiot here then get the solance to Gallop. "We approached you in good faith in order to save those people. As I understand matters, you took delivery after sampling the whiskey. Quite a lot of it."

"Exactly. By the time I took delivery, I was drunk, and simply was not of sound mind. Under Ograte trade rules that invalidates the contract. And worse, I felt quite bad the next day."

I put my hand on my forehead and tried not to yell. "You decide to get drunk, get a hangover because of that choice, and then use it as an excuse not to pay your bill. And cause billions of deaths."

"I would not have put it so crudely. It's not that I don't feel for them. Perhaps the Gallopians have something else they'd like to trade. Maybe accepting my sovereignty. I've been looking to expand my holdings and an entire world would be nice." Meaning she'd control every aspect of their lives and their only purpose would be making her a profit. "It's better than dying. You should ask them what they prefer."

I gritted my teeth and took a deep breath. "Planetary

democracy. Too many people incapacitated by the toxin to get enough votes to pass a measure to get you an answer in time."

"Pity. Just remember if you want my trade in the future you should come up with something that doesn't have such negative side-effects for the drinker."

"We'd be happy to sell you water." At a sizeable mark up. "Bad choices on your part do not relieve you of your obligation to settle your debts. Now pay or return the merchandise. Failure to comply puts you in violation of your contract with us."

"Are you threatening me?"

"Just stating the matter simply." Ogra's trade regulations had strict penalties for threatening a trade lord. "That way, I'm certain you understand."

"Since your Startender colleagues were foolish enough to release your swill to me in my impaired condition without first getting their payment, this loss is your own fault. I should actually bill you for the cost of having that toxic beverage hauled off."

I forced a smile. "We'll take it away now if you'd like."

"Why, so you can inflict it on some other unsuspecting customer? I think not. I will keep it and not pay you a thing. If you don't like it, sue me. Oh wait, you aren't Ograte citizens. You can't. A pity. I do wish there was something I could do for you."

And as easy as that, we had her. "Actually, there is."

"I was just being falsely polite."

"We were engaged in business negotiations. By Ograte trade regulations, any offer of assistance made must be followed through on, regardless of the result of said negotiations," I said. Their trade regulations are tens of thousands of pages long which is why it took even Loki a while to get through them. We'd been hidden in orbit for two precious days putting our plan together. Sun and Coyote mixed with the locals and learned what they could and the lot of us prepped for the ultimate con. "And that is something a non-citizen can take to the trade board. Especially since, as you were told by Bast, we would be using Veritasian verification to record all interactions."

Watching Vapella struggle not to squirm was entertaining. She muted communications, but we could see her yelling at her lawyers to find her a loophole to the loophole we outsiders should never have known about. Several minutes later, three of them groveled and bowed before the trade lord, having been unsuccessful in finding her an out. "What do you want?"

"That was cutting it close."

Obviously, Lord Vapella wasn't used to dealing with off-worlders familiar with Ograte trade law because both her eyebrows shot up and she frowned. "Excuse me?"

"By the third million and thirteenth stanza, you have a limited time to respond to my request without giving insult. Another moment and…"

Our hookup was clear enough that I could see her jaw clench. "That would have been… unfortunate."

"Actually, it was pretty close to call. We could review our recordings to double check the time to make sure you aren't in violation."

I could see her glare off screen at her communication techs. Assuming we had been ignorant of the statute, I was betting they hadn't timed it.

"No need, Head Honcho Murphy. I will hear your request for aid."

"We aren't asking for much, just your hospitality. We've come a long way to settle this matter. My crew and I could use a break planetside before we head back to Gallop." I let that hang in the air. "We request your hospitality according to Article 45,022 of the Ograte Trade Code. Or we could take that same break going before the Ograte Trade Commission to see how they feel about the violation. Or possible violations as I still haven't checked the time."

I could practically see the wheels spinning in her head, calculating gain and loss. Article 45,022 meant we were the trade lord's guests, with Vapella responsible for our room, board, entertainment and all other expenses we incurred as long as we stayed in her holdings. Vapella was weighing the cost of a fight with the board vs. the cost of us as her guests.

"How many in your crew?"

I choose my words carefully. "You can see us all here." Most ships needed crews much larger than ours, but they weren't built by Vulcan.

Vapella was silent as she counted and did the math. The entire crew was in the main bar, our version of the bridge.

If this bunch couldn't handle Vapella, we deserved to lose our lunch money. The problem is the people on Gallop didn't deserve to die.

Assuming she realized Foster was a crew member, there were only nine of us. Normally, not a large number of guests for someone with holdings the size of Texas.

"I suppose I could have you as my guests," conceded the trade lord.

"Article 45,022 guests," I specified.

Vapella sighed. "Yes. You won't be any trouble now, will you?"

I had a ship full of tricksters and Vapella had stolen from us and in the doing, endangered billions. It was a stupid question. Still, we were recording this. "I can assure you we will be making the most of our visit."

"I'll send the port clearance for your ship to land and I'll send someone to pick you up. Of course, all my vehicles and staff are rather busy, so it may be some time you'll have to wait." So the games began. "And I understand clearance can sometime take days before a landing is allowed." Two salvos in the same breath. Not bad, but compared to my crew, she was an amateur.

"No need for either. Expect us at your estate shortly," I said.

"You have teleportation capabilities?"

"Not exactly." Scientific teleports were dangerous and expensive, and even in space few realized magic was real so they didn't expect others to use any. It was our one real advantage here. "See you soon, Trade Lord." I ended the transmission and the view screen returned to being a mirror.

"Eric take us in in dust mode."

We've yet to encounter another ship that works the way one of Vulcan's barships does. It's not that they necessarily break the laws of physics, it's just they know more loopholes.

In dust mode, we were small enough to get past Ograte sensors and battle platforms and went down into the atmosphere. The heat of entry was shunted and stored as thermal energy, although at our size it didn't amount to much.

Eric located Vapella and zoomed in. To call Eric a pilot was a lot like calling a sun a light. While mildly accurate, it left out a lot. Eric was a melog, a mechanical life forms originally created by Vulcan. Melog could learn, heal, reproduce and even had souls. I happened to be visiting Vulcan's island when Eric was born, just in time to be involved in a war on Olympus.

The barships were built with special interfaces so melog could operate them as extensions of their own bodies, much like a molten suit of armor. Luckily, there are several asteroids in our solar system where gold is relatively easy to mine so when mixed with other, more mystic versions of the metal, the hull was able to be made from a gold alloy similar to that of the melog. Unlike the gold people, the hull was fluid and able to change shape and size at the wishes of the pilot.

The gold ball searched Vapella's estate until we found the trade lord. We waited until she was alone in her office. She seemed to be reviewing some data that was geared for her eyes only. Our sensors of course made copies. Eric had us hover in dust mode in front of the trade lord, even do some acrobatics, but she didn't notice. Eric then enlarged and molded the hull into a version of his head and cleared his throat. Vapella looked up and saw a floating gold face and let out a startled yip.

"We're have arrived," announced Eric. "Let joy be unconfined. Or at least let out on bail." Frighteningly enough, Eric considered me one of his role models.

Vapella rose to her feet slowly, unsure of what was happening and wondering why one person, or rather one part of one, was announcing himself as a 'we'. "How... interesting. Your head detaches. And flies. How quaint."

"Not exactly detaches," said Eric, molding the hull into a replica of his body.

Vapella was surprised, but struggled not to show it. "Where is the rest of the crew of *Fools' Glory*?"

Eric lifted a finger to indicate one moment, then put the same finger down his throat. After some gagging noises, the jaw expanded and out plopped Bubba Sue. The gremlin stands on the short side of four feet, but she always likes to make a big entrance. This time she hit the ground and rolled into a somersault, landing on her feet.

Next there was a knocking from inside Eric's ribcage. Vapella tilted her head like a puppy hearing a high pitched noise. The golden chest expanded and a door opened allowing stairs to fold down. Loki, Riga, Coyote, Savannah, and I walked out and down the steps.

Vapella may have been impressed, but she wasn't amused except perhaps by my sci-fi spaceman outfit. "An interesting fashion choice, Head Honcho Murphy." I nodded and stroked my head fin while Coyote snickered. "Is this all of you?"

"Almost," I said. Eric put his thumb in his mouth and blew on it. A tooting noise ensued from his posterior and out popped Sun WuKong. The master shape changer came out small and grew before he hit the ground. Vapella looked confused and mildly repulsed. No one off Earth seemed to understand the reference that'll we'll let you get away with stiffing us *when monkeys fly out of my butt*. Probably for the best or she'd spook before we balanced things out.

I held out my hand, which was filled with seeds. "Our one friend is sentient vegetation. Planting these seeds will allow him to partake of your hospitality. Do you mind where I plant them?" Foster liked to plant new bodies on every world we visited, just in case he ever needed them. He was almost killed once by worshippers who smoked his leaves.

"It doesn't matter. I'll have dirt brought to you. Now if you'll excuse me..." There was an implied dismissal that we ignored entirely.

"We've tried, but so far it hasn't taken."

Vapella worked herself up to a particularly fierce glare. "I have places to be."

"So do we, but as you are the only one here to show us our quarters as well as the recreation facilities available..."

"And food," said Riga.

"And entertainment," purred Savannah.

"And food and entertainment. We would like you to take care of that duty," I said.

"I'll have my servants see to your needs. I will even supply one of my servants with a lation stone so he can understand you. I assume that away from your…" Vapella gave Eric a none-too-subtle once over, up one side and down the other. "…ship that you will have trouble understanding him. Unfortunately, I have no lation to spare for the rest of you."

"No worries. Each of my crew has one."

"They do?" Vapella's voice cracked. Lation stones were very rare and extortionately expensive. The one she wore on her wrist was the size of a marble and probably cost what she paid out to her entire staff in annual pay. And I meant all of those in her holdings, not just her estate. And it could be broken down in order to give hundreds of those same people a lation stone fragment that would translate for each of them, like the Startenders had, but I doubt the idea of sharing without profit had ever occurred to Vapella.

"Of course. I thought you were a wealthy trade lord." In truth she was one of the poorer trade lords, as well as one of the newer. Even so, a trade lord was the equivalent of a billionaire robber baron back home. After doing some shape-shifting of his own, Sun WuKong's mixing with the locals had let him know that Vapella was very sensitive about being on the low end of the trade lord totem pole. "I'm surprised you only have the two."

"Yes, well, I have more on back order."

"Ah." I said and let it hang. The reason a lation is so rare is they are produced by the garba, who pass them the same way and with about the same frequency as a human passes a kidney stone. "Good luck with that. Now if you will get on with the tour."

"I told you that is a task for a servant," Vapella said.

Loki made a 'tsk'ing sound. "As per the three million and twentieth stanza, only staff that are present at the greeting of honored guests may be utilized for orientation purposes."

"But I didn't know you were coming."

Loki's brow creased and the trickster frowned. "But Murphy

told you we would see you soon. Did you not believe him?"

"I…" Vapella stopped short. She was no fool and her guard was now up. It was too much to expect her to take the bait. Insulting an honored guest's integrity is an offense punishable by heavy fines, half of which is paid to the insultee. "Of course I did. I just misunderstood what he meant by soon."

Loki nodded. "Be that as it may, only you are available to orient us to your holdings. Let us begin."

"We want to see everything, so it shouldn't take more than half a day," said Sun.

"Speak for yourself. Some of us want to see and smell everything. Maybe mark a few things. That takes much longer," said Coyote.

"And I'm sure I'll have oodles of questions about your *magical* technology and I'll need detailed technical answers," Bubba Sue said. "I'd also like the chance to examine and play with some of it."

The trade lord could feel her day being sucked away. With us taking up all of her time she wouldn't be able to pay attention to her dealings, which could prove financially disastrous.

Suddenly, her body language transformed and Vapella was all smiles. She turned on the feminine wiles, which having been enhanced by advanced surgical techniques was very impressive. Her voice became softer, radiating friendliness. "Head Honcho Murphy, I loathe to fail you as host, but I would be most appreciative if you would allow me to gracefully decline this task. What can I do to make this happen?"

"Pay for your whiskey and give us the solance," I answered. It was a last chance for her to make things right.

"Besides that." Pity. Vapella would regret her choice.

"We would have to be given free rein in your holdings. Otherwise we might do something, go somewhere, or interact with someone in a way that would cause offense." And end our favored guest status.

"Or eat too much of the wrong thing," said Riga.

Still in friendly mode, Vapella laughed at the dragon in human form. "A little thing like you? Feel free to eat all you want."

Riga did her best gee-gosh expression. "You mean it?"

"Of course I do." Bubba Sue started to speak, but Vapella cut her off. "And you can play with whatever tech you like." The trade lord turned to me. "As long as the lot of you stay out of my private quarters, do not interrupt me, or damage any of my holdings, you may do whatever you want. Do you agree?"

"I agree not to enter your private quarters while your guest." We had already gone through them before we even made contact. "Or directly interrupt you or directly damage any holdings."

"Directly?" The word had raised an alarm.

"Well, if we walk into an area and all your staff throw themselves at or attack a member of my crew, or if our unrelated actions have a negative effect on either dealings or property, we can hardly be held responsible, can we?"

"I'd prefer the word 'directly' be removed."

"I'd prefer to be paid."

"You won't rescind the term?"

"It's a deal breaker."

"You will adhere to the directly term?"

"Of course."

"Fine." The friendly woman vanished without so much as a puff of smoke and the trade lord returned. "This office is part of my private quarters. Please vacate it immediately. Contact a servant to deal with any of your needs."

And thus we were dismissed and the chaos in Lord Vapella's holdings began.

We spilt up in order to cause more "indirect" damage. We hit up servants for maps. Not that we needed them, but it would help any denials later. The beauty of the lation was they were embedded in our Startender badges, which were made of the same gold alloy as the ship. The lation allowed anyone touching metal connected to it to use the translating properties, and Bubba Sue had recently rigged a quantum connection through one of Vulcan's pocket dimensions from our badges to gold bands on our wrists, which extended into a rod. Anyone touching the rod or any metal it touched could understand us.

Ogra's setup was akin to the illegitimate child of a feudal system and capitalism. All the people who lived in Vapella's holding were basically her vassals. Sure, they earned salaries, but most of it was paid back to Vapella for food and rent much like the old mining companies on Earth. Instead of selling their souls to the company store, they leased them long-term to the trade lord.

It wasn't slavery, but the people didn't have many rights. Sure there were rules governing how long they could work and protecting them from hazardous working conditions, but they had to do what they were told. They even needed the trade lord's permission to marry or have children. On the positive side, there was very little poverty in a trade lord's holdings. Those without personal wealth or a job were not allowed to stay long and were banished to other parts of the planet, basically slums.

Riga's part was easy. She went to the nearest restaurant. Once her status as an honored guest was verified, she was seated and the staff took her order.

"When do you expect the rest of your party?" asked the chief waiter.

"That's just for me," replied Riga with a smile. She shared her father's skill with mastering new spoken languages.

The waiter stood in stunned silence. "But the amount of food…"

"Don't worry," Riga said, patting his hand and smiling before transforming into her dragon form. "It's just an appetizer. I hate deciding on a meal on an empty stomach." Riga smiled again, only this time her mouth was as large as the table in front of her. "I'd hate to eat the wrong thing by mistake because I was peckish."

Her food was ready in record time.

I planted Foster's seeds around the city, which the trade lord had modestly named Vapellan Prime. As an elemental, Foster was able to accelerate his growth and control the form his body took.

The shape was limited only by his imagination.

I planted the main concentration of seeds near a sewage and water junction. It took Foster about twenty minutes to grow roots through the casing that were long enough to tap into the fertilizer and from there another ten minutes to reach the water pipes. In less than an hour, the streets above had become a jungle. It was no coincidence that that area was the transportation hub of the city.

Sadly, for Vapella at least, it happened during travel prime, which was the local term for rush hour. The only difference was the system was run so efficiently that there was rarely much of a delay. If someone missed their connection and was late to work, they were penalized for it. No excuses were tolerated or accepted.

Foster had managed to change all that. The shuttle tubes all came to a halt, unable to get past the branches and limbs.

It took only ten minutes for those in charge to decide to clear the streets and the tool of choice was an industrial vaporizer, used to clear rubble in case of an accident or carve tunnels through mountains.

Four of the natives started clearing the brush and were rewarded with screams of pain that shook that part of the city. The men stopped, unsure of how to proceed. The matter was complicated further when the tallest limb turned toward the men and spoke.

"Why have you tried to kill me?" demanded Foster. He had long ago learned how to make leafy diaphragms to push air around so he could talk. Loki had taught him a few sentences in the native tongue so he wouldn't have to worry about using a lation. He could understand since one of his bodies was touching his badge elsewhere and due to his nature, it was able to work.

One native spoke up. "You are blocking the way."

"But I am an honored guest of Lord Vapella. Is this how she treats those she offers hospitality to? By trying to have them killed while they sleep?"

The men shut down the vaporizers and calls were made. When they learned that a sentient plant was indeed an honored guest of their trade lord, one fainted and two soiled their pants. Until Ograte trade law, Vapella's stead holders were considered by extension to be acting for her. Such a large infraction left the four of them subject to her wrath.

No attempts were made to restart the commuter system as the cries of the giant plant echoed between the street canyons.

In the crowds that now stood and waited, Eric the melog walked, *Fools' Glory* still molded to look and act like his body. His gold skin was attracting much attention. To show off as much skin as possible, his molded body wore the equivalent of a Speedo.

"Why are all of you just standing around?" he asked, extending bits of the hull for others to touch and understand him through his lation stone.

"The plants have stopped our transport. We are unable to get to work. What manner of creature are you to be made of metal?"

"I am a melog. My name is Eric and I am an honored guest of Trade Lord Vapella."

The entire crowd was now paying attention now and they had moved closer, each touching some of the extended gold tendrils. Using the ship's sensors, he had heard all the rumblings and worry of reprisals from the trade lord for their being late to work. Almost as one, the stead holders decided to try to do anything they could to make the honored guest happy in hopes he might put in a good word for them with Vapella.

Eric addressed the woman who had spoken to him. "What do you do?"

"I maintain the machinery for an assembly line."

"Do you like it?"

"I suppose. It's not like what I think matters."

"Of course it does. What everyone thinks matters," said Eric. "If you don't like it, why not do something different?"

"It is not permitted."

"Why not?"

"Because that is how things are. My career was chosen for me when I was still a child."

"What would you like to do?"

"I've always enjoyed working with children. I think I would have made a good teacher."

"I've always felt that people should be allowed to try to become anything they are willing to work toward."

"How can that be done? The trade lords control all the schools, jobs and money."

"But they are few and there are millions of stead holders. Without the masses to help run things, I would think any trade lord would have great difficulty keeping things going," Eric said.

"But to get rid of a trade lord is revolution and all the other trade lords, even their enemies, would move in to crush any rebels."

Eric laughed. "Who said anything about revolution? That would be wrong, but isn't negotiation the very lifeblood of Ogra? The masses may not have the money, but they have the numbers. Why back on my world they have these things called unions…"

Dogs may have had more paintings of them playing poker, but Coyote was no slouch. He was rather skilled at most forms of gambling as my current spaceman attire attested to. In fact, he claims credit for the idea of starting casinos on reservations as a way of getting back some of what his various peoples lost.

Quite on purpose, he stumbled across a weekly gambling game involving several of the higher ups in Vapella's holdings. Those involved were not put off by a talking canine. Ogra had been trading with other worlds for centuries and even those who had never met an alien knew they existed in various forms.

Those involved were familiar with how a lation worked, even if they never had the opportunity to use one before.

"So you want to get in on our game?" asked one, smirking to his fellows.

"I think so, so long as the stakes are big enough," replied Coyote.

"What do you have for money?"

"I'd be willing to put up my lation as collateral." The eyes of the lot went wide. It was if someone had walked into a nickel and dime card game and put the Hope Diamond on top of the chips. "What about you folks?"

"I… own a factory," he lied. "I'll be willing to put up a week's output."

"Sorry. I thought you were serious." Coyote turned and slowly walked away.

"Wait. I'll put up the factory."

Coyote turned back and remade the lation connection. "Can the rest of you offer comparable stakes?"

One of the women grabbed the man and pulled him aside. "You can't put up the factory as collateral. You don't own it." She assumed because she whispered she couldn't be heard. I suppose she couldn't be expected to realize how keen the trickster's hearing was.

"You think he owns that lation? If he were that wealthy, where's his entourage and security? He's a member of some trade delegation out wandering about and the stone belongs to whoever he works for. He has no idea how to play Scrimba. We'll tell him how to play, but it takes years to do it well. There's no way he'll beat us. And if he should win, he'll never collect. Non-citizens can't sue citizens."

Of course, Coyote kept the fact that he held honored guest status to himself and the fact that they were actually acting in their trade lord's name, whether they realized it or not.

Each of them agreed to put up whatever aspect of the holdings they were in charge of overseeing.

Coyote tried not to grin. "I'm never played Scrimba before. Could you please explain all the rules before we start?"

"The gentlemen win again!"

Loki and I had also decided to take the gambling route, but had done so at one of the casinos owned by Vapella.

"When you're hot, you're hot," I said.

"Well, I am a fire god," said Loki, blowing on his fingernails and buffing them on his shirt.

"I'm pretty sure it's the trickster aspect that's winning here," I replied. We had been playing for hours and hadn't lost yet. We were partners in Chell, a local game incorporating the chance of craps, the strategy of bridge with the skill of both bocce and dodge ball. I had spent the time we were hidden in orbit studying the game and practicing, but I still wouldn't have made it this far without Loki. I had barely avoided a broken arm and leg and I had bruises that would take weeks to fade. The head fin had come in handy, deflecting a ball that might have knocked me out cold. I had to lower the force field of my badge to play, as the rules did not allow them.

"The casino boss is trying to call Vapella again," said Loki.

I shrugged. "Bubba Sue is still experimenting on the communication systems."

Loki grinned. "Well she did say she could play with whatever tech she liked."

"Not a terribly wise thing to say to a gremlin. It's certainly not our fault if her playing is blocking all but select incoming transmissions to the trade lord." The last time the manager had managed to reach her central office was to verify our status as honored guests. We were already owed more than the casino had paid out in entirety over the last five local years. If we had been anyone else, we would have been cut off and escorted out several fortunes ago, but the casino boss was loath to offend honored guests without the trade lord's permission.

"Looks like she's had enough," said Loki. The casino boss had grabbed one of the employees and was giving him a message to deliver to Vapella in person. "Think we should quit while we're ahead?"

"Nah. I heard there's a few snarls in their commuter system too. Let's go another round."

Sun WuKong is a force to be reckoned with on any world. The Monkey King had the power to lay waste to most of Vapella Prime before the locals could stop him. Despite that, he's not overly prone to violence without provocation. He's very hard to hurt, to the point where's there's a pool as to whether he could survive a nuclear blast. I hope we never have to find out, but I've got a hundred bucks on yes.

Today Sun had walked into a bar in one of the rougher parts of town and ordered a drink by pointing, not even trying to take advantage of using the lation.

The bartender, a man having nowhere near my people skills, charm or wit, was demanding payment. Sun was telling him, in Mandarin Chinese, that he was an honored guest and the trade lord would cover the drink. The man started yelling. Sun reached for the drink and the man grabbed his wrist. Sun made a token effort to redirect the man's hand toward the gold band so he could understand the Monkey King. Instead of allowing the gentle touch to move him, the bartender slapped him across the face. Aliens had next to no rights in a conflict with the locals, so they were used to hitting first and asking questions only if it came up sometime later.

Sun rolled with the blow so the man didn't break his hand. A bouncer made a grab for the monkey from behind and Sun allowed the man to not only lay hands on him, but seemingly throw him into a wall.

"I just want my drink," said the monkey.

Instead the bouncer threw him again into a patron, who threw him into the next. This game of monkey pinball continued for several more patrons.

"I come in peace. Take me to your leader and she'll take care of things."

The bouncer had had enough fun and was planning to give him the bum's rush, but this time when he tried to grab Sun, the Monkey King turned. It was just a slight movement, but just enough for the bouncer to end up going past his target.

Angry, he tried again, And again. And a few more times to boot. Each time he got madder, until he was charging like a bull. Sun moved one last time and the man went rolling out the front door. Sun would have preferred it be a window, but the locals used energy fields instead of glass. The amount of force needed to send the guy through it would have turned his bones to pulp.

The rest of the bar got into the scuffle and Sun, a martial arts master who had been practicing for centuries, just weaved and spun so his opponents hurt themselves without him even touching them.

Moments later, the local cops rushed in, about a dozen or so. Sun stopped moving. "Thank goodness you're here. I'm an honored guest of Lord Vapella and all I wanted was a drink and these men attacked me."

The cops didn't have lations. No need since there was just one language for all citizens. Vapella also failed to inform her police force of the identity or even the existence of her honored guests, a huge lapse in her hospitality duties. Of course, Bubba Sue would have blocked the transmission even if she had.

Instead of assessing the situation, they attacked Sun with clubs and electric prods reserved for use on non-citizens.

"I think if we could just sit down and talk this out like civilized beings, we can resolve this without violence." The blows kept raining down on the monkey, until finally one of the cops smacked him across the nose with a club, breaking the baton in half.

"Ouch. Okay, this is the last time I ask you to stop." Two more cops broke their batons, this time over his head and shoulders.

Sun hit each of the three cops who had broken their clubs on him in rapid succession, knocking each one cold before turning on the others who had been beating him.

"Fine. You want a fight, I'll give you a fight, but no more Mr. Nice Monkey." Sun took on the rest of the cops except one who had the good sense to run to the far end of the bar and out the door. The rest of the patrons, about thirty in all, turned on Sun, but didn't fare much better.

Outside the lone cop was using his communicator to call for backup. Bubba Sue made sure that emergency services weren't affected by her blackout.

"How much backup do you need?" said the officer on the other end as a table hit the window hard enough to break the energy field and shatter it into splinters. Several unconscious men followed, each landing on the curb.

"Everyone." Sun stuck his head out the window and saw the runaway cop. The Monkey King smiled and waved before jumping through the opening. "Send everyone you've got. And hurry."

The messenger from the casino got through and members of Vapella's personal guard were sent to escort Loki and me to her command center. Not to mention the casino boss.

"How could you allow them to win so much?"

"My Lord, I verified that they held honored guest status. You so rarely bestow such an honor so I assumed you were aware of your guests' whereabouts and intentions. I did try to reach you no less than twenty-two times."

"Communications here have been erratic at best today. How much did they win?" When she told her the amount, Vapella fell backwards into a chair. It was over one thousand times the amount the whiskey was worth. In Earth terms, Loki and I were billionaires. "How could two off-worlders be that good at Chell?"

"We're good at games," I answered. On our way in, I signaled Bubba Sue and communications had gradually begun to come back online.

"Lord, we have several calls coming in that need to be brought to your attention," groveled a communication lackey.

"I doubt they are as pressing as this matter."

"They may be. One of your women honored guests has eaten enough food to feed Vapella Prime for three days."

"How is that possible?"

An image of Riga at the restaurant came on the main view screen.

"Apparently she transformed into a large reptile."

"You did tell my daughter she could eat all she wanted," said Loki.

"You didn't tell me she was a dragon!"

"You didn't ask," I replied.

Which is when Coyote walked in. "Where do I collect my winnings?"

"What, he was at the casino, too?"

"No, my lord," said the casino boss, bowing lower. His eyes hadn't come off the floor since we were escorted in.

"I was playing Scrimba with some of your muckity mucks. They bet several of your businesses, and when they lost they started betting real estate."

"My stead holders don't have the right to wager anything of mine."

"Actually, when dealing with section 45,022 guests, all stead holders act as extensions of their trade lord. They all speak in your name," said Loki.

"But I didn't authorize it!"

"You didn't have to," I said.

Vapella turned to her gaggle of lawyers. "Tell them stead holders cannot speak in my name!"

The lowest ranking lawyer was pushed forward by the others, looking like he wanted to curl up in a ball and cry. "Actually Lord Vapella, in this instance the off-worlders are correct."

"What!"

"There is an obscure sub section…"

The view screen changed from Riga's pig-out feast and the face of the head of Vapella's police force appeared.

"Lord Vapella, we have over five hundred officers down." The top cop did a double take, looking the trade lord up and down. Thanks to Bubba Sue's technical wizardry, every time Vapella talked on any view screen on the planet, she appeared totally nude.

"Are we under attack? Has Lord Terwon actually moved on us?"

"No, my lord." The top cop looked down and covered his eyes.

"Look at me when I'm talking to you."

"But I'm not sure I should be doing that

"You have a problem looking at me?"

For all he knew, seeing her nude could be some sort of test or new eccentricity. "No, my lord."

"Then tell me what is happening. What kind of force is being brought against us? Something off world?"

"It is all because of a single individual."

"What kind of weapons does he have?"

"He is unarmed, except for a large stick that he pulled from behind his ear when we sent a tank after him. It seems to grow and shrink at will and is denser than any armor we have."

"A stick? He beat a tank with a stick?"

In all fairness, it was a magic stick.

"Yes, he took off the hover engines and flipped it over on its top."

"With a stick!?"

"Yes. Then we sent in an airstriker."

"Against one person with a stick?"

"Yes, but he met the striker in the air."

"The individual with the stick can fly?"

"Actually, he seemed to float on a cloud." Cloud dancing is one of the martial arts Sun's mastered. "And he downed the striker, but he made sure the pilots weren't hurt. Even carried them to the ground."

"What about the striker? Those cost money."

"Destroyed. Along with a building."

"What!" yipped Coyote and screamed Vapella.

The cop hit a button on his end and Sun WuKong appeared, in a lotus position sitting on a cloud above a street filled with unconscious bodies. Sun was good enough that none of them would be seriously hurt. Behind the Monkey King, a building was demolished.

"Thank the stars," said Coyote. Vapella turned and glared at the canine. "I'm just happy it wasn't one of mine."

"None of them are yours!" She turned back to the top cop. "How many were killed?"

"Not a one. The individual bit hair off his arm and spit it out, making duplicates of himself. The main one then grew to tremendous size and stabilized the structure until his duplicates had cleared everyone out of the building." Like I said, Sun was a force to be reckoned with, with powers that defy description. And conscription. "I was calling to ask your advice on how to proceed."

"Don't you think you should have consulted with me before things got this far?"

"Especially since you were attacking an honored guest," Loki added in the native tongue.

The face on the screen went pale. "Honored guest?"

"Forget that. Why is this the first I'm hearing about this?"

"We've been trying to reach you, but your communications were down and with the chaos at the Central Junction…"

"What's happening at the Central Junction? I want it onscreen now."

The top cop was replaced by a scene of a literal urban jungle and the speakers boomed with moaning.

I tried to act surprised and angry. "What have you done to Foster?"

A comm jockey spoke up. "Apparently, some engineers tried to clear some vegetation from the transport lines with vaporizers without realizing the plant was sentient. Or an honored guest. He has been screaming in pain ever since"

Vapella just screamed.

"You tried to kill honored guests?" Loki shouted in the native tongue.

"I didn't try to kill anyone, but that could change any moment."

"Actually, my lord the same sub section applies…" said a lawyer meekly.

"Shut up. He's a plant. How bad could he be hurt?"

"Your compassion is underwhelming," I said.

"And your crew is laying waste to my city!"

"We've maintained our end of the agreement. We have harmed nothing directly. All damage was done by your people attacking us. Tell your forces to stand down on Sun and I'll make sure he doesn't defend himself against any more of them."

Vapella relayed the message to her people and I contacted Sun. The hovering police we could see in the distance floated away. Sun lowered himself back to the ground and a single floating camera followed him back into the tavern. When he reached the bar, he reached behind it and picked up the bartender who had been cowering behind it. Sun placed the man's hand on the armband. There was no resistance this time. "As I tried to tell you, I am an honored guest of your trade lord and this is all I wanted."

Sun dropped the man and picked up the glass, which somehow was untouched on the bar. The Monkey King downed it in a single gulp.

"No wonder you're all so cranky. That was pretty bad booze."

Vapella was shaking her head.

"We're going to help Foster. While we're gone, ask your lawyers what the penalty for wounding an honored guest is."

As we left, I heard them tell her.

"Any penalty, up to and including loss of trade lord status."

Vapella's screams weren't as loud or disturbing as Foster's, but they did bring a smile to my face.

As did the next call. "They want to talk to me about a union? What in the blazing pits of despair is a union?"

The trade lord spent the next few hours trying to calm the chaos, all the while wondering why everyone she spoke to on screen was looking at her so strangely.

"I need a break. I'll be in my pleasure chamber, breaking in the three pure." Vapella was wealthy and able to choose the jobs her stead holders had. She had an eye for beauty and picked many for her concubines. At present she had seventeen, eleven men and six women, at her work-based pleasure chamber, three of which were virgins she was saving for a special occasion. It was amazing how the gift of a beautiful virgin could help seal a business deal, but after the day she had, she was giving them as a gift to herself. Right after her four strongest massaged her from head to toe.

When she got to her pleasure chamber no one was there. Confused, she walked down the hall following the sounds of carnal pleasure, and lots of it. The noises led her to a conference room and when she opened the door, the sights that greeted her made her freeze.

The trade lord's world seemed to be going in slow motion.

All seventeen of her concubines were in the conference room in various stages of undress, most of them curled up in contentment, smiles on their faces from received pleasure. On the center of her conference table, Savannah was engaged with her three virgins, two men and one woman, somehow managing to pleasure each of them at the same time. It was a creative use for her horns, hooves, and tail.

"What is going on here!?" the trade lord shouted, but the quartet on the table went on about their business as if she hadn't spoken. In a fit of rage, Vapella lifted up an edge of the table, flipping it on its side. The impact with the floor was enough to put a damper on the activities.

"How dare you…"

"You said if any of us needed anything, we should see a servant and boy did I need this." Savannah was more comfortable naked than she was clothed and had very few inhibitions. She rubbed her hands over herself as she spoke. "And since I wasn't sure if the pleasure chamber counted as your private quarters, I brought everyone over here to the conference area."

"How could you get all of them to…?"

Savannah shrugged. She didn't see the point in explaining about the mystic pheromones her people gave off that both acted to induce desire and reduce inhibitions. "Well it took most of the day, but we managed. You mustn't do a very good screening for concubines. These three never even had sex before, but we've fixed that. Several times."

"Get out of here!"

"I'd love to, but I hate to stop before I reach an even hundred and I just have one more to go."

"A hundred what?"

Savannah rolled her eyes back, then shivered and moaned in anticipation. "What do you think? Of course if you'd care to join us, there's always room for one more."

The chair narrowly missed the she-satyr's head, so she took off running naked, her hoofs making good time on the tiled floor

After everything we did, Vapella wasn't about to give us anything, so we had to take her to the Ograte World Court. Our only way in was because our honored guest status gave us temporary honorary citizenship. We were able to convince the Trade Court to hear our case immediately. I'd like to say it was because of the urgency of the situation on Gallop, but Bast had to resort to blackmail using information her cat agents had gathered on the judges. Vapella lied and tried to twist everything around, even doctoring some footage to help make her case.

We hadn't been bluffing when we said we were using Veritasian verification to record everything. Loki acted as our attorney, quoting parts of the trade law even the judges had to look up. It was enough for the court to release the solance to use while the rest was sorted out.

We left Loki, Coyote, Savanah, Riga and one of Sun's bodies behind to deal with everything else on Ogra and got the solance to Gallop.

Luckily, since we'd been there before, the Transworld got us back quickly. Everything on Vapella Prime had taken a little over eleven hours. Twelve hours after we first made contact with Vapella, Hermes had the solance. Almost fourteen hours later, the anti-toxin was being distributed. It was most effective by injection, but with Kaye's help, Hermes had also made a gas-based version that was sent through the holo-projectors.

The Gallopians started to recover, but it wasn't total. Some of the very old, very young and sick… it was too late for them. They had already died. And there were some in places we couldn't find, where the gas didn't reach. We lost them too. All in all, only one tenth of one percent went off to dance with John Thanatos. It doesn't sound like much, but it was still three million people we didn't save.

Despite the loss of life, the Gallopians were grateful to us. We got medals, a parade and were made honorary citizens. There was talk of a monument. We tried to decline, so we'll see if it happens.

Of course we still had a problem – what to do with Davin. We had no prison. After much debate, we decided to turn him over to the Gallopians for trial. There was some more debate about whether this would violate our Startender oaths since they would be executing him if – and let's be honest, it was really when – he was found guilty.

The trial took three days. In the first event of its kind I'd ever heard of, the entire population was the jury and voted. It wasn't unanimous – a tiny fraction still found him guilty but were against capital punishment. At the end of his trial Davin was found guilty and condemned to immediate death.

The traditional method on Gallop was decapitation by sword. There was much debating about who would have the honor. It was offered to the Startenders, but for obvious reasons we declined.

They choose a soldier, gave him a ceremonial blade and put Davin on his knees. He was given a chance for last words and went into a rant about how he would finish the job he started and they would all dance with death.

As the soldier lined up his blow – Dagonet assures me decapitation can be a messy business – Davin rammed his head back into the blade, cutting his own neck. As the blood flowed down his neck, Davin burst into flames which reached out to envelop the executioner, leaving behind a pile of ashes.

To the untrained eye, Davin had been incinerated. Fortunately, the Startenders had several well trained sets of eyes. In particular, Hex and Gani had spent time studying the wards Davin had carved into his body and soul. Even for the two experts, it was an education. They had managed to neutralize most of his dark protections, but they would have killed lesser-skilled mages. There was one, however, that they were unable to even touch.

It was a good thing we hadn't resorted to try to torture him. He hadn't figured on being caught by people like us. If we had spilled even a drop of his blood, the fiery explosion would have been many times greater than the one at his execution. The idea behind it was it would kill whoever was torturing him and teleport him to safety.

Had Hex or Gani tried to remove it, the backlash would have killed them and taken out a part of the barship. The teleport would have assured that Davin got away anyway.

We never let him know we knew about that ward. We made sure the executioner would be protected from the blast by Hermes whisking him away before the flames hit him and let it happen.

No, we weren't stupid. Gani had figured out how the teleport worked and did a test run to see where it would take him. Once we knew that, we simply prepared for his arrival.

Davin had a bunker back on Hiven with a lab, grimoires and weapons. I guess he figured his pal Alom would be there strip-mining the world and hook him up with supplies to wipe out another world.

Instead he found Quan, Hiven's sole survivor, waiting for him.

Davin laughed and lunged at her, his hands reaching for her throat. The slayer of worlds passed through her.

"Illusion!" he spat, picking himself up to grab a weapon from his bunker, only to find it had been stripped bare. He unlatched the door and stepped outside into the Hiven night.

The bunker door slammed shut behind him.

Davin looked around him and assumed he was alone, but then heard the flapping of dark wings. Six black-winged graveyard angels came down from the sky to surround him in the air.

"Your presence here is the worst desecration of any grave that I could imagine," Mica, Moni's mother, said.

Davin snorted. "I don't fear any of you." He bit off the tip of a finger and started drawing symbols in the air. The trail of blood burst into flame and with a wave he sent it up toward the lasa.

Moni waved a hand and the dirt beneath her rose up to bury the blood fire that otherwise could have destroyed her, even through the shield of her badge. He had tried it on Sun WuKong and it had actually burned the Monkey King during his capture, an incredible feat.

As I'd mentioned, in an Earth cemetery, a graveyard angel could part the dirt over a grave. The entire world of Hiven was a grave, which meant Moni and the other lasa had an incredible amount of control over all aspects of the entire planet.

The other five lasa moved their hands and stones flew to batter and bloody the world-killer.

"I thought Startenders did not kill," Davin said, stumbling to his feet.

"My daughter is the only Startender among us, killer," Mica said. Moni had floated back to watch but not help. "Lasa have always been able to avenge the dead."

Davin raked his nails along his chest and arms, bloodying himself. "I still have more than enough power to kill the six of you."

"Perhaps you do," Mica said. "But we are not the only vengeance-seekers you face."

"I'm hardly worried about craven Startenders, cowards who are afraid of a little death," Davin said, weaving spells in the air with his blood.

"You do not face Startenders. My mother told you the truth about lasa avenging the dead, but I have always found it best when the dead can avenge themselves."

"What nonsense are you spouting, you winged…" Davin stopped speaking at the sound of a multitude of footfalls approaching. As a group, the lasa lowered the walls of dirt that surrounded the killer of worlds to reveal hordes of Hivenites marching toward him.

Davin laughed and clapped in glee. "More dancers to send to death."

The lasa chuckled. "They have already stepped out with the Reaper," Moni said. "We have brought them back now to dance with you."

"A few reanimated corpses? A few moments work to dispatch." Davin punched the air towards the approaching dead, reducing them to globs of goo, then laughed.

"I don't think you know the meaning of the word few," Moni said. She hit her badge. "Everyone, light it up."

A longer-lasting variation on magnesium flares shot into the night ski, illuminating the surrounding countryside. Every available bit of ground had a dead Hiven on it, walking toward their killer for a little payback.

Davin's cool was gone. He tried to run, but he was in the center of a wave of Hiven people, looking to crash onto his shore.

"No! Get back! I am the slayer of your world. You have no power over me!"

Just because someone says something doesn't make it true.

Davin was the most terrible villain I'd ever met or even heard of, but that didn't mean he was going quietly into his dark night. He fought, first with blood magic, then with stone, fist and bone. It took the dead Hivenites almost an hour to take him down. Since he had already triggered the soul ward to escape his Gallopian execution, he was trapped. And even if somehow he did manage to reset it, it would only transport him back into his bunker.

As Davin fell, Moni broke off from the other lasa and flew up to where *Fools' Glory* hovered, along with several other barships. Just because there didn't seem any way for the slayer to escape from his vengeful dead didn't mean we were taking any chances.

My remaining crew, along with Sun and Bubba Sue, stood on a platform watching what happened below.

Moni floated in front of me. "Murphy, your presence is requested below."

I was confused. "Davin?"

Moni shook her head. "A friend."

Back in the old days in New York City, Moni would fly me around by wrapping her arms around me from behind and holding my belt. I was still wearing my shiny jumpsuit and the utility belt. "I don't know if this belt is strong enough to hold my weight, even using the badge to lighten me."

"No need." Moni held out her hand and I took it. Power poured though her fingers and lifted me up and into the night sky. The graveyard angel flapped her wings and slowly towed me down toward the surface.

Davin had gone limp. Many hands held him and many bodies pulled. There was a scream and one of the killer's arms came loose from his body. The rest of his limbs and head soon followed.

"So he's dead?" I said.

Moni pointed down where the walking dead parted for a

skeleton of a man who looked like them in a dark robe.

"Does that answer your question?"

John Thanatos in alien Grim Reaper mode looked up at me and nodded. I nodded back and watched as the spirit-form of the slayer formed at Death's feet, screaming.

When he realized the dead had stopped attacking him, the screaming ended. Davin looked down at his torn-apart remains confused, then gradually realized what had happened. He turned to see the Grim Reaper, who suddenly shifted shape into a tiny skeleton on his knees and bowing in front of the slayer.

John appears like the dead picture him, so apparently Davin believed Death worshipped him. It took less than a second for John to shift back to his Hiven skeleton form.

"No need to thank me, little Reaper," Davin said as if he was speaking to a servant.

"WHY WOULD I DO THAT?" Death said,

"Because of all I have done for you. For all those I have sent to your cold embrace to dance with you. I made sure you did not grow lonely."

"YOU CUT SHORT THESE LIVES OF YOUR OWN ACCORD, NOT FOR MY SAKE."

"But I sent you so many at once."

"BUT AHEAD OF THEIR TIME. I DO NOT NEED ANYONE SENT TO ME. ALL COME MY WAY EVENTUALLY."

"You do not seem very grateful."

"I AM NOT."

"I have slain more than anyone else who has ever lived. You must be impressed."

"NOT REALLY. AND YOUR DEATH TOLL, WHILE PLENTIFUL, IS NOT THE HIGHEST."

"You lie!"

Death simply stared.

"Where is my reward?"

Death grinned. "TO PARAPHRASE THE LASA, I DON'T THINK YOU KNOW WHAT THAT WORD MEANS. YOU DO NOT GET REWARDED FOR EVIL. YOU GET PUNISHED."

"Nonsense. Let us dance so I can move on to my paradise."

John moved his scythe so it wrapped around his bony waist and became a gun belt with a pair of six-shooters, then winked at me.

"IF YOU WANT TO DANCE, WE SHALL DANCE." Hands made of bone pulled the guns and the right one shot at the slayer's spirit feet, causing the dead slayer to hop up on his other foot. "YOU ARE NOT DANCING. GO ON, DANCE." John shot at each of his feet in a rhythm like a gunslinger had done in a western we had once watched together. Dead Davin danced in a frantic, ungraceful mess.

"YOU HAVE POSED A QUANDARY FOR ME. I HAVE NO LESS THAN A DOZEN AFTERLIVES BEGGING TO PUNISH YOU. I THINK WE MAY HAVE TO START WITH THE MOST CREATIVE OR SEE IF THEY WILL JOIN FORCES FOR YOU. TIME TO BEGIN THE REST OF YOUR ETERNITY."

Davin vanished. John Thanatos put his six-shooters back in their holsters. Death turned and tipped his hood at me like it was a ten-gallon hat, then vanished after him.

I nodded, then realized Moni and the other lasa were staring at me.

"What?" I said.

"Master Thanatos is not noted for his sense of humor. Yet for you, he did… that," Moni said. "I don't think you have any idea how amazing that is."

I shrugged and chuckled.

"What's so funny?" Moni said.

"Just imagining what he's got planned when my time comes." Moni squinted like I was an idiot. I hadn't gotten that look from her in years. "Not that I want to go today, but it will happen someday."

"An enlightened attitude. What are you picturing?" Moni said.

"First, a skeleton wearing Groucho Marx glasses with eyebrows, moustache and nose. Then…"

CONSTELLATION PRIZE

We showed an edited recording for the Gallopians so they could rest easy knowing that the man who tried to destroy their world was no more. The fact that it leaked out to other star-faring races was nothing we did. However, we suspect the bastarts at Cynosure may have had a paw in it in order to build up the Startenders' rep.

The other lasa convinced Moni that her time would be better spent with the Startenders, so she left them to lay Hiven's death to rest. Oddly after what they did, not all of the dead went along with it. In fact, multitudes joined in to help and developed a primitive sentience.

Things on Ogra got complicated. We won our court case in no small order. When all was said and done, we had acquired 91% of Vapella's liquid holdings between the games of Chell and Scrimba. Coyote's gaming mates had bet eighty two percent of the city, assuming they were playing with an idiot. He even managed to get them to bet both the whiskey and the solance. We got the rest of her holdings awarded as damages for her breaking of section 45,022 and the other obscure subsections Loki managed to dig up. Not to mention the fines for indecent exposure—it turns out no one even told her about the view screen issue until she was in court.

Vapella was wiped out and the Startenders ended up owning everything. Without her holdings, Vapella lost her trade lord status. She was left with enough to buy passage off world, which was more than I felt she deserved after indirectly causing so many deaths on Gallop by not honoring our deal, but the Startenders oath limited our options.

Collectively the Startenders now qualified as an Ograte Trade Lord. We've been offered many deals by the other Trade Lords to buy our holdings. We're trying to determine what would be best for the people involved, especially since none of us have any desire to rule anything. We even managed to finagle permanent citizenship status for all Startenders, which would protect us in any future dealings should we sell everything off. Plus, the other lords figured it would make us more willing to sell, especially since we wouldn't have to worry about another lord trying to take advantage of us being non-citizens.

Somehow I didn't think that any Trade Lord messing with us after this was going to be a problem.

On the opposite end of the spectrum, while she was waiting on Ogra, Savannah made a fortune selling the recording rights to her day in the conference room, the profits of which she graciously shared with all her new friends. None of them will ever have to work as a concubine again, unless they wanted to.

And I got to take off my shiny gold jumpsuit and head fin. The bet with Coyote had run its course.

I was about ready to take a real furlough for myself, when Eric came in to my office.

"Boss, you okay? You're eyes are leaking," Eric said.

I nodded and wiped my eyes. "First chance I've had to be alone. Just thinking of the dead on Gallop. Trying to think of what could have been done different to save some or all of them."

Eric nodded. "Come up with anything?"

"Not with the cards we were dealt. What do you need?"

"You are going to love this. I've been going through the scans of the probes we used during the Cron affair." One of our first missions to get an alien race home past a Goblin Empire blockade so they could spawn the next generation. "Most are still out there mapping more of the universe so we can transworld more places. One found something very interesting."

Eric put a tablet in my hand. I was only basically proficient in chemistry thanks to my time at the Startender Academy, but even I recognized what these elements made up. "There is something in the cloud that is C_2H_6O?"

Eric beamed. "Not something. The entire cloud."

"Are you one hundred percent positive it's C_2H_6O not CH_4O? All the other clouds we've come across have been methanol, not ethanol," I said.

"And they've been far larger, two to five times larger than our solar system. This one is a fraction of that size, but it's definitely ethanol," Eric said.

"Hot damn. Set course. I want to be absolutely sure."

The probe had already sent back coordinates for the transworld drive. Minutes later *Fools' Glory* arrived outside the cloud.

"It's beautiful," I said.

"And has all the colors of the rainbow. That's got to be a good omen, right?" Eric said.

"Right." Rainbows had led those in trouble to Bulfinche's Pub in the days before Manhattan was sunk. "Send out more probes."

"How many?" Eric said.

"How many do we have?"

"Twenty."

"Save one for emergencies and have the rest check out the cloud, inside and out. I'll go get a sample myself," I said. I went to the nearest airlock with a booster harness and jumped out. Our badges' protective fields were better than spacesuits and the harness had dozens of small "blowers" to provide momentum and steering in the void of space.

I entered the cloud and swam through the colors. It was magnificent. I took samples of each color as there were chemical variations in each.

I went back to the ship and to the main barroom. Bubba Sue and Sun had left, Foster had body jumped and we hadn't been back to Ogra to pick up the rest of our crew yet, so it was just Eric and me.

I had found eleven different samples in my brief foray into the cloud, so I lined up twenty two shot glasses. I poured each by color.

"Are you sure it's safe boss?" Eric said.

"The readings say it is and the badges won't let any poison through." I slid a red shot to Eric and took one for myself. "Sláinte."

We took a sip. The sensors said it contained ethyl formate. "Mmm. Tastes almost like raspberry rum."

"You realize this means we're about to become really rich," Eric said. I nodded. Startenders had rules for commerce and as the ones who discovered the cloud, Eric and I got a very large share of what was coming, as did the Startenders as a whole.

"Boy are the rest of the crew going to be sorry they weren't here, especially Coyote," Eric said.

"No. he won't. If you have no objections, I say the finder's share should be split evenly between us and the rest of *Fools' Glory's* crew," I said.

"Sure."

"However that doesn't mean I can't get my pound of fur," I said, hitting my badge. Coyote's image came on the nearest bar mirror.

"Murphy, I see you are out of your Lame Gordon duds. Calling to tell me about it?" Coyote said.

"Nope. Calling to see if you are willing to double our stakes on a new bet," I said. "You win, I double my time in that getup. You win, you do the same stint in a collar, sweater, with me designing your fur-do." Like a hairdo only with fur.

"What, you learning to like that outfit? What's the bet?" the fleabag said.

"That within a year I can figure out a way to recoup the brewers' losses," I said.

"With Paddy's help, that's a no brainer. How about a month without any input from Paddy?" Coyote said.

"No input on the idea, but he can help with business matters. And six months."

"Two."

"Three," I said. "I'm not going any shorter."

"Sure. Three months from now."

"Great. How do you feel about a pink fu-fu sweater?" I said, then told him what we found.

Coyote cursed in a bark, but the lation translated it anyway. Then he sighed. "I'm a canine medium."

"I don't understand why ye are making all of us head light years out into the galaxy for something ye could tell us back on the NYC II," Paddy griped. "And why Dion and I have to be blindfolded. Knowing the pudgy man's history as I do, I'm more than a bit nervous to not be able to keep an eye on him."

"You were too short to ever be my type," Dion replied. "And I've had several wonderful experiences blindfolded." The Greek god of wine and orgies made make Savannah look like an underachiever back in his heyday. "Live a little. Besides, Murphy would never let anything bad happen to you."

Savannah snuck up and whispered in Paddy's ear. "Besides it's not Dionysus who you should be worried about cutie." Paddy jumped when she put her hand on his knee.

"Savannah…" I said, motioning her away by pointing with my thumb.

"What?" she said with mock innocence.

"Murph, we're here," Eric said.

The pair were turned so Coyote was in front of them when the blindfolds came off.

Paddy and Dion chuckled.

"You made us come all this way to see the fleabag decked out like a French poodle with a pink sweater?" Paddy said. The rest of the crew had helped me with Coyote's grooming and I felt it was at least as embarrassing as the getup I had to wear. "Ye could have done that on Startender Station."

"We wanted to show you this," Loki said, nodding to Eric. The entire ship went to clear mode so it looked let we were standing in space. Several of the brewer's startled, having never witnessed the effect before.

"'Tis a nice view of a pretty cloud, but what's all the fuss?" Paddy said, but Dion had simply stiffened up as he literally stared out into space. "I don't get it. Is it a rainbow thing?"

Riga handed him a tablet with the formula of the main part of the cloud and its size. The old leprechaun's eyes went wide and he looked back out. "'Tis beautiful."

Then the old friends who once made all the booze sold in the finest pub the Earth has ever seen turned toward each other and embraced to the point where the much taller Dion lifted Paddy off the floor, normally a dangerous act. Then they started laughing like a couple of kids and, still holding hands, started jumping and dancing in some cross between a traditional Greek dance and a jig. After a few minutes the two, arm in arm, skipped toward the nearest airlock. Oddly, neither of them tripped. Impressive considering the floor and walls were all transparent.

Eric looked at me and I nodded. As soon as they reached the airlock, Eric let them out. The pair spun and danced in the ethyl cloud, swimming somehow without any propellant. Probably some power of Dionysus in regards to alcohol.

We watched from the bar and could hear their laughter and gasps of pleasure over the comm.

Walt, the apprentice brewer stepped beside me. "Won't they die in space?"

"Nah. Startender badges gives them all the comforts of home," I said.

"I don't understand what's going on or why you brought us. It's amazing to be out in space and see this, but why all the fuss over some multi-colored cloud?" Walt said.

"We couldn't have saved the Gallopians without all of you giving away your whiskey and we wanted to say thank you. First, we went to Ogra before picking you up and we managed to get back most of the whiskey. About seventy-five percent." Vapella had already blown through the rest.

"That's great news," Walt said.

"But that cloud is even better news," Loki said.

"Why?" asked Angie, another apprentice brewer.

"Because that cloud is made out of pure booze," Riga said.

"You made it?" Angie said.

"More like found it," Eric said.

"We've found other alcohol clouds, bigger than our solar system, but it wasn't the drinkable kind. This is," Savannah said.

"You mean we can put that in a bottle and sell it?" Walt said.

"Yep. And if I know those two…" And I did. "They will come up with a hundred more ways to mix or distill it into the most wonderful drinks this side of anywhere. And because of what you did, you will be involved in what gets made, both products and profits."

"How big is it?" Walt asked.

"Big enough that any other ship from Earth not made by Vulcan would take decades to cross it," Eric said.

"How long will it take to run out?" Angie said.

"It will last my lifetime," Coyote said. "And we will be able to sell it on a galactic scale. We are all going to be rich enough that it almost makes up for me having to wear this getup." The brewers started to jump and dance a bit on their own.

Coyote looked up at me. "But payback's a bitch, Murphy."

"So was your mother," Loki said.

"Coyote, as far as I'm concerned we're even. Do you really want to have a prank war with me?" I said.

"You're mortal. I'd decimate you," Coyote said.

"He's Murphy. Everybody likes him. Nobody much likes you, fleabag," Loki said.

"I like him," Savannah said.

"What does that have to do with the price of steak in Dallas?" Coyote said.

"Murphy would simply ask for help and people would come out of the woodwork," Loki said.

"Actually I can handle him myself," I said.

Riga put a hand on my back and stroked it like I was a child. "And it's so cute that you believe that too. Let Dad handle this, Uncle Murphy."

"You wouldn't be facing Murphy, but Murphy and all his friends. ALL HIS FRIENDS." Loki's voice got deep and scary for that last part.

"I see your point. We're even, Murph," Coyote said.

"Great. Now how about all of you help me pour some shots for the brewers here." There were a hundred of them after all. "We collected lots of samples." Technically the probes did. "I recommend starting with the pink. I named it T-Belle because it reminds me of my late wife's hair."

SAVING TOCK

We got a priority one distress call from Buzz. The garba was the head honcho of the *Bitter End*. The barship was parked in the Watering Hole, a real bar on the planet Traven. The same bar we'd sort of won then sort of took from a bunch of killer robots after they wouldn't honor our wager.

As the most heavily traveled and populated known world, a lot of people pass through Traven. A lot of those people were looking for help. Some of them found it by coming into the Watering Hole. It didn't have the advantage of rainbows leading the troubled to the door like Bulfinche's Pub had in the days before New York was sunk, but some of the troubled still managed to find it, which has let us help quite a few people along the way.

Now we had to help someone who could have been one of our own.

"They're going to kill Tock," Buzz said from behind the bar.

"Who's going to kill him?" I said.

"The Empire." There was no need to state it was the Goblin Empire.

"And we know this how?" Loki said.

"Me," said a goblin that I recognized.

"Rem, what's going on?" I said to Tock's nephew. Rem had gotten into some trouble his first time out as commander of a goblin cram. It was the first mission for my crew of Startenders and how we ended up with the Watering Hole, not to mention saving a bunch of folks from slavery along the way.

"Tock's brother failed at a mission. The Great One..." Quiet speak for Gob, the scum god who ruled the interstellar Goblin Empire. Same guy who'd risen to power by slaughtering the rest of his pantheon and taking the helm of the Empire for himself. Ever since he's been out conquering other worlds for their natural resources, the most important of which – at least to him – was new worshipers. Each new believer expanded his power base. He is the most powerful divinity that the Startenders know of this side of the creator. You didn't want to mention the name of somebody with that kind of juice unless you wanted to risk them being able to listen in on your conversation. Or worse. "It was determined that Tock's brother had betrayed the Empire and the Great One sentenced him to death. Then he sentenced his entire bloodline to make an example. Anyone within three generations of him is now marked for execution. My uncle, the general, got most of the non-bloodline family out, but he himself stayed behind." Rem held onto the metal rail that ran along the bar. A small fragment of a lation stone was embedded in the metal, so anyone touching it would be able to understand any language spoken, making conversations possible.

"Why?" Buzz said.

"He's offering himself up in place of the rest of his family. Uncle is one of the highest-ranking generals in the Empire. Tactically, he's probably its best. That, and the first family member the divine guard took into custody was his daughter."

"Tock has kids?" Loki said.

"Child, singular."

"But I thought you goblins bred in litters," Buzz said.

"Typically, we do. My blood aunt, Uncle's wife…" Tock was married to Jade, his second-in-command back during the Karma Affair. "Became pregnant. Jade was too stubborn for her own good. The Empire doesn't recognize maternity leave and expected her to be able to be combat-ready up until she gave birth. In fact, she gave birth during a firefight, laying down cover fire so the troops under her command could get to safety. She caught a stray round that killed her. Tock went back for her just in time to hold his wife as she died. Then Uncle took his blade and tried to save his children. They were expecting seven. My uncle cut seven tiny, lifeless corpses from the woman he loved, and tried to resuscitate them while holding off the enemy. Six times he failed, but on the seventh he was rewarded with the cries of my cousin's grasping for life. He named her Tada, which means joy of the survivor."

"So Tock's not leaving without his little girl," I said. Loki and I exchanged a look. Terrorbelle had died protecting our daughter

Elsiebelle. I would move heaven and any planet necessary to protect her. Loki had a lot of kids, most of which had fallen into the category of problem children. All of them were killed at Ragnarok, with the exception of Riga. I knew he felt the same way about Riga that I did about E-Belle.

"I guess we'll have to go in and get both of them out," I said.

"Murphy, you've said some crazy things in the past and done things a madman wouldn't even dream of, but you're talking about going to the Goblin Throneworld. It can't be done," Buzz said.

"You're only saying that because it never has," Loki said.

"Wait a moment. Am I understanding you correctly? You're considering risking your lives in a doomed attempt to save my uncle and a child you've never even met before?" Rem said.

"Your uncle is a brave and honorable man who helped us once when we needed it to save a world," I said.

"You hired my uncle and his cram as mercenaries." The Goblin Empire has an odd view on supporting their soldiers in-between battles. They don't believe in it. Feels it makes them weak, so it is up to the soldiers to support themselves. Most become mercenaries. Tock started out charging us full rate on Karma, but after seeing what we were doing, lowered his price to little more than what his cram needed to get by because he was proud to be fighting for what he considered a noble cause. He even gave Buzz a full escort to take down an old one that was in danger of rising. "Even had you not paid him for his services, any debt of honor you had was repaid when you helped him rescue me and my cram in this very place."

"Wait a second," Buzz said. "If you didn't want us to rescue your uncle, then why did you come to us?"

"Because you were his friends and I thought you deserved to know. I hoped you would hold a memorial service to honor his memory. My uncle was a great man. He deserves that much and he will not get it in the Empire he dedicated his life to serving."

"Your uncle deserves more than that. He deserves to live," I said. "Hell, he'd be a Startender right now if his obligation to the Empire hadn't prevented him from joining us."

"But I still don't understand. Tock was only doing his duty

after you hired him."

"Tock helped us save an entire race of people. In one battle on Karma, three hundred and sixty-four men, women and children were slaughtered by the invaders," I said.

Rem tilted his head. "In war there are casualties. People die."

"These weren't casualties, they were people. I can tell you the names of each one," I said.

Rem made an incredulous face, then realized I was serious. The goblin looked towards Buzz and Loki as if questioning my mental state and ability to lie.

"Trust me, he can do it. He honored one of them each day of his native year –" True. I put up a name behind my station at the bar every day to remember. "–saving the last day for his first wife," Loki said, then started to examine his feet. It was a sore point for him. At that point in the campaign he had made a break for his freedom. If he hadn't, some of those people would have likely survived.

"But going to the Throneworld of the Empire is certain suicide," Rem said. "Why would you even considering losing your lives in attempt to do something that can't be done? Why throw away your lives on a fool's errand?"

I smiled sadly. "There's more than one reason for the name of my ship."

Buzz started pacing the bar. I meant it literally. Back when Bulfinche's Pub sat above sea level, Paddy Moran used to have a ramp on the inside of the bar that so he could stand on it and look like he was normal height. Buzz was much shorter than the leprechaun and simply stood on the bar itself. "I owe Tock a lot too, Murphy, but the kid has a point. Why throw away lives on a suicide mission?"

"Because he deserves better."

"A lot of people deserve better. And worse, for that matter, but that doesn't mean they're ever going to get it. The universe sucks," Buzz said.

"True, but sometimes you just have to stand up to the universe and tell it to do otherwise," I said. "Besides, with the resources at the Startenders disposal, maybe it won't be suicide. And either way, it's the right thing to do."

"And that, ladies and gentlemen, is why I will follow Murphy anywhere," Loki said.

"But do you have to follow me everywhere? It gets a little bit creepy," I said. "You've totally ignored that restraining order."

Loki smiled. "I thought we were still playing follow the leader."

"That was years ago when our daughters were kids. That game's been over for more than a decade," I said.

"And it didn't dawn on you to tell me that? Did I at least win?" Loki said.

Rem looked from the Norse trickster and back to me, then at Buzz. "Are they making jokes at a time like this?"

Buzz chuckled. "Yes. It's how they deal with stress."

"I deal with stress much better than Murphy does," Loki said.

"That's because you cheat and deal from the bottom of the deck," I said.

"So they aren't really going to attempt a rescue?" Rem said.

"Oh no, that they were serious about," Buzz said. "Wait here. We have Startender business to take care of. Gentlemen, join me in my office."

The Bitter End was parked inside the Watering Hole. Easy enough to do with a morphing hull. We followed the garba inside to his office. It was simply decorated, but Buzz had adorned the walls with pictures of the people he and his crew had helped. The first picture was of Karma and the second was an image of the cron glowing and dancing in space, mating as they headed toward their home world. That was the first time we crossed the Empire. As difficult as it had been to stop the goblins then, I knew this was going to be a lot harder.

"Buzz, I think this is blue button worthy," I said.

"It is, but let's start smaller first," Buzz said.

"I guess you'd be the expert on small," Loki said.

Buzz had picked up some Earth customs and stuck his tongue out at the trickster, and sent out a few calls. I preferred using the bar mirrors, but Buzz liked holograms. A few moments later Buzz had four faces floating in front of us. Bast, Paddy, Vulcan, and Jan, one of the Karmans we'd saved way back when. In fact, Jan was the Karman who'd gathered the rest of us together to save her people.

I told them what I was planning on doing.

Vulcan let out a long whistle. "That's a tall order."

"There is no way we can win a war with the Goblin Empire, so is it worth it to risk starting one over one man?" Bast said.

"One man and his daughter. A man who was offered membership in the Startenders. And if the Startenders can't take care of our own, then what good are we?"

Paddy sighed. "We've got to do this with ultimate stealth and have the prisoner gone before he realizes it. Preferably without him knowing it was us. Last thing we need is Big Nose…" With all the people in the Empire uttering Gob's name, the odds are lower of him taking notice of any one utterance, but the name being said in a system outside of the Empire might attract his attention. Simply not worth the risk. "And the Empire raining destruction on us. Or on…"

One of the worries with the Startenders going out and meddling in the universe was someone or something would follow us home. Earth didn't have any interstellar fleets of its own, only the Startenders. Our barships and Startender Station's starshots – one person defensive ships that can't travel outside of our solar system – were the only real defenses our planet had. We had less than twenty barships – Vulcan and his team were working on more, but each ship took a lot of resources, both mystic and scientific, so we couldn't just churn them out. There were over ten thousand starshots, but they were far more limited in design and function, built with planetary defense in mind. In short, we made a big effort to make sure that the bad guys in the universe didn't know about Earth or its location.

"I agree with Murphy. Tock helped save my people. Someone needs to save him. However, Paddy is also right that we need to do it smart," Jan said.

Bast sighed and shook her furry head. "Murphy, you're really planning to step in it this time, aren't you?"

"Looks that way. What do you know about the Throneworld?"

"Even Cynosure has limited intelligence on the seat of the Empire. We do know that Big Nose can sense any intrusion of another divinity into his system, let alone his world. He can sense any bastart five generations or closer to me. Those that we have gotten on world must remain in feline form because of the risk of Big Nose sensing a shape-shift. He can sense the use of any major magic on the world. Despite his PR to the contrary, Big Nose isn't omniscient, so he can miss things, but there is no way of guaranteeing he is distracted enough at any given time," Bast said.

"So no magic at all?" I said.

"Magic objects could be cloaked, but people using anything more than a minor spell would be very risky," Bast said.

"That is going to limit the rescue team." I thought about it. I needed Startenders who could get by with limited to no magic.

My crew was going to have to stay behind on this one. Unfortunately, so was my ship. Barships were our only edge in the universe. We couldn't risk one falling into Gob's hands. If he was able to reverse-engineer the magic and technology and build weaponized versions for his military, they could quite simply become unstoppable.

While my crew are some of the finest folks I know, they're not exactly noted at staying under the radar. And with the exceptions of Eric and me, are gods or children of gods. They'd be noticed by Big Nose for sure.

"After what you did on Rchaic, our intel is your intel. I'll have what we have sent to you within the hour. Within three, I'll have my best analysts get you a half dozen ideas on how to get in and out safely."

"Thanks."

"So Murphy, who do ye want on the team?" Paddy said.

It was a good question. I thought about it and once I figured out who I wanted, I had a dark thought. If we didn't make it back, a lot of honchos were going to get promotions. My picks were all head honchos of other barships.

My first pick was Nellie Moran. I'd known her since she was in pigtails. I helped raise her. When she was a little girl, she decided she wanted to be a ninja. Then she found out that ninjas were assassins and decided to change her definition of what a ninja was so she could still be one. In all honesty, I'd say she succeeded. Even named her barship in keeping with those values. *Perdu* means hidden or remaining out of sight. Like me, Nellie's only human, but she's spent her life honing her skills. She can get in and out of almost anywhere undetected. Yeah, she does have a couple of magical items that help her along these lines. One of them is a pair of black boots with wings on them, of the same type that Hermes and Kyna wear. In fact for this mission, I was wearing an old pair of Hermes' cowboy boots. The ability to fly might be crucial to the rescue mission. While our Startender badges could negate gravity, we didn't yet have a means of propulsion that worked well on a planet. The harnesses with the blowers only worked in space. The former Pink Reaper was working on the problem though.

Nellie was a much more skilled flyer than I was, although I'd learned a lot of the theory from watching Terrorbelle teach our daughter how to fly. Nellie also had a piece of Hades' helm in a baseball hat. The death god had thrown a bet in order to give it to her. It allowed her to remain invisible for an hour at a time. It then required another hour to recharge before she could use it again. I was counting on her to get us in and out undetected.

I'd asked Xen to join the crew. He was a former planetary AI in a cute robot body that had more power than a military starship. Unfortunately, he had encountered Gob before and the goblin god had made mystic arrangements to specifically scan for him if he ever entered the Throneworld's solar system.

Of course I wanted Sun WuKong, the most versatile and powerful of the Startenders. Unfortunately, the Monkey King was a god and an extremely powerful one at that. He'd never get onto Throneworld undetected, so I went for Sun WuKong lite – Rumbles.

I first met Rumbles when he was a clown working at the circus. His shtick was dressing like a boxer. He really had been a Golden Gloves boxer. Rumbles held several black belts and was an Olympic gold-medal fencer before he joined the circus. It made sense that he named his ship *The Big Top*. On an adventure to help out Loki way back, Sun ended up training Rumbles and Jane the monkey princess in mystic martial arts.

Rumbles ended up with part of his clown makeup tattooed to his face, but he still considers it a small price to pay to gain the mastery that he did, including becoming adept at cloud dancing, which gave him the ability to leap over small buildings and fly.

Both Rumbles and Jane are Startenders. I thought the world of Jane. She had a huge heart and a quick mind, but Rumbles was bigger and stronger, not to mention a better fighter and I needed muscle.

My next pick was somebody who had done it all and survived to tell the tales. Sir Dagonet, known as the Infinite Jester, was the head honcho of the barship *Excalibur*. The former knight and jester of the Round Table was quick on his feet and an excellent tactician. The fact that he had an invisible sword named Hayden that could injure even a god didn't hurt either.

The last member of my crew was Hex, head honcho of *The Accursed*.

I'd explained the plan to them and to their credit, they all agreed to help.

"So, how do we get there? Are we hitching a ride with Hex?" Rumbles said.

"Too big a risk of being noticed," I said. I'd checked with Bast. Dagonet's sword, the flying footwear and other minor mystic objects could be shielded, but mystically transporting on to the world would be like blowing an air horn in Gob's ear.

"Nexus?" Dagonet said.

I nodded.

"It has to be quick because it could still be traced back to wherever we start from, so we don't want to do it from a barship or anywhere in our home solar system," Nellie said.

Hex smirked. "I think Murphy already knows that and figured out a way around it."

"Right you are. We're going to use the Traven troll guild."

"That will cost a fortune. Where are we going to get the money?" Dagonet said.

"It's not as much as it could be. The guild maintains a permanent nexus for use of the Empire so we don't have to pay for opening and closing, just passage. Plus, Pace gets a discount." Pace was one of four troll Startenders and a genius in quantum geography. He revolutionized the way the troll guild worked nexi, getting people further using less energy among other things. Part of his licensing deal gave him a discount when using a guild-controlled nexus. "Luckily, Big Nose was too cheap to pay the guild the exclusivity fee. And Pace chipped in." Pace was the troll equivalent of a multi-millionaire. "Still, it'll cost most of the profit the Watering Hole has made since it opened."

"Ouch. I bet you Paddy's crying over that one," Rumbles said.

"Not a peep, since it's for good cause. However, Buzz hasn't stopped weeping about it. Since we don't have to open a nexus, there won't be any mystic noise on the other end and Big Nose can only trace it back to Traven." Traven was located on a hotbed of natural nexi, allowing its natural nexus access to more worlds than any other planet, which is why there were so many different races of people there. It's easy to travel to other worlds when you can do it on foot. It was also why the troll guild had their headquarters there. Many trolls have the magical ability to open up or control a nexus between worlds. It takes less energy to control a nexus than to open one. On Traven they are a power to be reckoned with. "We are paying the extra fifty percent anonymity fee, so the guild won't give us up. Bast figures even Big Nose won't push it too far with the guild. Otherwise, they might block any nexi to or from Throneworld, which means if Big Nose needs to get off-world in a hurry, he'll be up a creek."

"Cynosure's intel is about a week old." One of the goblin guards had let a cat in, then gave it a saucer of something to drink. It was one of Bast's more distant descendants. "Both Tock and his daughter Tada were alive then. Big Nose put them in adjoining cellblocks. Close enough to torture each other with the knowledge of how near the loved one was, but far enough away that they couldn't hear or see each other."

"I don't like Big Nose already," said Nellie.

I nodded in agreement. "We got lucky. The Traven nexus opens up only about twenty miles away from the prison. We should expect it to be well-guarded. The prison is well-run, well-thought out and well-guarded. Worse, it has its own magic detectors, so if we try to use anything mystic to sneak in we'll set off alarms," I said.

"Wait a second. If this prison is so impenetrable with the magic alarms, how did one of the bastarts get in?" Rumbles said.

"Bastarts have two natural forms – humanoid and cat. Neither requires an active output of magic to maintain, only to change. The cat simply walked in with the change of shift," I said. Our shape-shifters were either gods or needed to use magic to maintain a form, so having them go native or feline wouldn't work.

"And we can't do that because?" Dagonet said.

"They check the guards. They'd notice extras," I said.

"So we find a couple of guards when they're off-duty, knock them out, use makeup that can make us look like them and walk in with the rest of the shift," Nellie said.

"Problem is, that would be violating our Startender oath. Big Nose would execute the guards for allowing themselves to be replaced. We might as well kill the guards ourselves," I said.

Nellie creased her brows, then raised them. "Could this fall in the category of no other option?"

The Startender oath had a loophole, allowing the taking of life to save a greater number of lives.

I shook my head. "Five of us means five dead to save two."

"How the hell are we supposed to get in, then?" Nellie said.

"Get taken prisoner ourselves?" Dagonet said. "I've been in prison far too many times, so what's one more?"

"I thought about it, but it's a big place. Odds are we'd be put far away from either of them. My crew and Bast's agents came up with an idea. We pose as priests of Big Nose. His clergy wear monk robes with hoods, so we'd be able to impersonate them," I said.

"Why hasn't it been done before? It sounds too easy," Nellie said.

"Actually, it's not," Hex said. "Big Nose runs a theocracy where many religious offenses are severely punished. One of the most serious is impersonating one of his priests. Unless they had a death wish, none of the natives would risk it. Most goblins would never even consider it as a possibility, so they wouldn't even ask for ID. It's perfect. You come up with it, Murphy?"

"Actually Loki and Coyote did. Basically we suit up and go through the nexus," I said.

"What about whoever is guarding the other side?" Rumbles said.

"I can answer that," Dagonet said, holding up a small bag of glass marbles and a metal tube with a button on top. "*Excalibur* was on Earth duty." We have two barships permanently stationed on Earth and two more rotate through. "Murphy asked me to pick up something from Kaye Chandler before I came. No magic, just knockout gas. She's also a bit annoyed that you didn't pick her for the mission."

I sighed and passed out the marbles, keeping a few and the tube for myself. "I thought about it." Kaye was well past the century mark and unlike many of the other older Startenders, the former Pink Reaper owed it to science rather than magic. "But was worried her fear gas would ruin our element of surprise."

The pink gas absolutely terrified almost anyone who breathed it in, human or alien. Problem is, sometime the victims were very loud and vocal about their terror. Goblins running away while screaming in terror would attract attention.

"She is more than a one hit wonder," Dagonet said.

"I know, but I went with my gut on this one," I said.

Eric dropped us near the Throneworld nexus on Traven. Once the trolls on duty verified we had paid, Nellie went through, first and fast. She made sure anyone on the other side was unconscious by the time the rest of us came through.

Nellie and I took to the air to make sure there was nobody else nearby. I was especially proud of myself for not throwing up. To me, nexus travel has always felt like going through electrified gelatin. It makes me extremely nauseous.

Dagonet unrolled a small carpet that floated two feet off the ground.

Certain magical objects didn't give off much of a background signal, including flying shoes and magic carpets. Plus they were cloaked on top of that. The *Excalibur's* honcho Ganieda used to work with Terrorbelle at Nemesis and Co. and had been a member of the king's council back in Camelot. She was also the twin sister of Merlin. She's had this flying carpet for centuries and had loaned it to us for the mission.

"If we damage this, Gani will hurt us," Dagonet said.

"I'll make her a new one," Hex said.

"This was the first major magic object Gani made herself and it was better than the one her brother made. A new one won't replace the sentimental value," Dagonet said, climbing on the carpet. Rumbles and Hex got on behind him.

Hex cast a minor distraction spell, so that anyone who happened to look at us flying through the air would automatically look somewhere else and ignore us. He claimed he crafted the spell to work the same way so if Gob sensed it, he'd instantly notice something else much more interesting. Oddly enough, a side effect of the curse made it hard for Hex to focus on us for a brief period.

We flew low enough so he would be picked up by their version of radar and landed a short distance away from the prison. Dagonet rolled up the carpet and stuck it under his robe and we all walked up to the prison like we owned the place.

As a magí, Hex was able to tap into any form of magic, including the type the garba use to speak any language. He made sure that he was especially fluent in Goblin Prime before we left Traven. "We are here to see the condemned ones on orders of his greatness."

"Which would you like to see first, holy ones?" the goblin guard said, bowing, so he didn't look into our faces, a religious offense and thus standard operating procedure.

"Take us to the disgraced general," Hex said.

We were led through the prison, not even having to bother with the indignity of being searched.

A goblin jailer opened up the cellblock gate and started to come with us. Hex held up his hand to stop him. "This is between us and the condemned."

The jailer bowed his head, looking at the floor. "Of course, holy one. I will wait here until you need to leave."

We walked down the cellblock, which was empty accept for Tock. Solitary confinement was probably part of his punishment. We stood in front of his cell, the metal door of which had only a window so small that Buzz wouldn't be able to fit through. Tock turned toward the solid back wall as we got to the front of his cell.

"Go away priests. I have no need of you," Tock said.

"Okay, if that's the way you feel, but it's rather rude considering we've come such a long way," I said in broken Goblin Prime.

Tock turned and his eyes went wide. "Murphy! What in the forty-seven hells are you doing here?"

I noticed he still had on his ring with the lation stone in it, so he'd understand me no matter what language I spoke.

"We're here to bust you and your daughter out," I said.

"This is insanity. It's impossible. It's…"

"Yeah, I've heard it all before, but we made it this far, so I'd like to get going as quickly as possible. Gentlemen," I said.

Rumbles examined the lockbox with his hands, searching for weak points. Next he folded his fingers up and smashed his palm at the metal, actually cracking it. Dagonet got the tip of his invisible sword through the crack and sliced through the bolt with much effort. I yanked the door open, pulled out another robe from under mine and handed it to Tock.

"This is sacrilege," he said.

"What's Big Nose going to do? Have you executed?" I said.

"Good point." Tock put the robe on and shut the cell door behind him.

We walked to the exit and hoped the jailer couldn't count.

"Open the door," Hex demanded. The jailer did and bowed as he walked by. I took up the rear. As I passed him the jailer's head popped up. Damn, I guess he could count.

"Are you daring to look at us?" I said in Goblin Prime, hoping my accent wasn't too bad. I gave a nod to Nellie and she silently sprinted ahead of us and around the corner in the blink of an eye.

"Apologies, holy one, but weren't there only five of you going in?" the jailer said.

"They are only five of us now," Hex said. "You must have miscounted. We permit you to recount."

The jailer cautiously looked at us, so we bowed our heads so our faces were hidden. He actually lifted up his fingers when he counted us. Twice. He got five both times.

"It's so odd. I could've sworn that there were six of you."

"No matter. Better for you to be sure than neglect your duties to the Great One," Hex said. "Now take us to the disgraced general's daughter."

"I cannot."

"What!?" screamed Tock. The jailer bowed so far his head almost touched the floor. Tock moved toward him, but stopped when I placed my hand on his shoulder.

"I'm sorry, holy one. I would if I could, but while you were in with the former general, the Great One sent for the daughter himself. Apparently he has moved up her execution."

Tock pushed past me and grabbed the jailer by the front of his shirt and lifted him off the ground. "Tell me where they took my daughter!"

"General Tock, you've committed sacrilege!" The goblin was more shocked by the wearing of the robe than the escape.

"I'm going to commit murder in a moment. Where did they take her?"

"To the Great One's palace."

"How long ago?"

"Five minutes." A nice feature of lation stones is that they switched all the local units to ones the wearer understood.

"We might still be able to catch them," Dagonet said, unfurling the flying carpet.

Rumbles jabbed his fingers into the jailer's upper spine, rendering him unconscious.

"Dagonet, put it away," I said.

"Murphy, it's my daughter," Tock pleaded.

"We're going to get her back. But if we use that in here, it will set off the magic alarms and the place will go into lock down with us inside. We'll never get to her in time. We have to walk out the way we came in," I said.

We couldn't risk assuming that the goblins didn't count us when we came in. Nellie was a good head shorter than me, so she got under my robe facing me, her arms hugging me and her feet standing on my boots. Dagonet was shorter, but broader and heavier.

It was slow going and difficult to walk. If I used the boots to lessen the load, the alarms would have went off. Our cloaking was good enough to hide the objects, but not powerful enough to fool the magic sensors if we used them. After a while my feet hurt, but we made it to the front gate with all the goblins doing the requisite bowing. As we neared the exit, one female goblin looked up and noticed my girth. "I guess they keep you well fed, holy one."

"The Great One is good to those who serve him," I said in Goblin Prime.

Apparently my pronunciation was a little off because she started to look up toward my face. I moved my sleeves to block her view. The others were almost at the gate.

"Why is this still closed?" Hex said in a harsh tone. A guard rushed to open it.

The others got out and kept moving, but the one guard stepped in front of me.

"Pardon holy one, but I need guidance," the guard said, bowing in front of me.

I stopped and Nellie started poking me to keep moving.

"Speak," I said.

"I have been proposed to," she said.

"And?" Gob's priests were not the nicest of people, so I was polite and nothing more.

"He is a teacher. Not the worthiest of professions. And a bit beneath me. I'm worried what my parents might think."

"Do you love him?" I said, careful of my pronunciation.

"I do."

"If your parents speak ill of him, ask them how one who

teaches the ways of the Great One to the young can be considered unworthy by any of the faithful?" Religion was taught in all aspects of goblin life.

"Yes, even my father would have to concede that. Thank you, holy one."

I walked on as if her gratitude was as beneath me as her boyfriend's profession was below hers.

Once outside, I let the flying boots lessen my load, but the streets were more crowded than when we went in and I had to keep walking for almost twenty minutes until I found a place deserted enough to fly up to a roof.

"Nice job. Father Mike would be proud," Nellie said, coming out from beneath my robe.

"Thanks."

We both took off into the skies. We had studied a map of the city so we knew where the palace was. We hovered about a block away from it to get our bearings.

"Where do you think the others are?" Nellie said.

There was a boom as a wall blew out from about the three hundredth floor in the palace. It was the largest building the city, towering over everything else, none of which exceeded one hundred stories.

"If I had to make a guess, I'd say over there," I said and noticed there was a man with white hair and a beard falling along with the rubble. "Save Hex."

Nellie was already diving toward him. She was the faster and more experienced flyer, but we were still a ways away.

Things hadn't gone well for our team. I later found out that right before Hex blew out the wall that the magí had body-slid the team into the throne room, hoping the element of surprise would be enough for them to get the drop on Gob.

It hadn't. After the initial attack, Rumbles and Dagonet were on the floor, barely moving. Hex was down on one knee, but glaring at the god Gob. The goblin god was enormous and energy crackled around and over his skin.

"Slow Mo."

Hex's spell made the goblin god move much slower. From the floor Dagonet rolled over and pointed Hayden. Although Gob couldn't see the invisible blade move, he felt wounds open in his shoulders, abdomen and knees. Gob was tough. He grimaced, but that was it. The energy blast that he shot toward Hex seemed to move pretty fast. It was more than his personal shields or those of his Startender badge could handle, although it deflected enough that the magí kept breathing as the mystic explosion smashed him through the wall.

I raced toward the hole to try to help.

"Give me my daughter!" Tock screamed.

"You dare make demands of your god?" Gob said. And I do have to admit that the moniker others had given him was appropriate. He stood at least twenty feet tall and his nose was bigger than my torso.

"I served you faithfully my entire life. And I've asked for nothing in return. You know I had nothing to do with my brother's treachery and Tada had even less. I am still your humble servant. In exchange for my years of serving you and the Empire, I beg you to spare her and you may take my life instead."

"May? The lives of all of my subjects are mine to do with as I see fit. And the duty you refer to was nothing more or less than what was expected of any of my subjects. I owe you nothing. However, I owe your family for what your brother did to me."

"My brother is dead by your hand. This cannot hurt him. It makes no sense, Great One."

The goblin pointed his finger at Tock and a bolt of dark purple energy shot out toward the goblin. I dove down to shove Tock out of the way. The blast caught me in the back, but my badge's shields held and saved Tock, even as we were both flung across the room. Dagonet used Hayden again and seven new wounds opened, but Gob used a giant metal club and beat the knight into unconsciousness.

The he turned back to Tock. "Do not tell me what makes sense. I have decreed that your entire bloodline shall perish from the face of the Empire. You two are the last that remain." His nephew Rem was on Jade's side of the family. "I should kill your offspring first knowing that will bring you the most pain and then I will send you to join her."

Tada floated into the room in a bubble of energy. She was little more than a toddler. Rumbles flew up on a cloud and used his body to disrupt the energy flow between Gob and the sphere. There was an explosion of light. The bubble popped, the former clown screamed and both Rumbles and Tada fell.

Despite his injuries, Tock managed to get beneath and catch the little goblin girl. Rumbles rolled as he hit the ground. Gob smashed an enormous foot down on top of the former clown. Rumbles leapt up and managed to punch Gob's enormous nose and it bent halfway across the goblin god's face. Rumbles followed it up with a kick to an eye and spun so his elbow hit the enormous forehead. The force of the blow snapped the giant god's head back slightly. Gob swung a clawed hand at Rumbles, who was now standing on a cloud which spun him away from the blow, but right into a punch from Gob's other hand, which knocked Rumbles from his cloud and onto the floor. Gob moved faster than someone that big should have been able to and again stomped his enormous foot down on top of the former clown. Rumbles got his arms up in time for a two-handed block, but the force of the blow smashed him through the floor to whatever was below.

I hovered, trying to figure out options. There was only one that made sense – we needed to get out now. I wished I could just draw the sigil for Gani's elevator, but someone with Gob's power would likely sense it and use it to trace us back to Earth.

Tada wrapped her arms around her father's neck and squeezed. "Papa, I'm scared."

Tock rose to his feet and stood defiantly facing his god. "I love you, my daughter. We will be together on the other side."

Gob smiled. "And that's where you're wrong. You shall not escape Gob even in death. I control the underworld from the forty-three heavens to the forty-six hells. I will ensure that you will never see each other again."

Gob reached down and tore the child from her father's arms.

Tock tried to stop him, but it was like a spider trying to fend off an elephant. The girl's fearful cries filled the room. I knew I didn't have the power to stop an angry god, but I wasn't going to let him take a child, especially the daughter of a friend. I dove in and took hold of Tada's arms and tried to pull her away. Gob swatted me across the chamber with a flick of his finger, like I was nothing more than a gnat. My badge cushioned my impact against the wall, but it still took my breath away. I turned and flew back to try again, but I was too late.

Gob simply squeezed the girl like she was a balloon he was trying to pop. And pop she did. The crunch of her rib cage collapsing echoed in the chamber along with the little goblin girl's last cry.

"No!" Tock screamed.

The goblin God tossed the small corpse of Tock's daughter at him. He caught her and fell to the floor weeping, cradling her tiny battered body in his arms and stroking her hair.

The goblin god towered over Tock and laughed.

I hung in the air, looking for something to hit him with. Then I realized that I hadn't used the Pink Reaper's gas marbles. I threw a handful and they burst on his face. Amused, the giant goblin inhaled deeply. Nothing happened except he blasted me again with the dark purple energy. I managed to fly out of the way so it only tagged my arm, but it was enough to ground me. The blast that I had taken for Tock had damaged my badge's shields. They deflected some of his vile mystic energy, but some got through. I curled up into a ball and threw up from the pain. My body felt like it was being eaten from the inside out.

"I will give you a moment to savor what I've done before I end you, like I did your flying friend."

"I will destroy you!" Tock shouted.

Gob laughed. "That's just what I was about to say."

It was hitting the fan so hard the fan's blades had disintegrated.

"Murphy, we're here," Nellie said through the comm in my ear. I couldn't see her so I guess the baseball cap was in play.

"Hex with you?" I whispered.

"Yes, but he's barely conscious," she said.

"I'm fine," Hex said over the comm.

"You able to evac?"

"Yes." At least that's what I think he said as he coughed up something that sounded nasty.

"Get Dagonet." The boots flew me down through the hole in the floor, which was good because I doubted I could stand. Rumbles was trying to crawl out from beneath the rubble on the floor below us. I pulled and flew him up then put him next to the Infinite Jester.

"You think your tiny magi has the power to leave when I don't wish it? I am Gob, master of the universe. I can block any mystic plan he may think he has to escape. I may not see him and the other intruder, but I can smell them."

"Over your body odor? Now that's impressive." I said.

"You wish to die first, I presume. There is no other reason to insult the Lord of the Goblin Empire. Your death wish is most impressive."

Good. Gob was angry and focused on me. I waved bye. Still invisible, Nellie flew to Tock, wrapped her arms around him and his dead daughter, then touched her badge. An instant later, they were gone.

"What?!" Gob said, stunned and having trouble figuring out what just happened. Now visible, Hex used the goblin god's distraction to body-slide Rumbles and Dagonet out of the solar system before Gob could stop them. Hex was so skilled he was able to slide just an instant before the god could sense the power build-up. Unfortunately at those kind of distances, Hex could only safely body-slide one person on each arm.

Nellie and the goblins had left courtesy of the Hermes Express. Hermes had figured he also could only safely carry two, although I suspect Tock wasn't letting go of his daughter anytime soon.

The incursion and exodus of another god to and from his home solar system so rapidly had taken Gob entirely by surprise. As fast as Hermes was, the trip was far from instantaneous. Hermes said the round-trip had taken just over eleven seconds. It was in our original plan as an emergency backup.

This original plan called for the odd men or women out to

hop on either Hex's or Hermes' back so we'd all be able to get out, but if I had tried to piggy back on either, Gob would have suspected something and likely stopped the escapes.

So we needed a distraction and said distraction had to stay behind. It may sound noble, but it wasn't. It was only fair. I asked for everyone's help and I wasn't about to live with anyone else's death on my conscience. I still blamed myself, at least partially, for Terrorbelle.

So there I was, spending some quality terror time alone with the most powerful lesser god in the universe. To say Gob wasn't happy was the understatement of a lifetime. And quite possibly the end of mine.

"It seems your friends have left you to my mercies, and I assure you I have none."

Gob blasted me with more of his dark purple energy and my badge's shields fell. And so did I.

I wasn't sure I could move, but I forced myself to my feet. At least I assumed they were my feet because I couldn't feel them anymore.

"That's great. After what you did to Tada, I'm not feeling too merciful either. Here's what's going to happen. You are going to let me walk out of not only your palace, but your system."

"Your paltry speed god won't be able to pull that trick again. I'll stop him while he is still planets away."

"You might, but then I would have no choice but to destroy you."

Gob's laughter rocked the entire city, maybe even the planet. "You are a mortal with a badge and boots that are but magical toys. A breeze would knock you off your feet. You are no more a danger to me than a speck of dust."

"You'd think that, but you'd be wrong. And bacteria are smaller than dust and they have wiped out civilizations. I have a story to tell you. A while back some of us encountered a group that was a spinoff of the Nil." A twisted cult that wants to bring about the end of the universe. "They called themselves the Void. I believe you're familiar with them."

The goblin god became very still. Which was good, because I was bluffing my posterior off to get out of this using some information I'd gotten from the bastarts at Cynosure and making up the rest as I went along.

"As you know, one sect of the Void had found a way to destroy manna." Again, not exactly true. Manna was the mystical energy that gods used to sustain themselves. It fueled their power. "Which is why you killed them."

A Void sect had attacked the Throneworld. Gob had indeed killed all of them, but witnesses described him stumbling during the battle to the point where his own troops had to intervene in order to save him. Afterwards, witnesses said he appeared confused about the reason for it.

"While energy is neither created nor destroyed, it can be changed into other forms. These members of the Void had figured out how to transform manna into hydrogen gas, rendering it useless to any god. The Void decided to start out using their weapon on the greatest collection of manna in the known universe – Throneworld. But they bit off more than they could chew."

"Why bore me with a story I already know?" Gob was trying for uninterested, but I wasn't buying it. If he wasn't curious, I'd be dead. Bast guessed that he never figured out why he had a power loss. I was just making something up to fit the facts.

"Because as you know, one of the Void cultists escaped." From the fiery energy that burst from Gob's eye sockets, I'm guessing he had no idea. Which made sense since I was still making the story up, channeling everything that made me a writer for the most important tale I'd ever told. "We came across him when he was trying to pull a scam on some lesser divinities to get them close enough to destroy their manna and then them." I took the metal tube with the button I had kept from the marble bag out of my pocket. It was actually a tiny detonator to trigger the gas marbles if we had a need to plant them and wait until someone walked by instead of throwing them. "The cultist you failed to destroy was actually the brains of the operation. He developed several manna eaters, small devices that can infect an entire world. Which is why no divinities are assisting us on planet. This way, I can detonate them anytime." Gob's finger started to glow. "And yes, you could destroy me and the detonator, but my colleagues would simply send another signal. It might just take a while to get here from so far away, so I guess the question is whether or not you believe you can find all the manna eaters we hid before that signal arrives."

Gob didn't look like he was feeling lucky.

"Now that we're in the same room, I can tell you that it will absolutely destroy every last bit of manna on this world. Of course, such a wise being such as yourself has no doubt stashed manna on many other worlds throughout the universe, just in case of an emergency such as this."

Manna was far more valuable than gold or jewels. No god would do such a thing, because manna left unclaimed could be sensed and claimed by any other god as their own. Any manna out of arm's reach was too far. Plus, Gob was noted to not leave Throneworld. It was his place of power. Leaving it would weaken him substantially and mean more risk to him. It's why he sent troops to conquer other worlds instead of doing it himself. That and things like fighting battles would use up manna, something Bast was certain Gob did not like to do.

"How long is it been since you had to deal with the tropes of mortality? I wonder – once you are powerless, how long do you think it will be before someone you or your Empire crossed and angered comes gunning for you? I mean, once the universe realizes you can be harmed and even killed. Perhaps even one of your own subjects, looking to gain power or avenge a loved one that you slaughtered? You'd be able to rebuild a sizeable supply after many years, but you only gained enough to seize control of a mortal empire by slaughtering your own pantheon and stealing their manna for your own. That's a trick you can't do twice."

Gob started to move his arms into a defensive position. He was buying it.

"How long would you guess it would be before someone found out you were a fraud? Don't guess. Not long at all, because my colleagues would make sure the entire universe knew." I played with the detonator in my hand and grabbed it between my fingers. "I've just activated what my people would call a dead man's switch." Even I wasn't stupid enough to tell him we were Startenders or from Earth. Maybe he wouldn't find out. It was a long shot, but one I was still going to take. "You can kill me, but then I let go and the manna eaters will be deployed. Or if you destroy the switch before it triggers, it's just a short wait until another signal gets here. If you survive, I feel confident someone else will finish the job for me. So what's it going to be, Gobby? You going to let me go or learn to enjoy life as a mortal?"

The entire city shook in his anger.

"Oh, I planted several manna eaters in your city alone. If there is any retaliation against Tock or my people or even any of your own people, one of us will activate them."

"How do I know you won't leave and activate them anyway?"

"Simple. I give you my word that I will not activate any manna eaters on your world." True enough since I couldn't turn on an imaginary device if I wanted to. "Unless you give me reason to."

"So I am just supposed to take your word?"

"Yes. And really what choice do you have?"

"If you really had manna eaters, why not use them before now?"

"Because a side effect of manna turning to hydrogen gas is any spark would cause an explosion. You have so much, it would blow up most of the city, which would have killed the people we came here to save. But the girl's dead now, so if I'm dying, I'm not going alone. But like you, I want to live."

Gob opened his mouth and I held up my hand.

"Stop. I don't need to hear the speech where you swear vengeance on me. It's been overdone. Let's both just go on with our lives. My group will be kind enough not to spread the word of this happening. But we have also manufactured a lot of these manna eaters. Should anything ever happen to us, the enemies of the Empire will receive one each to deploy or reverse-engineer, so it's in your best interest to insure that nothing ever does. Don't bother to see me to the door. I'll see myself out," I said, flying out the hole in the wall. I didn't look back, mainly because if he was going to vaporize me, I didn't want to see it coming. That and someone as confident as I was pretending to be wouldn't feel the need to check behind him. Nothing happened to me, but the ground below rocked so hard, parts of buildings fell.

Better get while the getting is good and before he changed his mind. I hit my Startender badge. "Evac now."

Less than six seconds later Hermes grabbed hold of me and extended his badge's field around me. Another six and I was out of Gob's system.

It took a little longer until I was back in the Traven system and on board *Fool's Glory*. Hermes told me while he was waiting for my call, he managed to snatch Tada's soul and lead her away from the goblin pantheon's underworld. Part of his power as a psychopompos lets him lead the dead into an afterlife. Hermes brought her to Pluto – the god, not the former planet. Pluto has a soft spot for kids and although she couldn't come back to the land of the living, it did get her out of Gob's clutches.

Tock was still weeping and was kneeling on the floor, holding his daughter's body. The others and my crew stood silently, their heads bowed.

Tock looked up at me when I walked in. "I meant what I said, Murphy. I will destroy him."

"Someday, but for now, morn your daughter. And when you're ready, there is still a place for you here among the Startenders," I said.

Tock bent down, kissed his daughter's head and stood up. "I'm ready now."

"Excellent." I realized I had been running on nothing but adrenaline and willpower. "I think I need a nap."

Which is when my legs collapsed. Hermes caught me an instant before everything went black.

RECOVERY

When I regained consciousness, it was like coming back from nothingness, as if I'd ceased to be. I tried to remember what happened, but the pain overwhelmed me and I screamed. My eyes opened and were attacked by icy daggers of light stabbing into my skull.

"He's awake," said a voice that registered as Loki.

"You figured that out from the screaming, did you?" That wiseass could only be Coyote.

"Ye have to do something. The lad's in agony." The brogue was unmistakably Paddy Moran.

"We're trying." It was a female voice. I turned towards it and saw white hair. Maybe Ganieda.

"Big Nose affected him with quietus. This is the toxic magic he used to knock off the rest of his pantheon. The only reason Murphy's still alive is because he's mortal. The stuff goes after magic and manna. It separates it from the host and lets the caster of the spell absorb it. Murphy has none, so instead it's just attacking his flesh." I recognized Master Hex's gravelly tones. His voice had gotten a lot coarser since he came back from the dead.

"Give him something for the pain." That's one voice I'd never mistake. Through the pain, I was comforted knowing my daughter was nearby, but it wasn't enough for me to stop screaming.

"Too risky. We sedate any of his systems too much and he might not have the strength left to fight off the mystic infection," Hermes said.

"If we don't do something, he'll die from the fight," Paddy said. "Hold him down. Loki, lift up his head.

I felt strong hands grip my head and hold my mouth open.

I saw the old man's face blurrily in front of me. "Murphy, this should help ye. 'Tis Mosie's blend."

Before our favorite psychic shuffled off his mortal coil, he was in a lot of pain. He'd been drinking since he was a kid in order to keep his psychic visions at bay, and constant imbibing of alcohol damaged more than just his liver. Mosie had some very painful years leading up to his actual death. The saddest part about it was he still couldn't stop drinking alcohol even though he knew it was killing him. Without the booze he would see all of time laid out in front of him and would go comatose and insane. Paddy, Dion and Hermes had made up a special blend of cream, whiskey, brandy and some other nutrients to maximize Mosie's system's strength, and still give him enough alcohol to stay drunk.

"It should give ye strength and we upped the alcohol to knock ye out so ye don't hurt so much."

I nodded and forced myself not to scream while Paddy poured the concoction down my throat. The taste was magnificent, but you'd expect nothing less from the boss and the Greco-Roman god of wine. I coughed and threw up a little of it, but then Paddy gave me another. Then another. A warm sensation flowed through my body. It didn't get rid of the pain, but lessened it enough to let me stop screaming. The booze was kicking in and it wouldn't be long before I was unconscious.

I saw Elsiebelle's face in front of me as Loki let go of my head and gently put it down on a pillow. I looked around and realized I was in the hospital section of Startender station.

"Dad, you know I love …" My daughter was cut off by Paddy putting his hand over her mouth.

"No lass, 'tis not the time for goodbyes," Paddy said.

"I just want him to know that I love him," E-Belle said.

Paddy wrapped his arms around my daughter and hugged her. "And you don't think he knows that ye love him? In fact, don't ye think he knows that all of us love him? We may tease your father because of his idiotic sense of humor, but Murphy is a smart man with a gift for seeing the best in people. He knows. But if we all start telling him how we feel, it will sound like we're saying goodbye. He might give up the fight and then he will be lost to us. So don't burden him by telling him things he already knows. Instead give him something to fight for."

E-Belle sniffled, wiped her eyes on her sleeve and nodded her head. "Dad, there's something I never told you. I've been working on writing a story like you do. I don't think I'll ever be the author you are, but I have just about finished a story about something that happened with me and mom back when I was a kid. If you don't get better, you're never going to be able to read it. If you get better, I'll even write a story about you and me and mom."

I tried to speak, but everything I said was coming out slurred so I just nodded my head and gave a thumbs up

Hermes came over and held my face between both his hands, forcing me to look into his eyes. "Murphy, Paddy's right. You need to keep fighting. Big Nose's quietus infection is bad and if you give up even for a moment, that's going to be the endgame. I've got an idea, but it's risky. If it doesn't cure you, it may kill you. It could do both. Do I have your blessing to try?"

Again I tried to speak and gobbledygook came out, so I nodded and waved my hand in the vague imitation of a cross symbol like what Father Mike might do. Hermes smiled, then I tried to lift Hermes' wallet, but I was too slow and sloppy. It's a thing we have. Hermes used to constantly steal my wallet until I managed to be able to do it to him. Neither of us had tried it in ages.

Hermes saw my pitiful attempt and laughed. The god of thieves guided my hand into his pocket, placed my fingers around his wallet. When he put my arm back on the side of the bed, his wallet was in my hand.

"You can hold onto that until you're better," Hermes said.

I tried to ask what happens if I don't make it, but it came out gibberish. I tilted my head sideways and managed to scratch my finger across my throat.

"If you don't make it, then you can keep it."

I chuckled, nodded and held the wallet close to my chest as I passed out.

I had only a vague recollection of waking up long enough for someone, I think it was Loki, to pour Mosie's Blend down my throat before I faded back off into oblivion. It went like that for a while – drink, pass out, repeat.

In between the repeating, there was nothing – no thought, no dreams, no pain. I was nothing. Then I fully woke up and there was no more pain. It was dark, but I could see a light in the distance. I had nothing else to do, so I followed it straight into something that looked just like the bar at Bulfinche's Pub. And by bar I don't mean the entire pub, just the actual bar itself that we served drinks on. Reflex and instinct kicked in and I walked toward the serving side until I realized there was already somebody back there. The familiar face didn't look old enough to drink.

"Peter?" I said.

The little boy put a glass on the bar, poured cream-colored liquid in it then slid it towards me.

"Hi ya, Murphy."

"If I'm seeing you, does that mean I'm dead?"

Decades back, I'd tried to find my first wife Elsie in the afterlife, or rather afterlives. In doing so, I upset a large part of the supernatural order. It all got sorted out, which is how ended up becoming friends with the Grim Reaper.

Peter helped me out on part of my quest. Like me, he'd lived in the apartments upstairs at Bulfinche's. We'd taken him along with some other kids – who became Paddy's kids – in off the dangerous streets. Peter was adapted by the Changs, a wonderful family. Sounds like a happy ending. Would have been too if he hadn't been slaughtered by a sadistic and evil cross-dressing vampire who thought she was doing the world a favor by killing a kid with Down's Syndrome. She was one of the few people Paddy ever endorsed killing.

Peter became a spirit guide, a lite version of a psychopompos like Hermes. Guides help the recently dead get their emotional affairs in order then move on to an afterlife.

I didn't want to die. I wasn't done living yet, but I'd survived a dozen times that I should have died only by sheer luck and stubbornness. It had to run out sometime. At least I knew I had friends on the other side, and I'd be reunited with Terrorbelle and Elsie again.

I was a little disappointed that one of those friends was a no show, especially after how the Grim Reaper helped me on the

Cyndicate ship. "So is John so busy he can't be bothered to greet me in person? I was expecting something special. At the very least, Groucho Marx glasses."

"Thanatos sends his regards, but regrets he could not show up in person. He didn't want to speed your death," Peter said.

If you hang around gods, mages and other mystic folk long enough, you learn a few things. There are points in people's lives that are not fixed by fate, where they can take one of a number of paths. That includes dying. People often have an option, not unlike Quan, the last survivor of Hiven.

"If Death himself came too near, it might eliminate your option to live," Peter said.

"I'm not dead?"

"You're mostly dead," Peter said. I laughed. "What's so funny?"

"You never got to watch the Princess Bride when you were alive, did you?" Peter shook his head. "It'll take too long to explain and I don't have true love to fall back on." Actually, I was fortunate to find real love twice, but both my loves were on John's side of things. "So am I going to become all the way dead?"

The young boy shrugged his shoulders. "Hard to say at this point, but you still have a chance to live."

"Like 50-50?"

Peter shook his head. "More like 98-2."

"Those are great odds," I said.

Peter frowned. "For dying, sure."

"Oh." I sighed, picked up the drink in front of me and drained it. It tasted and felt real. I didn't bother to ask how the bar or drink could be in whatever limbo we were in. I'd tried asking similar questions in the past, but those who know the answers just don't want to share. Or maybe they can't.

"So what do we do? Just wait?" I said.

Peter nodded. "At least this way you get to spend some time with me. That's not such a bad thing, is it?" Peter pulled a clown nose out of his pocket and put it on his spirit form's face. Nellie and several of her crew had made sure Peter was buried with it back when they were all kids. That action somehow let him have a spirit version of it. And over the years, the kinder had sometimes been able to see him in the living world.

"Seeing you again is a very special thing. It's kind of weird to be on this side of the bar, so I might as well enjoy it. Pour me another Mosie's Blend, even if you don't look old enough to drink or serve alcohol."

"Paddy didn't worry about such things in Bulfinche's Pub, and this is a doorway to the afterlife. Rules from the living world don't have to apply," Peter said.

"Fair enough, but I have a question. You've been dead for decades. If you were alive, you'd be older than I was when we first met, yet you still look like a kid. Why?"

"I tried being a grownup for a while, but I didn't like it so much. I'm more comfortable being a kid. Even though I have the years to be an adult, I never was one when I was alive. I really have no proper frame of reference as to how to be one. I do make a good kid."

"You always were. You loved to play pool. Pity we don't have a table," I said

Peter smiled and snapped his fingers, then pointed behind me. "Who says we don't? You can rack them, but I get to break."

After a few games of pool – all of which I lost – I wasn't in the bar that wasn't Bulfinche's anymore. It seemed like I was finally dreaming. That or I was suddenly floating in space in an old fashioned space suit. In real life I wouldn't need a suit, just my Startender badge.

"Good luck," a voice whispered and my insides suddenly seemed to explode. Dark purple energy burst out from every opening I had, from my mouth and nostrils to the two down below.

The quietus energy shattered the faceplate of the spacesuit and ripped the lower part to shreds on the way out. Things suddenly got very cold as I faced down the darkness of the void before falling into darkness all my own.

I opened my eyes expecting to see Peter or John. I was pleasantly surprised to have other faces greet me.

"Is he going to make it?" Paddy asked.

"He's not dead. That's a good sign," Hermes said.

"What do I have to make? Because I feel horrible, so whatever it is, it's probably not going to be done well," I said and tried to sit up. My entire body exploded with pain, knocking me back down on the bed

"Daddy!"

My rib cage was suddenly being crushed by Elsiebelle's arms. My daughter was nowhere near as strong as her mother, but she was still several times more robust than a human woman. The pressure on my chest increased threefold as Savannah and Riga got in on the hugging action. I hugged them all back for a moment until the pain it was causing got the better of me.

"Ladies, I'm having a little trouble breathing," I said.

"C'mon, show some decorum. You're not scared little girls, you are Startenders. Get off the man," Nellie said. "Show some dignity." My daughter and my crewmates had no sooner let go of me when Nellie took their place, her arms wrapped around me and her head on my chest.

"Definitely very dignified, squirt," I said.

"Shut up, Murphy," Nellie said as she squeezed me tighter. I looked down and saw tears rolling down her face. She turned to look me straight in the eyes. "Don't you ever do that to me again!" I rubbed the ninja's head. "Next time that happens, I'm the one staying behind. Are we clear on that?"

I helped raise Nellie and her sister and brother. There's no way I'd let her take a danger just to save me. However she was stubborn enough to make that argument unwinnable, so I just said, "I hear you."

Loki raised the head of my bed up to a sitting position and put his hand on my shoulder. Paddy messed my hair and couldn't stop grinning, but his eyes were red and moist.

The small room was full. I turned my head to my left. My two godchildren waved at me and said in unison. "Hi, Uncle Murphy."

John was the firstborn child of Ryth and Mathew, a succubus and an angel who ran away together during an apocalypse attempt we managed to stop. I had delivered John without his mother tearing me to shreds. It's a long story, but it's why he's named after me. Both his parents are Startenders and John was in the Startender Society. He'd become a medical doctor, specializing in mystic illnesses.

My other godchild Pixie had been delivered by Terrorbelle and myself. She grew up in the same apartment building as Terrorbelle.

My entire crew was there alongside the rescue team and Tock. So were the rest of the staff from Bulfinche's who lived on Startender Station – Dion, Demeter and Kamile. Hermes stood in the corner, grinning. His wallet was alongside me in the bed. I smiled and nodded to him. He nodded back.

"Thanks."

"Anytime," he said.

I threw the wallet to him, but my body wasn't up to the task. It fell after only about three feet. Luckily Hermes was fast enough to catch it and be back against the far corner so fast I didn't even see him move

"It's so nice to see so many people keeping watch for me to get better," I said. Everyone laughed like I'd said something funny, which was a better reaction than most of the times I was actually trying to say something funny.

"What's the joke?"

John walked up and hit a button. The wall slid open.

"Uncle Murphy, I'm be taking over your case from Hermes now that you're out of the woods, so I will state that while you do need your rest, there are still a few more people keeping watch for you. Why don't you say hi to them and then you're back to bed rest."

My bed was on wheels, so Loki pushed me out into the corridor, only it wasn't so much a hall as it was a handball court, filled with dozens of people. The crowd gave a cheer and I tried not to swell up too much as I said my hellos. Apparently every Startender in the system who wasn't on duty was there, not to mention a number of friends who lived on the station. Plus some former refugees from an international incident I had helped cause who now lived on the station. There were view screens linked to the main barroom of every barship we had and The Watering Hole. Everyone waved and shouted my name. I waved back, trying not to show how hard it was to move.

While it was great to know that I was loved, the simple truth is everybody who had been waiting for me had lives and duties of their own. Loki and Elsiebelle would have stayed if I hadn't insisted that I'd be okay.

It turns out that Hermes' idea worked, but had come close to killing me. Startenders tried to get the quietus toxic magic out of me, but even Hex and Ganieda had come up short. Apparently quietus attacked anything mystic. Even Vulcan couldn't figure out how to get it out of me. Everyone was stumped until Hermes came up with the idea of using something as bait to make it crawl out of me.

The problem was that a good portion of Startender Station and our barships utilize magic in their structure and there was a risk that the quietus would go after other mystic sources of energy if they tried anything onboard.

My Startender badge had been utterly destroyed, which freaked Vulcan out. He didn't think it was possible and he was worried that the quietus allowed Big Nose to scan the badges. Further investigation revealed it just absorbed power, not knowledge or physical structure. Vulcan was working on building me a new badge. Apparently he, his gremlin wife Bubba Sue and Kaye Chandler were trying to work in some upgrades, but the badges use up a lot of resources and it would be weeks before my new one was ready.

I didn't think the time frame was going to be a problem, because it would be at least that long until I was in good enough shape to go back out into the field. I was luckily to be able to walk at all. The quietus tried to eat me from the inside out. If it wasn't for me spending ten plus hours a night in one of the Pink Reaper's healing chambers I still wouldn't be able to move around at all. Since it was technology-based, there had had been a debate about whether or not to use it on me earlier on, but the big brains were worried that the healing and destructive energies would get in a tug of war and tear my flesh apart. That, and in the past when it was used to try to help someone with cancer, it not only strengthened the person, but also the tumors.

It turns out that my dream of being in a spacesuit wasn't a dream at all. Hermes' plan had involved him taking me out to the asteroid belt and leaving me to float in space. Vulcan had designed a trap to hold the energies so they couldn't attack someone or something else. The problem was coaxing that dark magic into the trap. With a mouse, they would've used cheese. Since this thing was attracted to magic they used the most concentrated form available – manna.

I was wondering where they got enough to bait the trap. We had a number of gods in the Startenders whose very existence depended on having an ample supply of the stuff. Most of them would be more willing to give up a limb than manna. As it turns out every Startender that had access to manna donated a little bit. Each bit by itself was rather insignificant, but put together it was enough for a couple decades of existence for a god. Hermes left Vulcan's trap near me, set a timer for it to open and then got out of range. He would have been a more tempting target than the trap. After a stunt I'd pulled when we invaded a sovereign nation to save some refugees awhile back, Hermes ended up having one of the strongest reserves of manna of any deity in the solar system.

Another interesting aspect of the quietus is that it would remain safely contained in my body, at least as long as I lived. However the moment I died, it would be set free to head off in search of more magic and manna to absorb for its master.

Which got me to thinking that Big Nose may not have let me go entirely because of my bluff, but because he knew that what he infected me with would eventually kill me and go after my friends. We had to start planning for the next time a Startender faced him. This time we had the element of surprise. Next time, he'd have an idea of what to expect and we wouldn't get off this easily.

Fortunately for me, Vulcan's trap worked like a charm. The quietus went after the manna and the trap clinked shut around it. So far, it seems to be holding. It stayed in the asteroid belt in case the trap failed. It won't be able to hurt us from out there.

Of course, it still tried to do as much damage as possible on the way out of me, shredding the helmet and neither regions of my space suit. Despite what you might've seen in some movies, a body in space doesn't explode from the difference in pressure. Lack of air and heat are more than enough to kill a human. And therein lay the risk to me. If the quietus wasn't contained by Vulcan's trap, Hermes wouldn't be able to safely get to me without risking his own life and power. I have no doubt he'd risk his life for me, but for Big Nose to absorb his abilities would make the goblin god even more powerful. There was nobody in his pantheon with the same power set as Hermes. To have Gob be able to travel the universe in the blink of an eye would likely mean death or enslavement for billions if not more.

Since the trap held, Hermes got to me before I died, extending his badge's field to provide me air and heat long enough to get me into one of the Pink Reaper's healing chambers.

I wasn't stable enough to risk taking me out of it for three days. All told, I had been out of commission for about ten days.

Physical therapy had become my life, but I only got about three hours in every day. The rest was left up to me. For decades, Hercules had bugged me to get in better shape and I mostly humored him. Then when I was in Startender Academy I went through a physical regimen that would put any boot camp to shame. When I graduated the Academy I could do at least a hundred push-ups in a row.

I finished eleven and had to collapse onto the floor and wheeze to catch my breath.

I thought I was alone until I heard the applause and I looked up to see Theodore Sappo leaning on his mop and clapping his hands. "Getting better, Mr. Murphy. That's two more than yesterday."

"Thank you, Theodore. I've still got a way to go. And I told you to get rid of the Mr. and just call me Murphy."

Theodore laughed and started mopping the floor. "I could never do that. You're one of the mighty Startenders. And you personally saved my life in that refugee camp. Then you folks took me in and gave me a new home and job. Startenders even managed to find homes for the fifty thousand of my countrymen all over the world. I could never address you informally. Now excuse me, for I have to get back to work. Mitch is not working today," he said.

"Is he sick?"

"Yes. When one works in the medical ward with sick people it's bound to happen."

I managed to get off the floor without pulling on the bed. It was a major accomplishment. "Then how about you let me help you? Where do you keep the other mop and bucket?"

"Mr. Murphy, you are a Startender. You can't be expected to mop floors and clean toilets," Theodore said.

I laughed. "Do you know what I did before was a Startender?" Theodore shook his head. "I was a bartender in the greatest pub in the world. In addition to serving drinks and helping people, I mopped my share of floors and much worse. Cleaning toilets is nothing. We used to run a program for the homeless and I often had to clean out the porta potty. That ancient monstrosity was far worse than any mere toilet."

"But you're a patient. You're supposed to be focusing on your recovery."

"All I'm doing is focusing on my recovery. I'm going stir crazy. Besides I thought you'd be happy to not have to do twice your normal workload."

My godson walked by in his white lab coat. He was an amalgam of both his parents in pretty much equal parts. He was built like his father, but had his mother's face and hair, although his eyes were from his dad.

"John, is there any medical reason I shouldn't help out the cleaning shift?" I said.

"No reason. Have fun."

"But Dr. John, I don't want to get in trouble for having a Startender do my work," Theodore said nervously.

My godson laughed. "Both my parents are Startenders. My father washed dishes in the same pub where my uncle here tended bar. No Startender is going to be offended that one of their own was willing to do some hard work."

We tried to get across what the Startenders were and what the Startenders weren't, but many people have in their mind how the people in charge are supposed to act and sometimes they don't quite believe what we tell them.

"Your father put you through medical school washing dishes?" Theodore said.

"No. My mother made the big money." Ruth had made millions starting with a phone sex service and then branched out into similar Internet services.

"I'm still not sure," Theodore said.

John pointed to a closet. "They keep the cleaning supplies in there."

I got a mop and a bucket on wheels, filled it, then got to work.

More time passed and I was bored out of my skull. It was driving me crazy to sit around and do nothing all day except exercise. It occurred to me that I had taken very few traditional vacations in my life. Not that I didn't get out and see the world, but in almost every case I was doing something.

Fool's Glory was on put on Earth assignment and Loki had been running things while I recuperated. As acting head honcho, Loki was entitled to pick who would be his temporary honcho and had come to discuss it with me as I spent a few hours walking around the station to build my strength and endurance back up. Eric, Savannah, and his daughter Riga were all qualified for the position, which is why Loki was surprised when I made my recommendation.

"Coyote?! You can't be serious," Loki said.

"I've been told it's one of my major personality flaws," I said with a grin

"The fleabag is lazy, undisciplined and refuses to take things seriously," Loki said.

"Exactly. But he's also smart, incredibly loyal and about as cunning as they come. At times he doesn't play well with others." In fact, several other Startenders had mentioned to me on more than one occasion that they wonder how I was able to control him. The simple truth of the matter is there is nobody who could control Coyote. Convincing him or setting a good example on the other hand had worked pretty well for me.

"Coyote's been around for thousands of years. In all that time, he's never really been trusted to be in charge of anything. On occasion he's connived his way to the top of a few heaps, but he's never been asked by people who truly knew him. I think it would be good for him and maybe good for all of us. He might come up with an entirely new way of doing things that might work better than some of things we're doing now," I said.

"You make him sound like he's a 16-year-old being offered the keys to the car for the first time," Loki said.

"In a lot of ways, Coyote is. Despite his age, he's never really moved past the rebellious teenager stage. Not unlike someone else when I first met him."

Loki frowned. "Are you comparing me to the fleabag?"

"You do have some personality quirks in common. However you grew up with a family. A dysfunctional one, but a family just the same. You had responsibilities to shirk or complete as you saw fit. Coyote has been a loner most of his existence. And early on, he treated a lot of people very badly. The ones that are still around remember that. Even the ones who weren't know his reputation, so their trust of him is conditional."

Loki nodded slowly. "That's something I can certainly relate to. What you say makes a lot of sense. I've come to like and respect the fleabag."

"Oh that's nice to hear," came a voice from behind and below waist level. "I hope I'm not interrupting a private conversation," Coyote said.

"If we wanted private, we wouldn't have said your name more than three times," I said. While best avoided with adversaries, it's the easiest way to get a friendly divinity to show up.

Coyote had changed in a lot of ways over the years, but his nature not so much. He knew in the past he couldn't be fully trusted so on some level he tended to view others the same way.

"Look, I don't need any pity or favors from either of you,"

"No you don't, but that doesn't mean you're not going to get them," said Loki. "With Murphy's permission I'd like to offer you a position."

"You want me to be number two. Let me tell you, Coyote is nobody's number two." I started to speak and Coyote shot me a glance. "And no poop jokes Murphy. It's beneath even you."

"Actually I wasn't going to offer you the honcho position," Loki said.

Coyote stopped acting arrogant and annoyed. Instead he seemed deflated and sad, his haunches hunching forward. "You weren't?"

"No. I was going to suggest that you take the position of temporary head honcho with me acting as your number two."

"I guess you're both going to be feeling flushed," I said. They both ignored me

"You'd give up your chance to be in charge of *Fools' Glory* for me?" Coyote said.

"I would fleabag, so long as you gave me your word that you'll do the best job you could at it," Loki said.

Coyote was standing straighter than I've ever seen him stand before. "You have my word. But what about the Startenders Council? I'm not so sure they'll approve of me being a head honcho."

Coyote was right. He would face a battle to become a head honcho. "This is only a temporary position until I'm well enough to come back," I said. "I get to make the recommendation of who tends my barship. Since you gave your word that you'd give it your all and since Loki has no objections, consider yourself temporary head honcho of the barship."

Coyote yipped and did something quite out of character

– a backflip. Then he got a hold of himself and looked up at me. "Thanks, Murph. I won't let you down."

I smiled. "I know you won't, fleabag."

"That's enough lollygagging here, Loki. We need to get back to the ship and go patrol or something," Coyote said.

Loki looked at me, smiled and then rolled his eyes. "Murphy, I hope you're right about this."

I thought about all the havoc that could happen and became more than a little nervous about the ship, but all I said was, "Me, too."

Coyote and Loki left to go to *Fools' Glory* and I continued walking around the station. I walked in a loop around our Central Park, the multi-leveled center part of the station where we had a large part of our vegetation and farming, not to mention recreation areas. After I did five laps on each recreation level, I went to the tubes and shot up to the next level. It was kind of fun and took a while to get through the ten rec levels. During lap three around the fourth level, Tock fell into step alongside me. "Greetings, Murphy."

"Hi, Tock. How's the Academy going?"

"Surprisingly challenging. I've been paired with the yumin."

"That's Herschel. Good guy. I recommended him and you for the Academy."

"I can see similarities in sense of humor between the two of you."

"That's what Manuk Manuk said."

"I still cannot believe that you know the hatching goddess. Even Big Nose is wary of her. On more than one occasion, an invasion of the yumin home world was suggested and Big Nose would not even entertain the possibility."

Interesting. "So to what do I owe the pleasure? Did you just wander by or were you looking for me?"

"I sought you out."

"Good job finding me." Startenders could be tracked by our badges, but my new one was still in the shop. Although everybody on the station had multiple ways to be kept track of, a cadet from Startender Academy wouldn't have access to any of them. Although if they were as good as we hoped they were, they would be able to figure out a way.

"Not really. You have been walking the same pattern around the station for the past week. Under other circumstances I would say it was a dangerous habit, but here on the New York City II or Startender Station – why you have two names for it I will never understand – it seems people don't have as much to worry about. I must say I am truly impressed at what you all have managed to set up here. I have not come across or heard of anything similar to it. To be welcomed into the group charged with its guardianship does me honor. However I'm having some reservations about whether your choice in including me was wise and I wanted to discuss them with you."

"No problem long as you don't mind walking as we talk. Shoot."

The lation stone's translation abilities were amazing, but not infallible. Tock crinkled his eyes and tilted his head. "You just survived almost dying in an attempt to rescue me and my daughter. Why would you want me to fire a weapon at you?"

"Just an expression. It should be translated as tell me."

Tock nodded. "First, my presence here endangers the Startenders, your station and your very planet. Big Nose, as you call him, does not forget or forgive. He will be coming for me. And likely for you for having bested him."

"That's something we considered. But if he's looking for me, what difference does it make if you're around when he gets here? Besides, Bast has Cynosure working overtime to spread rumors that Big Nose let you go in exchange for your years of service and the fact that you were the one who turned your own brother in," I said.

Tock stopped short and his brows were trying to lift off the top of his gray-green forehead. "But I did no such thing."

"We know that, but when you're dealing with politicians and divinities, what people believe to be true is actually far more important than what actually is true. They have also included in the rumors that you and your brother do not share the same father and so you are not of the same bloodline, which gets him out of having to save face because you're still alive."

"But we were littermates," Tock said.

"Something that the average person in the Empire would have no knowledge of."

Tock began walking again in silence for a while, mulling it over. "Yes, if that's what people believed, for him to come after me would make him look as if he had changed his own edict. It would weaken the false belief that he was infallible. It might work, at least in the short term. However, I'm also concerned about whether or not I can live up to what a Startender should be. I am a soldier. I have been one my entire adult life. I've been taught to fight and to kill. As an officer and a general I have trained myself to be able to direct others to be killed in such a way that I kill even more of the enemy. If you figure in all the battles I've been in or overseen, we're talking about hundreds of thousands of casualties on both sides that I'm either responsible for directly by way of leadership or a much smaller number that I actually killed in battle myself. My presence could be a detriment to how the Startenders are perceived, and frankly I don't know if I will be able to keep to the no killing part of the oath I will have to take."

"I think you will. When we fought on Karma, you were able to direct your entire cram to battle with a heavily-armed enemy and minimize casualties." Any deaths of an enemy would physically hurt the native Karmans. Their world's magic literally made violence hurt them more than the one they were fighting, which is why the invaders were having such an easy time of conquering and enslaving until we got there. Unfortunately, since we were asked to help by Jan, our actions hurt her and those who sent her to find help. Killing the enemy could have resulted in the innocent dying. A challenging condition to fight a war under. "In fact your cram was able to not kill in most of your battles, something that goes against all your training, yet you did it. I have no doubt that you have the strength of character and discipline to be able to do that as a Startender. You have a very strong sense of honor. I know back on Karma, fighting for a good cause meant something to you. Now you can devote your life to fighting for good causes. I think that's something that you not only want, but will thrive doing. Not to mention the fact that your knowledge of the universe will help the rest of us be better prepared out there."

We walked in silence for an entire lap, before he slapped me on the back. "Thank you, Murphy. I needed to hear that. I will endeavor to make both you and the Startenders proud."

"I wouldn't have recommended you if I thought otherwise," I said.

Up ahead I saw Theodore near one of the air ventilation shafts, which was odd because as a janitor in the hospital he had no reason to be there.

Even odder, no alarms were going off.

Protocol demanded I use my Startender badge to report the activity before getting involved. A danger to the station could kill almost eleven thousand people. Only I didn't have a badge, and as a cadet neither did Tock.

"The tube behind that vent handles air circulation for a large part of the station. He's got no reason to be there," I said to the goblin.

"Here's why I'm worried about my future as a Startender. My first instinct was to attack him to stop him, but Startenders can't do such things," Tock said.

"We could if we were sure of what he was doing, but as a resident on Startender Station he has rights and is also innocent until proven guilty. Back me up and let's go find out which of those he is," I said.

I motioned and Tock and I came at him from separate angles.

"Theodore, what are you doing?"

He stiffened then turned toward me. "Mr. Murphy. I didn't expect to see you here."

"You know you're not supposed to be in there." We were not idiots. Crucial systems had security monitors, motion sensors and alarms, any one of which should have stopped him.

"I'm just curious and trying to learn all I can about my new home," Theodore said.

I moved closer and noticed jugs of cleaning supplies at his feet. He had a groundskeeper pushcart, which explained how he got so close. It had security bypass codes to allow the groundskeepers to care for all the areas in the park. The bypass was put in the equipment instead of given to people, since there were multiple shifts and jobs changed and it was harder to sneak around with a huge push cart than a personal badge. We were going to have to rethink that one.

Just because I was badgeless didn't mean I couldn't call it in. I kicked a ground sensor. An alarm went off and the vent snapped closed.

"You're not a very good liar. What you're really doing?"

"I am sorry for this, Mr. Murphy. You saved my life, but not those of my four children. I thought they died in the camps, but I was sent a video showing they're still alive."

"Who sent it?" I said.

When Theodore told me, my blood didn't actually boil, it just felt like it did.

"Dicky did this?" That was my little nickname for the former Supreme Exalted Dictator for Life of the country we invaded last year to save fifty thousand refugees from being slaughtered by Dicky's armed forces.

"How could he do that? He's on trial at the International Criminal Court in the Hague for war crimes and crimes against humanity." Happens when attempted genocide gets recorded on video for all the world to see.

"He still has many in my home country who are loyal to him. These men claim to be members of his death squad. They told me if I did not commit a terrorist act on the station that killed at least a hundred people that they would rape and butcher my children. I had no choice. But maybe if I kill a Startender that would be better than a hundred regular people and they'll let them live."

Theodore lifted three bottles of chemicals, one of which was bleach. From my practical chemistry at the Academy I knew the cleaning supplies he had with him could be mixed together to make a chlorine gas. Crude, but still deadly. And honestly, the amounts he had would likely be cleaned out by our environmental filters before it did much damage. At least that's what I hoped.

I took a deep breath and moved to take him down. Before I could, Tock kicked Theodore's outer knee inward. There was a crunch and Theodore collapsed. Tock and I managed to catch the three jugs before they hit the ground.

Theodore curled up into in fetal position and began weeping. I didn't think it was the pain in his knee that was causing his tears. "What's going to happen now?" he sobbed.

"Now we find and save your children." Tock had taken the words out of my mouth.

"I don't understand. I just tried to kill you and other people. Why would you help me?"

"Because that is what a Startender does. They help people and they rescue children. At least if there's any way possible to do it."

Tock nodded at me when he said that last part. This had been our first real conversation since his rescue. I had wanted to ask his forgiveness for my failure to save his daughter Tada. That nod told me as far as he was concerned there was nothing to forgive. We had done what no one else in the universe would have. I knew the man. All of the loyalty the goblin once had for the Empire and more now belonged to the Startenders for what it was worth. As far as I was concerned, that was worth a lot.

After searching Theodore to make sure he had no more surprises, our station police arrived including the chief, Jason Cervantes. Jas had long ago won his ongoing bet with Paddy that had him dressing in women's clothing. After doing it for so long, Jas found he rather liked the comfort of skirts. Running a police force as a man in a dress was not as big a deal as it would have been thirty or forty years ago, but was still problematic. He compromised by wearing a kilt with the blue and gold Startender colors and a matching pair of boxers underneath.

Years ago when he was on the NYPD's payroll, I helped Jason work a case to catch a serial killer, but that didn't make me a detective. Jason was, so I let him take over and followed in his wake.

Startender Station had Internet access. Sure, we had filters and security, but tried to give the citizens as much freedom as we deemed safe. The devices used to surf or receive and send email used Earth-based operating systems. The rest of the station used a variation of something Vulcan had developed years ago and which had been refined by him and several other Startenders. There is no chance of an outside virus getting into our system because there was no connection. That and no one outside of the station even had any idea how our system worked. Even when Startenders surfed the net, we used unconnected tech.

It seems these former members of Dicky's death squad had been working hard to find people still in their country with connections to those who immigrated to Startender Station. The attempted genocide had been across ethnic lines between two groups who didn't seem all that different to me.

Not everyone bought into the hate. A family that was in the ethnic majority had hidden Theodore's children. Now that the country was enjoying the fruits of its first democratic election, those in hiding dared to come out into the light. Unfortunately, it didn't work out too good for Theodore's family as all four children were taken hostage.

Jason was able to trace the e-mail carrier to Theodore's county. The former death squad had been smart enough to send it from a café, so just retracing where the message originated wasn't going to find the kids.

Many Startenders had ways to trace people mystically, but for that we needed their genetic material. Even using Theodore's paternal half wouldn't be enough. We might be able to whip something up if we had a sample from his wife. Sadly, she had been killed in the camps, one of the many dead we weren't able to save.

The worst part was Dicky knew this would not make a difference in his trial. It was just his way to screw us over for taking him down.

"Murphy, we have a problem," Jas said. "According to the video Theodore was emailed, he had less than five hours to cause an act of terror before they execute one of the children."

"Time to bring this to the Startender Council," I said. Less than twenty minutes later, we were in the council room. The Startender

Council consisted of Paddy Moran, Vulcan, the Karman Jan and Kaye Chandler – the former Pink Reaper. The Low Council included the gremlin Bubba Sue, Bast and the kobold Kamile, plus whatever head honchos were in-system. At the moment that included Nellie and Coyote who was filling in for me. Most of the council seemed confused when Coyote took his seat, but when I didn't react, they ignored it. Jason and I brought them up to speed.

"What if we send out a press release saying that we have over a hundred dead, but leave out the details?" I said. "That would buy us time to find and save the kids."

"Absolutely not. We've made a huge deal about the world being able to trust the word of the Startenders. If we send out something that's a lie, it would undermine that," Paddy said.

"I agree with Paddy. The world would never again fully trust anything that came out of Startender Station and would assume when we back pedaled and said nobody was dead that we were merely covering up. Plus this is the closest an act of terrorism has ever come to succeeding. We don't want others to feel encouraged to try," Bast said.

Tock raised his hand and Paddy nodded at him. "There were times when the Great One –" Tock was furious with himself for using that term. "– rather the fecal bag that rules the Empire would simply stop all news from an area until he decided how he wanted to deal with a situation. Unlike your world, he controlled what people in the Empire learned entirely. On your world you at least have a few sources showing things, plus your Internet," Tock said

"It's a pretty good idea," Kay Chandler said. "It lets the kidnappers draw their own conclusions, without us having to actually lie or mislead. I say we do that." There was a quick unanimous vote. Paddy shut down all Earthside communications into and out of the station except through Startender badges.

"The problem left to us is how do we rescue those children?" Vulcan said.

"I assume Cynosure hasn't been able to locate them or we would've mounted a rescue mission already, correct?" Coyote said in an extremely respectful tone, far different than how he and Bast normally communicated.

It took the cat-headed goddess a bit by surprise. "True, but we are looking."

Coyote nodded. "And with luck, you will find them, but we cannot count on that. We don't have enough genetic material to trace them mystically, nor do we have a good technological way to trace them. What if we simply convince them to tell us where they are?" Coyote said.

"Exactly how do you propose we do that, fleabag?" Bast said.

"Simple, hairball. We have the father send them a message. We fake some footage showing dead bodies. Then we let him say he got away, but he only killed a couple dozen. That he'll kill the rest only if they allow him to speak to his children. That means they have to make a live connection. They don't seem to be computer geniuses or they would have bounced the signal around rather than using a public terminal. However, we can't be positive that they don't have that ability." Coyote turned and looked at Bubba Sue. "Would it be possible for you to send something hidden in the video feed so when it was broadcast on the other end, we'd have something to trace? If so, we follow that, hopefully saving the children before they're even done with their video chat."

All eyes turned to Bubba Sue, who had her tongue in the corner of her mouth, her finger on her chin and her eyes looking up at the ceiling.

"I could put out something in a high enough frequency that humans wouldn't be able to hear it, then use a carrier wave to boost the range so even at low-volume the sound would travel for miles. We would have to have ships in the area to find the signal and trace it back, but it should work." Bubba Sue stood up and ran toward the exit. "I'll get to work on it right now. I vote for whatever the rest of the fleabag's plan is."

"Will this terrorist help us?" Jan said.

"I think so. It's the only way he is ever going to see his children again," I said.

It was decided that we would use three of the four barships in-system in dust mode to triangulate the signal

"The problem with that is we'll need another ship to bring the rescue team to the hostages, but would be foolish not to have at least one barship on the station in case of emergency or attack," Kamile said.

"I could use my bike. Bubba Sue can transmit coordinates directly to my bike. And my bike has the only transworld drive that can be used planetside." I had a motorcycle with a sidecar that Vulcan built years ago. It had an earlier version of the transworld drive. It didn't have the bells and whistles of the new drives, but it could be used safely inside a planet's atmosphere and gravity field because the mass of the bike was a fraction of a barship. A barship couldn't use the drive on a planet without significant risk.

"But Murphy you're still recovering and ye don't have even have a Startenders badge to protect ye," Paddy said.

"True, but the bike has a force field of its own."

"Fine, but be careful. We almost lost ye once, we don't want to do it again," Paddy said.

I nodded. "Kaye, I heard you were a little upset that I didn't choose you for the rescue team on Throneworld. In this case, I could really use someone with your skillsets." Back in the pulp era, when Kaye worked as the Pink Reaper, she was able to sneak in and rescue kidnap victims on a regular basis. "Besides, we could get lucky and the kidnappers might have been exposed to your fear gas when we were rescuing refugees."

Just one exposure was enough to make someone scared when they saw the Pink Reaper, even years later. Sometimes just the color pink would do it.

I turned to Nellie. "And since we're going back in, we might as well have the original team, don't you think?"

"I'm in," said Nellie.

My plan was for Nellie to sneak in while Kaye stormed in to cause a distraction. With luck, I'd only have to play chauffeur.

Theodore agreed. I think he would've agreed anyway, but

Tock's promise to break his three intact limbs if he did anything to mess it up probably didn't hurt. Even though his homeland was a relatively small country, it still covered more area than the state of Vermont. The barships had to be fairly far apart to triangulate the signal. We launched thirty-six probes – a dozen by each barship – to augment their sensors.

Theodore sent an email with his cover story, claiming he found a terminal outside of the information blackout zone. It took them a half hour to respond by email saying they would make video contact in two hours. They were only eight minutes late.

It took us five minutes to find the signal and another forty-two seconds to triangulate. Under other circumstances we would've used Hermes for the rescue, but the truth of the matter was he was spent after working so hard to save the Gallopians, and then he had to get the rescue team off Throneworld and keep me alive. Add to that the manna he donated to the trap – a good third of it came from him – and he was exhausted and weak. It was too risky. His power might crash at the wrong time. Another week or so and he would've been able to do it in a blink of an eye, but these kids didn't have that long. Bubba Sue sent me the coordinates and a satellite view of the area. They were in a small village with nothing over four stories. I transworlded so we came out fifty feet above the building. Nellie jumped off and flew off to sneak inside, while the Pink Reaper simply stepped off and floated down. I called Kaye the Pink Reaper because she was once again wearing a mask and a cape. She held her oversized pink metal gun in her right hand.

Once inside the room with the hostages, Nellie dropped a pair of knockout gas marbles which shattered at the feet of the gunmen near the children, which knocked out the children, as well. Her badge worked better than a gasmask.

It was safer to gas everyone than risk one person being awake and able to shoot. Kaye didn't have that option in the old days. Back then, the Reaper's knockout gas sometimes proved fatal, but she's improved it over the decades. The children were in a different room than most of the gunmen, so the gas didn't work on them.

Despite being significantly over one hundred, Kaye Chandler

kicked in the front door. She's spent decades using her healing chamber and it made her strong and healthy even for a woman a third her age. She wore body armor on her boots and gloves that made her punches and kicks much more effective, kind of like having scientifically-designed brass knuckles. She went through the splintered wood, laughing like something out of a pulp novel. All still-open eyes were on her. Two men heard the sound, saw the pink cape and threw their weapons away, then crawled into little balls. Three more attacked her. Knifes and bullets were useless against her badge's force field. Even without the badge, her special cape would have stopped both. The Pink Reaper moved only three times, knocking out each member of the disbanded death squad with a single blow each. There had only been seven men holding the four children hostage.

Nellie and the Pink Reaper carried the children out and leaned them on my motorcycle. Kaye gave them each the antidote to the gas. *Fools' Glory* landed in a more traditional aircraft form than usual. A staircase came out and Coyote led a group of a dozen soldiers down the ramp and into the building. They placed the seven unconscious men in handcuffs to take them back to the capital.

The fleabag had suggested we ask permission before we invaded this time, which made Kamile, Dion and Dr. Sheriff – the top members of our diplomatic team – extremely happy.

The Startenders were national heroes, having gotten rid of Dicky. Despite the ethnic tension, most members of the group on top hadn't been thrilled with the country's kill-happy dictator. When Dr. Sheriff brought them Coyote's proposal to bring them in on the arrest, the new government agreed immediately. We gave them the video they sent Theodore for evidence. It turns out three of the seven men were wanted for war crimes, so this kidnapping would be the least of their worries.

The *Perdu* landed next, followed by a golden shuttle craft from the station. The door opened and Tock escorted Theodore out on crutches. Ismail walked out behind them and waved to me. I waved back at the former New York cabbie. Ismail was older than I was. As a member of the Startender Society, he and his family got regular nap time in Kaye's healing chambers and it helped slow the aging process.

At first we couldn't bring Ismail to the station. He'd been cursed to wander the tristate area by the mad god Poseidon. When he left the borders of New York, New Jersey or Connecticut, it caused him pain to the point that the stress would eventually kill him. Oddly enough, a short time after the destruction of New York City, the curse laid on him by Poseidon was lifted. We still haven't quite figured that one out. Of course we're still looking for Poseidon to make him pay for what he's done, but he continues to elude us.

Ismail loved being a cabbie, so now he flies one of the shuttles from the station to Earth. When the curse was lifted, he also lost his mystic ability to automatically know where his customers were going, but he says being able to see his family, including grandkids and one great-grandson, whenever he wants makes up for it. Plus the shuttle has a GPS that works in the sky as well as the ground, so he makes out okay.

Theodore limped over on his crutches and kissed each of his children on the head, then hugged them. Next he came towards me. "Thank you, Mr. Murphy. You Startenders saving my family is far more than I deserve. I'm ready to face my punishment and go to trial for what I did."

"There's not going to be a trial," I said.

"Then are you simply going to execute me?" he said.

I guess I couldn't exactly blame him for thinking that. After all, he had lived in a country where that's exactly what happened.

"Startenders don't kill unless there is no other option. There are plenty of other options here. Your children have been through a lot without losing their father, too. However, we cannot have you on the station. You are too great a risk. There would be a diplomatic nightmare to deport you anywhere else, other than here in your country of origin."

"But I would no longer be a danger to you. My children are safe and I owe you my loyalty," Theodore said.

"The Startenders saved your life and gave you a home. You already owed them your loyalty and instead you tried to kill people," Tock said. "If you'd come to the Startenders with what was happening, they would've done anything in their power to rescue your children and all of you would likely have gotten to live on the station."

"Will I be able to get my things from my apartment?"

"You have your miserable life and your children are alive. Be grateful for that much. Not everyone is so fortunate," Tock said.

Theodore nodded. Tock walked over to each of the four children and gave them a backpack. The backpack was Tock's idea. Each had a change of durable clothes, enough rations to feed each of them for a month and some currency for the emerging republic that they would be living in. It would be enough to make sure they had time to get settled. Tock also gave them each a signal ring and explained how they worked. The rings would allow them to contact the Startenders if they needed help. They're very expensive and paid for by the Pink Reaper, but she happily donated them.

I stood next to Coyote as the soldiers loaded the prisoners on *Fools' Glory*.

"Thanks, Murphy. You know I have a soft spot for kids," Coyote said.

"Don't thank me. You did great," I said.

"Well, I did promise." Coyote licked a paw. "I think I've got a little bit more respect now than I did before. Even the hairball told me I did good. I had the respect of the others as a trickster and Startender, but this leadership thing is different from that, isn't it?"

I nodded.

"None of the crew gives me a hard time like I give you. I mean making you dress up like an old movie spaceman? Why do you put up with it? Why did you even request me for your crew? I know no one else did and there are Startenders who don't serve on a barship. Why burden yourself with me?"

"We've known each other a lot of years. Way back when, there were people who saw something in me that I didn't see in myself. They believed in me which let me become the best person I could be. You're a pain in the butt sometimes, but underneath it all you have a good heart and you always fight for the underdog. And I like you," I said.

"You like me? People tolerate me, but nobody likes me," Coyote said with a smile.

"Savanah likes you."

"Savanah likes most everybody."

"More people like you than you realize. That doesn't mean they want you wreaking havoc on their ship either. Do you know when I first realized I liked you?"

"That Fools' Day when we stopped a nuclear Mysticaust?" he said.

"Nope. It was when you came in to Bulfinche's Pub with a drunk guy who you were conning money from in dribs and drabs to pay back to an old woman he'd swindled. You could've found a way just to take his money, but instead made him endure a portion of what he put that woman through to the point of inducing a phobia in him of pink elephants. Then you sold him a mouse for protection –and since he was drunk had him keep giving you money for it a half-dozen times by telling him he'd hadn't paid yet – then managed to have him run right into an actual pink elephant. It was beautiful. That's when I figured you out. You'd endured a lot and it was important to you to help other people who been through the same thing. You used the fact that the woman prayed to you for help as an excuse to help her. You're also the only lesser god I know who still answers prayers on a regular basis. That says something about you, too. Despite your issues about taking orders, I'm proud to have you in my crew and to call you friend," I said.

"Murphy, I appreciate that more than you'll ever know. As my way of saying thank you, I give you a one-time free pass to give me any order and I'll follow it. But just one. So are you coming back on duty?" Coyote said.

"I'm still not well enough. You watch out for my ship for the next few weeks, because I'll be back."

"I look forward to it. I'll probably even give you your command back," Coyote said with a wink, then climbed on board *Fools' Glory*.

Loki, Riga, Savanah and Eric stood at the edge of the ramp holding a sign and trying to look frightened.

It read *Help us! Come back soon!*

Loki winked at me, then they ineptly tried to hide the sign from Coyote.

The canine trickster laughed and told Eric to close the door. My ship took off and went to deliver the prisoners to the capital.

RAGE AGAINST
THE DYING OF THE LIGHT

We had five barships in the Delfina System. It was far enough away that folks on Earth had no inkling it even existed. Not that it was likely to exist for much longer. We were facing a crisis of epic proportions and it looked like there was very little the Startenders were going to be able to do about it.

We were still going to try.

Fools' Glory was hosting a strategy session with most of the in-system head honchos – Dagonet, the Infinite Jester of the barship *Excalibur,* Hercules of the *Argo II* and Rumbles of *The Big Top.* Buzz, the head honcho of *The Bitter End,* was up on the mirror over the bar from his post planetside. Around the table we also had Pace the troll and Vulcan. Paddy was sharing space on the mirror screen with Buzz. He was back on Startender Station.

Delfina had three inhabited worlds. Our crews were out trying to do what they could, but it wasn't looking good.

The system's sun was dying. No sun meant no life, which meant billions on three worlds were going to go into a very dark and permanent night. None of the planets were space-faring. We were looking for solutions to save everybody and hadn't figured out how.

"How are the plans for evacuation looking?" Paddy said.

"Not good. I've contacted the Yumin, the Dragonstars, the Gallopians and some other friendlies. Ships to help evacuate are en route, but they will likely arrive too late. Even if they make it, there are only so many who could fit onboard," Buzz said.

I sighed. "Savanah contacted the Mother Cron." A planetary intelligence that had the ability to teleport her children across galaxies. We had saved her latest generation. Savanah joined in the species-wide mating and made lots of friends. "She's willing to teleport ships, but will not accept any refugees."

"Why ships? Doesn't she just teleport her own people?"

Rumbles said.

"Yes, but only through space. The cron physiology allows them to survive in the void of space and even reentry. Mother Cron has trouble compensating for planetary rotation, gravity and revolution. It's much easier for her to move something through space. She can probably move millions if we have something to put them in. We'd only need life support, not propulsion. And the small matter of a place for them to go," I said.

"That leaves our barships. Using the inner cargo space stretched to the maximum extrusion capacity of all five barships, even figuring in the rest of our ships getting back from their search missions in time –" The rest of the barships were out hunting down worlds to take in refugees. Paddy had been working on the countries of Earth, but so far had no takers. "– we won't be able to save one percent of the populations," Vulcan said with a frown. The man was a consummate scientist, even if his science mixed with magic. He hated when there was a problem he couldn't figure out the answer to.

"Pace, what about you and the rest of the trolls opening nexi off the worlds?" I said. Pace was the Albert Einstein or Stephen Hawkings of his race. Maybe even the Vulcan. He mastered ways of inter-dimensional travel that no one else had even considered. He and Vulcan had been working together to build in more ways for getting around the universe into each barship.

"We can open a nexus. The problem is finding where to put twenty-one billion people. Most worlds won't accept them. Matching up their needs with the ecosystems, atmosphere and gravity is a nightmare. Dropping that many people anywhere, even on an abandoned world, could quickly eat up the natural resources and condemn them to a slow lingering death rather than a quick one when the sun goes out," Pace said.

"Jan has contacted Karma and the world is willing to take half a billion, so long as they agree to eat native food before they go through the nexus," I said. Their world has strong magic and a rather unique way of keeping itself and its people safe. It physically rewarded people for doing good and physically punished them for being bad. The Karmans had no use for physical defenses or a military, which is why they needed us way back when. Anyone that eats the food has their body chemistry converted and wouldn't be able to hurt a fly without harming themselves. "It's a start."

"We've all been contacting worlds we've visited," Dagonet said. "We have made arrangements for a few million if we can get them there. The other barships and Hermes are out looking for more."

"Murphy, what about Ogra?" Herc said. "Considering we own a damn city, we should be able to take some."

"We still have to be able to find places to put them and our claim there is constantly under legal fire," I said. "Still, we figure fifty thousand." But it gave me an idea. "What about Xen's home world?" The robot once ran a world as a planetary AI until they shut him off and self-destructed.

Buzz shook his head. "The Nimians were barbaric idiots. The entire world is uninhabitable for centuries."

"Then we should be looking at the worlds Davin slaughtered." Everyone's face got dark.

"The Goblin Empire claimed Brixton. Apparently your Cyndicate friend didn't want to risk exposure to the homicidal hallucinogen there. Big Nose didn't have as much concerns for his own troops. Your Cyndicate friend claimed the others," Buzz said.

"Alom works for us. We could order him to let us have the worlds he claimed," I said.

"Paddon is toxic," Herc said. "Too much of the atmosphere is still carbon monoxide."

"Then we figure out some method of cleaning it up," I said.

"Murphy, it would take years to fix it. Same with getting the poison out of the water supply of Hiven," Vulcan said.

"And Hiven is still covered with millions of corpses. The lasa had done a lot, but still have a long way to go. I can't imagine Alom cleaned up the corpses on the other worlds," Dagonet said.

"Actually he sold them. Subcontractors are constantly taking the bodies to markets," I said. Turns out there are several markets for corpses for everything from breaking them down to base compounds, using them for fertilizer, experimentation, target practice for soldier training or weapon testing, even people with twisted love lives, and that's just the tip of the iceberg.

It was my turn to sigh. I knew Vulcan was right, but was hoping one of us would come up with a brilliant idea to make it work. It was what we did best, but wasn't happening this time around.

"I think we might be looking at this all wrong," Rumbles said. "We are looking at evacuation. Maybe we should be trying to re-ignite the sun."

We all turned toward Vulcan. The limping god sighed. "Don't think I haven't already tackled that problem. We have neither the fuel nor the energy needed to light it back up again. Even if we had a full sun god to help out, it likely wouldn't work. For one thing, this wouldn't be their sun. For another, it would probably mean the god in question would have to be willing to sacrifice their life to save the dying star. I don't think we're going to find any takers."

"So our only solution remains finding worlds that are unpopulated but inhabitable, or more worlds willing to take evacuees," I said. "I suggest we pray that the other Startenders find some."

"We might as well check in with the Startenders on the ground. Perhaps one of them might come up with more ideas," Paddy said.

Oddly enough, the reason we even knew this was happening wasn't because of some interstellar distress call. It was something far more subtle than that. It was a prayer from a pair of children. Somehow, even from light years away, Coyote was able to sense the children's prayer and bring us here.

"Any good news?" I said as the reflection of the mirror over the bar split in three. Coyote's furry canine face took up the latest third.

"None. I just wanted to let you know that *Fools' Glory* will be taking on the children whose prayer we answered, as well as their family and friends."

Coyote had been better for a while after his stint as head honcho, but had slipped back into some of his old habits and has been back to giving me grief, but only occasionally. One of the disadvantages of having a volunteer, non-military chain of command. The fleabag must have been really worried because he added, "Please, Murphy. At least let me answer their prayer."

"Done. They'll be the first on board," I said. Sometimes you can't save everyone, so you have to start with those that are important to those that are important to you. My stomach was already in knots over the task of deciding who lived. And therefore also who died.

"One thing of interest. All the peoples on this world have a legend of a sunbird that will re-ignite their dying star. They say this happens every three hundred years. Same bird each time, so maybe it's some cosmic variation on the phoenix. A lot of the locals view it as so much hogwash, but considering who some of us are, I figured we should pay it some special attention in hopes that it's true. If it's real and if enough of the billions of locals believed in it, then it would have serious power in keeping to the no atheists in foxholes theory. Everyone would pray and believe out of sheer survival instincts." Twenty-one billion terrified worshippers would give a god some serious power and manna levels. If this sunbird was a god willing to sacrifice itself, there was a chance to save the sun.

"Okay Coyote, new priority. Have all the non-troll Startenders start searching the planet for houses of worship and libraries to research the legends and the actual physical presence of this sunbird. Since you seem to be the one most finely attuned, Buzz will join you when we're done here to help translate." Buzz still considers himself a devout coward, but never hesitates to help folks in need.

"Will do," Coyote said. "And Murphy…" The fleabag was choking on some words he couldn't manage to get out

"You're welcome, fleabag," I said and the trickster faded out.

In rapid succession we checked in with the other Startender teams on all three worlds with interesting results. All three planets, none of them whom had any direct contact with the other that we could find, all shared the same legend of a bird made of fire that would appear to re-ignite their dying sun. The orbits and therefore the planetary years varied, but some math showed that the numbers involved all matched up to the same timeframe, about three hundred Earth years. We had to find this bird.

"I hate to put a damper on this new found hope, but a star going out and being re-ignited every three hundred years is next to impossible," Vulcan said. "Most of the universe works on science."

"So are ye saying that it is hogwash?" Paddy said.

"No, but I know most of us are betting folk and I wouldn't bet on this with Murphy's money," Vulcan said.

I smiled. "You have a point. We won't stop working on the evacuations, but I'm willing to bet everything that the legend is true and that we'll find the sunbird in time." Honestly, I had my doubts but this wasn't the time to show any. Any hope of saving these people had to be grasped at. "How much time do we have?"

"Roughly one hundred and seventy-four Earth hours before the star becomes a supernova and moves toward becoming a black hole," Vulcan said. The inventor god looked down at his hands, which were neatly folded in his lap. "I sent out energy collectors. I'm hoping to siphon off as much of the exploding star as I can. It will give the Startenders a massive, practically unlimited source of energy and might protect the worlds from instant incineration, giving us a few more hours with the evacuations."

Vulcan was obviously feeling guilty that he thought of ways to better our situation while people were waiting to die. He had been abused by others in the Greco-Roman pantheon, but instead of continuing that cycle, he's worked hard to create wonders and help others. He was being eaten up inside by his failure to come up with a way to save the three worlds.

"Ye will do it, Vulcan," Paddy said. "Brilliance does not mean ye can solve every problem. And this one may yet be solved. Never give up hope. All of us know that. If any of ye need anything, ye only need call." Paddy said and the mirror went back to being a reflective service. The lot of us sat in silence. My fellow head honchos were men of action. Sitting around didn't set well with any of them. Still we were the leaders, which meant we couldn't always be on the frontlines. We had to figure out where the hat was in order to pull a rabbit out of it.

The extended silence went on too long. I knew it had to be broken, smashed into little bits and thrown out the nearest airlock.

"Pace, do we have measures in place to make sure none of our trolls go primitive?" I said.

Pace nodded. "We are being very careful. The amount of limbic energy needed to open up as many nexi as we need to evacuate worlds is dangerous, but we should be able to handle it."

Trolls used heavy-duty magic to open the gateways and if they ran out of that particular energy while working, their brains shut down. It makes them incredibly stupid, which they called going primitive.

A primitive troll on his own tended to go near bridges and tunnels because it reminded them of the gateways they could once open to other worlds, which explains some of the legends of them guarding bridges. Pace was primitive when we first met. He and his brothers were bounty hunters who followed Loki, Buzz and me to Karma. They ended up helping us save that world and we helped restore Pace to his normal self.

We didn't need any of our people going primitive, especially with so many lives on the line.

The mirror suddenly burst into life and Eric came on screen. "Murphy, long range sensors are showing a goblin moonship entering the system."

The other melogs burst on the screen telling their honchos the same thing.

"All ships go to dust mode," I said, then looking to my fellow head honchos realizing in a way I had superseded their authority. None of them seemed upset. Because of Vulcan's genius, we were able to shift the mass of the ships back and forth between the worlds in a pocket dimension which ran underneath and along the real one.

Each ship used a separate pocket universe. We had to maintain a certain amount of presence in the real universe, but it was minimal, about the same size as a golf ball. Golf balls are notoriously difficult to pick up on sensors.

"Why is the Goblin Empire here?" Pace said.

I came up with an idea that I didn't much like.

"Probably the same reason we are. Answering a prayer."

Everyone at the table cursed.

I broke into a cold sweat and it was all I could do not to run away screaming. I had been back on duty for a couple of months, but the effects from the quietus still lingered. And we keep waiting for Gob to move against us and were doing our best to stay off the Empire's radar.

"Okay, I'm not one to promote the expansion of Big Nose's worshippers, but if the moonship can save them, wouldn't life as subjects to the Empire be better than death?" Dagonet said.

I looked at the two gods in our midst. Vulcan had found alternate power sources, making him one of the most powerful Earth gods. Hercules' legend, much of it promoted by him, meant he had no shortage of strength or long life, but both still fell far short of Gob's power levels.

"Life is always better," Hercules said. "However, some of the goblin worlds live as little more than slaves.

The Goblin Empire had multiple strategies for conquering worlds, including sending out poorly manned space ships towards the outer limits of the known universe. Goblins breed faster than rabbits, so sometimes they simply crash and begin building and training the next few generations until they have enough to simply take over the local planet. It happened on Earth as well as in Faerie. Those cases didn't work out well, at least for the Empire.

"Big Nose could just be here to build up his energy reserves," Vulcan said.

"How?" I said.

Hercules sighed. "If that ship can convince billions on these three worlds that Big Nose can save them and they get all three populations praying to him, he will become even more powerful, even if they die."

"And if Gob manages to divert that manna, there's a chance that there won't be enough left for the sunbird to relight the sun," Vulcan said.

"Well, we're not going to let that happen," I said.

The next few seconds made my bold statement highly unlikely. Every living being in the system was hit with a telepathic message that was translated into the native tongues, but was mostly images and emotions. The emotional broadcast sent out hope and trust wrapped up in an image of Gob. The next sent out an image of a fiery bird trapped in a cage onboard their ship. The gist of the message let everyone know that they needed to worship Gob and to become one with the Empire, and in exchange Gob would free the bird and save the sun.

Even with the protection our Startender badges offered us, the emotional broadcast made me want to believe it was true. I can only image what it felt like to the unshielded natives of this system.

"This is not going to happen," Hercules said. "If he pulls this off, he will have taken three planets without firing a shot. There will be no resentment, only gratitude. Big Nose will be even more powerful when he comes gunning for us."

"Eric, do our sensors show Big Nose on the moonship?" I said, hoping Gob hadn't changed his policy of never leaving Throneworld. The moonship was not shaped like a moon, but was actually the size of a small one. It won most battles through sheer intimidation. It also mined asteroid fields as it went through systems to replenish the ship's resources and load up their hold with space debris. If a planet gave them any grief, the moonship let gravity do the fighting for them and released asteroid missiles to crash down on defenseless planetary targets. Enough of them could cause a planet to go into a state akin to a nuclear winter. A moonship also had some of the best weapon systems in the galaxy. Even barships couldn't stand up to them for long.

Eric, still planetside, closed his eyes. "No sign of that level of mystic activity."

"Good. He sent underlings to do the job. We've got a shot. We need to free the bird before the planets agree to the demands. Buzz, can I borrow Tock?" We'd pulled him and Herschel from the Academy in hopes that their knowledge of the universe would help us find homes for the people. Since Tock knew Buzz and Randor the troll, he went with the crew of *The Bitter End*. Herschel was with my crew for the same reason.

The garba nodded. "You can have him. What do you have in

mind?"

I smiled. I haven't commanded a ship of tricksters without learning a few tricks of my own.

As a former general of the Empire, Tock was an invaluable resource and we needed him now.

"I'm going to take a team and try to board that ship without them knowing it. Then we're going to find the bird, free it, and then probably leave a significant mocking message for Gob after hopefully having done everything we could to cripple the ship."

No, I wasn't bitter about what happened on Throneworld. Not at all.

Buzz smiled. "Oh, is that all?"

"Probably not. I'll need to get my crew back onboard for a pow-wow, but I imagine we'll need distractions."

The four other head honchos with ships in-system knew what that meant. They would have to engage the moonship to distract it from noticing us sneaking inside.

"Sure. What are friends for?" Herc said.

The crew on board the goblin moonship numbered in the six figures. They also functioned as an invasion force. We had no real chance of overpowering them as a whole, so we had to outsmart them. I chose the crew for this mission carefully, deciding to go old school.

Again, nothing against my regular crew. They were fantastic, but fantastic wasn't going to cut it. We needed the people who helped originate the term trickster on this one.

My first choice would have been Hermes. The ancient god of thieves could move at speeds undreamed of by most spacefaring races and was able to get into places impossible for anyone else. Unfortunately, he was unavailable. Because he could move between worlds in the blink of several eyes, he was out searching for new homes for the natives in case we couldn't stop the sun from going nova. So far he had succeeded in finding a few. Our plan, even with his help, was far from a sure thing. For all we knew the goblins were bluffing and didn't really have the sunbird in their ship. Pulling Hermes from his search mission could doom millions, possibly billions.

That didn't mean we still didn't have good candidates, and I was picking most of the heavy hitters from the team that helped me on Ogra.

My second choice was a gremlin raised in Atlanta, Georgia. Bubba Sue had mechanical and engineering abilities that didn't just border on mystical, they invaded it and took over the place and gremlins had a type of natural cloaking that let them remain unseen.

Next we needed power. Someone who could take on a battalion of goblins and win. Hercules could do it, but the Monkey King could do it better. And his shape-shifting abilities put Loki to shame.

And I had Xen too, but decided he would be best used in space. After all, his body had been built using parts of a starship and he had the speed and firepower of one. And the Empire apparently had warnings about him in their standing orders.

Coyote and Loki were givens. Shift shifters and tricksters would make sure when the plan went sideways – I always assume it was when, not if – we'd have options and quick thinkers to complete the mission. And the simple truth of the matter is I didn't trust anybody else to have my back as much as the Norse trickster. And since we were bring *Fools' Glory*, Eric was coming along to drive. Riga and Savanah were staying planetside to help matters there.

And I also had a cowardly reason for the three tricksters. The Startender oath was very specific about killing. It was a last option and to save more lives only. I didn't think I'd be able to kill a hundred thousand goblins, even to save three billion innocents. My gut told me Eric and Bubba Sue would feel the same way.

I knew the tricksters could and would if it was our last option.

The last member of our team was Tock. One thing you learn when traveling the universe and the otherworlds is that stereotypes about races are usually stereotypes for a reason. You also learn very quickly that a good many people of each race don't fit the stereotypes.

Tock was one of the latter. And he was looking for some payback for what Big Nose did to his daughter, so he had a personal reason for stopping Gob from getting this manna.

The team discussed the best way to gain access to the ship. I jokingly suggested going in through the trash chutes, to the rolling of eyes of those who had been raised with Earth popular culture. Tock was quick to point out that the majority of waste aboard the ship was recycled and that trash chutes weren't even an option because they didn't exist. The moonship was heavily fortified and had been evaluated from the point of view of someone trying to do just what we were attempting. There were no easy access points.

Teleportation wasn't an option. Most forms of it were blocked by shielding and wards that were intermingled to stop both magical and science-based attacks. Almost all attempts to gain entry that way would end in painful disintegration. In fact, shields and wards were up constantly, so first we had to bypass them. And I meant plural. Layers and sections of them, so if one shield fell there was another behind it to pick up the slack. Seven layers had to go down before getting to the armor plating was even an option.

It seemed an impossible task, but luckily Startenders thought the impossible was just the universe's way to issue a challenge.

There was a possible way in. An incredibly dangerous and stupid way, but one that might work just the same. It was going to involve quite a bit of danger for the other barships and Xen.

Energy weapons were mostly useless against the barships. Vulcan had designed the gold hull to absorb and re-channel energy, much like the drones he had sent to absorb the star's energy. If the sun went supernova, the barships would likely survive if they were far enough away. The hulls would simply absorb the excess energy. That does not mean that we wouldn't be destroyed if we were at the heart of it, but we could ride it out in the outskirts of the system. We'd keep evacuating until just before the first wave hit.

The Empire had decent intelligence. Not on the level of Cynosure, but still impressive, so they might already know this about us and could opt instead for projectile weapons. *That* was our way in. The shields had to be lowered to fire a missile, but the design was rather brilliant. The arrangement between layers had been designed so that the spacing between each level of shielding was a bit more than half the length of the missile. The system was timed so that no more than two layers of shielding over the launch point were down at the same time. This ensured that an enemy shooting at their weapon ports wouldn't be able to penetrate their defenses. However someone in a golf ball-sized ship could theoretically gain access by moving through each layer as it was dropped before finally gaining access to the launching tube. Best case scenario would be nine launches to gain access past the shields and the tube's outer and inner airlock.

That left the task of being targets for at least nine missiles to the other barships and Xen. The goblins had multiple warheads that were mixed between mundane and mystical and nuclear. The right combination would damage our hulls and get through our shielding, which was nowhere near as elaborate as that of a moonship. The other barships would have their hands full trying not get hit.

Another big problem was that their sensors could pick up golf ball-sized objects and let them blast us, which might not necessarily destroy *Fools' Glory*, but if the damage was bad enough we'd have to jettison our ship's physical link with this planetary system by pulling back into our pocket dimension. We'd probably survive, but would have to re-emerge at another of our drop zones elsewhere in the universe. It would take a while to get back, during which time the goblins could take the system.

Best not to let them see us coming.

Hercules made the *Argo II* look as large as possible, shuttling mass from their pocket dimension. Each barship had access to about two percent of the mass of the moonship but tried to appear even more massive by forming a thin shell around a hollow inside. By weaving a web of thin strands inside the shell, the barship would appear solid instead of a metal big balloon when the moonship pinged them.

As expected, the goblin ship ignored the hail. The *Argo II* was too insignificant to speak to or worry about. Hercules launched an asteroid that had been "conveniently" floating nearby. When it hit their shielding, it shattered into thousands of fragments. One of those fragments was *Fools' Glory* in dust mode. *The Bitter End, Excalibur,* and the *Big Top* shifted mass from dust mode to maximum size, seemingly appearing out of nowhere in a V formation with the *Argo II.* That alone should have worried the moonship. It was possible to slide into a system, but not quietly. A ship appearing suddenly should have set off all number of alarms. Because they were only growing and not actually entering into the system, those alarms would be silent. That would get the ship commander's attention.

"By what matter of insanity do you attack a warship of our Lord Gob?" said the commander, breaking the communication silence. The Goblin Empire was unusual that it did not give names to its ships, only designations. Gob apparently felt that such designations would endear loyalty among the crew to the ship instead of him, so that referring to them as his Lord Gob's vessels said loyalty would instead be focused back onto him. It was kind of a waste not, want not, recycling of belief system. And as it wasn't a secured communication, we could listen in.

"My name is Hercules of the Startender barship *Argo II.* I understand that you have the system's sunbird aboard your ship. I am here to request that you release it so it may perform its star-regenerating task. Please and thank you," he said with a smile.

The goblin commander's communication showed him with a very perturbed look on his face. "Why would we do that? Our demands have not yet been met and you have no way of enforcing your request upon us. Attack this ship again and we will vaporize you."

Hercules grinned. "That's not very neighborly of you. What happens if they don't comply in time? I bet you wouldn't release the bird, would you? That's just not nice."

"This communication is over," said the goblin commander, cutting off his transmission.

Hercules sent another asteroid at the shielding and the moonship went into battle mode. We had positioned the four barships in a formation to make sure that this particular launcher would be the most logical one to use. We had Xen floating silently in space, a secret and hidden weapon with the firepower of a starship, ready to defend or attack as the battle demanded. Our sensors picked up the first missile coming out. As the outer shielding went down, we went in.

I hoped the other barships were doing okay. They must not have been doing too badly because three more missiles launched. We did better than expected and got through four additional layers. Three more launches got us into the missile tube. Unfortunately, the goblin ship stopped firing.

To the best of our knowledge, no one has ever been able to hack or otherwise listen in on the communication channels from our Startender badges. We could listen in to the others talking, but it was too great a risk communicating directly to ask why the moonship stopped shooting. They might be able to triangulate or otherwise locate where the signal was coming from.

"Do you think they got the others?" Eric said.

"Not a chance," Bubba Sue said with a confident tone, but her eyes looked as worried as I felt.

"What do we do?" Eric said.

"I could go into the tube and try to force it open," Sun said.

Tock shook his head. "No, that would set off alarms and they'd lock down this section of the ship. Troops and weapons will be brought to bear right where we don't want them to be. We'd be trapped and the resulting backlash of radiation and mystic power from their attack could kill us," Tock said. Sun WuKong grinned. "Okay, most of us."

Bubba Sue stood up and rubbed her hands together. "Tock, I've got a few more technical questions for you." The gremlin and the goblin had an exchange that was far above my head about metal alloys, densities, electronic and mystical systems.

"Murphy, I think I've got this," Bubba Sue said.

"Then get us in," I said.

"Eric, let me out," Bubba Sue said.

"Yes, grandmother," Eric said. Technically, Bubba Sue had no genetic link to the melog. She was also present at Eric's birth. Long after that complicated day, she married Vulcan, whom the melog all called father or grandfather. After the nuptials, the melog adopted Bubba Sue as their mother and grandmother.

She had her badge, so Bubba Sue didn't need any other life support to go into the tunnel. She disappeared from our sensors. The gremlin had never configured them to pick her up when she disappeared. As she says, you can't blame a girl for displaying some self-preservation. A moment later the tube cracked open a hair's width.

Bubba Sue came back into the ship. Although we have a minimal amount of mass we have to maintain, our shape is fluid. Eric started elongating the gold hull into an extremely fine wire that was able to fit through the crack. We snaked our way through slowly, but eventually we ended up inside the moonship. We stayed in dust mode until we were out of the weapons room.

Eric shunted enough mass to open a door large enough for the rest of us to exit. When we stepped outside the barship, the shape-shifters all looked like goblins. And Tock looked like a goblin because he was one. Bubba Sue was nowhere to be seen, and Eric stayed inside, piloting the ship. I was outside too, but we had used makeup and facial prostheses to make me appear goblin as well. The Infinite Jester had spent time in Vaudeville and was something of a makeup expert.

One thing that most races have in common is a sense of the normal. That is to say what happened yesterday should happen today and tomorrow and in pretty much the same way. It's what makes surprise such an advantage.

A moonship is one of the most fearsome and deadly vessels in space. It makes those onboard overconfident because there are probably less than half a dozen other known ships that could harm them in a fair fight. None of those ships were in the Delfina system. Therefore they had only been on a low-level alert, despite our attack. And since the huge battle cruiser was so well designed, no moonship had ever been boarded without being attacked and breached. Even that was rare enough to border on the non-existent except for a one-time freak accident.

The goblins on duty in the ship weren't expecting trouble.

Tock let us know about day-to-day protocols and idiosyncrasies the soldiers likely observed. We moved freely about the ship, acting like we belonged there. The few times someone stopped us, Tock let loose with his PO'ed commander routine and we got apologies instead of interrogations. Without Tock, we would have been searching blind. Fortunately the mental projection the goblins had let loose on the system had the bonus effect of letting him know exactly where onboard the sunbird was allegedly being kept. It was near the center of the ship, not far from the bridge. As we got closer, security became more serious. We weren't going to bluff our way by these guys solely with the attitude of a former general. We needed a plan. Fortunately we had one and a host of contingencies in case it didn't work.

Thanks to the commander's broadcast to Hercules, we had a pretty good visual of what he looked like. It was enough for Sun to copy his likeness and voice. Unfortunately, since it only showed him from the waist up, Sun guessed on things like height and gait pattern. He decided to err on the side of tall. When we got to the door the goblins on guard duty went to attention and saluted.

"Open the door. I wish to check on our *guest*," the disguised Sun WuKong said in Goblin Prime. Our plan seemed to be working. The guards were so intent on watching their imitation commander that they weren't paying attention to the rest of us, which was good. Coyote was a little sloppy and my makeup looked better than his shape change. His eyes and ears were off. Loki had the golf ball-size barship tucked in his armpit so the goblins wouldn't see it. I wasn't sure where Bubba Sue was, but it looked like we wouldn't need plan B. That would involve us taking out the guards, followed by her bypassing their systems to get us in.

Inside there were another ten guards in a circle around an energy-dampening cage which held the sunbird. They hadn't been bluffing after all.

"The lot of you wait outside," the disguised Sun said, to the quizzical looks of the goblin soldiers. Undoubtedly, he had given them orders to not leave their posts upon fear of death. Although it was not looked favorably upon, goblin commanders had the authority to kill, maim or otherwise hurt those under their command.

"Did I stutter?" The soldiers double-timed it out.

I assumed the gremlin was with us. "Bubba Sue, we need to get the bird out of there."

"I'm working on it," a disembodied voice said.

The bird was sitting on a silver platform from which the energy cage went up. I took my hidden Startender badge and placed it so that it touched the metal, allowing the lation stone inside to translate for me. "We are here to get you out so that you can save the sun. We won't hurt you."

It was a long shot. I know a lot of intelligent animals. Heck, two of them were helping me on this mission, but that didn't mean that all animals could communicate. I took a leap of faith that the sunbird was one and felt more comfortable with her knowing what was going on. She must have, because she nodded.

Outside we could hear the real commander yelling and screaming at the soldiers for leaving their posts.

"Crap. Loki, time for plan D," I said. As far as plans went, we literally had all of the letters in the alphabet covered, as well as several numbers. Plan D was for distraction. The trickster had also been a fire god back in the day and he transformed into a reasonable facsimile of the sunbird. Loki flew out the door past the soldiers and down the hall. They took off running after him.

"Loki bought us some time, but we don't know how much," I said, as the energy field went down.

"Nice work," said Sun, still in his goblin commander shape as he reached into the cage.

Bubba Sue screamed. "No!"

Sun looked at his hand and slowly pulled it away.

"They have four more death traps, which may or may not be able to hurt you, but might hurt the bird. Actually, they might hurt you too."

Coyote took up position by the door, with the golf ball-sized ship floating next to him, which fortunately had left Loki's armpit before he transformed.

"Murph, sensors are showing another group of soldiers heading here. Intercepted communications show that the commander ordered them to come back and secure this room. We probably have less than a minute," said Eric's voice through our ear nubs.

"Bubba Sue, I hate to rush you, but …" I said.

"No worries. I work best under pressure," she said as the cage made about four different mechanical sounds in rapid succession. "Okay, I got everything I can find. There's no guarantee that I got all of them though."

"Then I guess I'll have to take my chances," Sun said, reaching in for the sunbird. It climbed onto his wrist like it was a parrot or a trained falcon. The Monkey King slowly pulled the flaming bird out. Bubba Sue had missed something. A bladed wall slammed down like a guillotine. Sun reached up with his free hand to grab hold of it, inches before it hit the bird. As soon as the bird was out, he let go and it slammed down. I got worried when I noticed Sun's hand was bleeding. That blade was designed to hurt a god and apparently it worked.

The Monkey King licked the blood off, focused and the wound closed.

"Eric, extrude enough of the ship to get us a door," I said.

The door appeared and so did Bubba Sue. The gremlin stuck her arm out and the sunbird left the Monkey King's wrist for hers. They both went into the ship with Coyote and Tock behind them. Sun didn't move.

"Come on Sun, it's time for Plan G," I said. G was for getaway.

The Monkey King didn't budge. "You know you're not going to get out of the moonship without someone staying behind. And a bartender isn't going to cut it. It's time for Plan F instead."

I probably don't need to spell out what the F stood for.

"Sun, you know we don't leave anyone behind," I said.

"You got left behind," he said with a smirk.

"It was my call. And it was different," I said.

"Not really." Sun reverted to his simian form and he was smiling. "You won't be leaving me behind for long. You'll be coming back. As a matter of fact, I bet you I can make the goblin commander beg you to take me off his ship."

To gamble against the Monkey King was a sucker's bet. However, like many tricksters, he did some of his best work trying to win wagers.

"I'll take that bet. No unnecessary risks though." Sun WuKong is notoriously difficult to kill, but he has been beaten before. And tortured. And imprisoned.

The Monkey King smiled. "As long as you realize our definitions of what unnecessary means may differ greatly."

I chuckled and nodded, then followed the others through the golden door that hung in the air. Once I was inside *Fools' Glory*, Eric closed the door, retracting the extrusion so we were golf ball-sized again.

We could use a drop zone to get out and it would have seemed logical to leave one elsewhere in the system so we had a quick exit. Moonships have superb sensors and we might need that trick another time against Gob. And if we used one inside their ship and emerged elsewhere in-system, their sensors could pick up too much information about how we did it and Big Nose might figure out how to counter or duplicate it. Or find a way to attack us through the pocket dimension.

Sun grabbed hold of the ship's extrusion like it was a football and ran with us down the hall. In comedy and escapes, timing is everything and ours sucked. Loki – still disguised as the sunbird – crossed Sun's path as we ran down the corridor so the squad of goblin soldiers were chasing after all of us now.

Eric grew the ship large enough to make a sunbird-sized door for Loki, and my honcho flew onboard. Eric slammed the door behind him with the goblins firing at us. Sun sprinted for the missile launch room. Our cover was long blown, so the alarms Tock warned us about had been triggered. Foot-thick security doors cut us off from the missile room. Sun keeps his size-changing metal staff about the size of a toothpick and wears it behind an ear. He pulled it out and smashed it against the junction of the doors as the goblin soldiers fired energy and projectile weapons at him, including needles that were incredibly tiny and designed to slip between molecules. They penetrated even his thick hide. I could see his face on the bar mirror. The Monkey King was hurt, but Sun made like he was ignoring them. It took him a dozen swings, but he made a crack where the doors met. Not big enough that it went all the way through, but just enough for Eric to adjust our extrusion to flow into the crack. The melog turned the barship into a high-tech jack by expanding our mass until the doors opened.

We got into the launch room, but the goblin soldiers were right behind us. There was no time to change the plan no matter how bad I felt about leaving Sun behind. We molded *Fools' Glory* to attach to the front of the missile in the firing tube. Sun raised a hand over the fire button. The goblin commander raised his hand and his troops stopped shooting. Pretty good idea, at least if they didn't want to risk exploding one of their own missiles where it would kill them and put a hole in their hull.

"You're trapped. I have overridden the security codes so that no one can launch any missiles without my say so. You are not getting out," the goblin commander said.

The Monkey King smiled and hit a red button. Apparently humans aren't the only ones that like making colorful switches. The missile hadn't gotten the memo about not being able to launch, mainly due to Bubba Sue's rerouting of that particular system on our arrival. The goblins couldn't stop the launch without risking the missile detonating inside their shielding, so we rode on the tip of the missile out into space.

We disengaged. I ordered Eric to push the ship into overdrive so we could get as far away from the missile and the moonship as possible, just in case the rest of Bubba Sue's handiwork didn't take.

I should have had more faith. The moonship started to chase after us then acted like it hit a bump in the metaphysical road and stopped short. We flew *Fools' Glory* within 100,000 miles of the sun. I looked at the countdown that we had put on the clock on the wall. We still had some time, but there wasn't that much of it. Fixing something during the last ten seconds on the clock was dramatic, but didn't leave much room for error. We had no idea how fast the sunbird could travel or even if the legend was true. We would still have days to get some of the people out if this failed, but a lot of the inhabitants of the Delfina system were going to die.

We brought the sunbird to an airlock and opened it. The fiery bird took flight and went out into space, its magic somehow keeping its skin aflame even in the vacuum of the void. It turned back and bowed its head once to us, then flew toward the sun. According to our sensors it was traveling at incredible speeds, but it didn't seem to be getting any smaller. In fact, if our sensors were right, it was growing in size, soon dwarfing the goblin moonship. The sunbird's image appeared to all three worlds with a telepathic broadcast of its own that made it clear that Gob had nothing to do with its mission and in fact, tried to stop it, effectively cutting the goblin god off from harvesting any manna here.

The sunbird hit the sun's corona and plunged into the heart of the star. All energy fusion seemed to cease as the entire stellar fireball went dark.

Several long, dark moments ticked by, followed by a blinding burst of light.

"Eric, get us out of here, just in case," Bubba Sue said.

I nodded, not about to argue with one of the designers of our ship.

The three planets shared relatively similar orbital distances from their sun, but somehow their paths went at different enough angles that they never came close enough in their solar revolutions to affect each other. The physics was a bit beyond me.

We figured once we got near a planet that we'd gone far enough. We went to clear mode with filters so we seemed to be floating in space, and watched as a star was reborn. Fiery plumes shot out hundreds of thousands of miles in the shape of the sunbird, who was now big enough that even the people on the planets could see her. I collapsed on my stool behind the bar. Luckily it had a high seat back.

The mirror chimed as the other head honchos called us.

"Looks like you did it, Murphy. Nice work," Hercules said.

"Thanks. It was a team effort. We couldn't have done it without everyone else," I said. "Are you all alright?"

"We're fine. The goblins realized the missiles weren't working and switched to particle beam weapons," Herc said.

"Murph, the goblin moonship is hailing us," Eric said.

I had forgotten in my relief that Sun was still onboard. I remembered our bet and smiled. "Let them wait a minute." After letting them stew I nodded for Eric to put it on the mirror.

"Commander, a pleasure to see you again. I must say, you have a lovely ship. We had a marvelous visit. Now what can we do for you?" I said.

"Lowling, you invaded my ship, disabled it, then stole our property and you have the audacity to ask what I want?" the commander said.

"Actually, the way we see it is *you* kidnapped an intelligent life form and held her hostage, endangering billions of lives. We only did what needed to be done to save those lives," I said. "I suppose it is all a matter of perspective and frankly, I don't like yours. And my name is not lowling. You can call me Head Honcho Murphy. Or great one."

"Sacrilege! There is only one Great One!"

The portion of the mirror where the goblin had been a second ago disappeared. I looked at Eric. "Sorry to cut him off, Murph, but we seem to have incoming. You all need to get down to the air lock."

The lot of us did. As we looked through the invisible shield that separated us from the void, a tiny ball of flame in the shape of an egg hovered outside. As Eric opened the outer air lock it floated inside, then once he closed the outer field and opened the inside one, I held out my hand and the flaming ball landed there, reverting to what looked like a plain old egg.

"Oh, boy. Not again." I had once been the guardian of an egg Manuk Manuk, the blue cosmic chicken, laid. One of her eggs hatched our universe and set off the big bang. The one I was in charge of did the same for a whole other universe, even if it ended with me sort of dying. I was lucky enough to get better.

I was understandably wary of accepting eggs from cosmic birds, but better us than the goblins. We'd figure out what to do with this one, too, and keep it safe. "Anyone have any idea what the gestation cycle of a sunbird is?"

"No idea, but we know it's less than three hundred years," Loki said.

"I guess we're going to be guardians of this thing," Tock said.

"We'll have to take special care to make sure Big Nose doesn't get it," Coyote said. "He'll be around in three hundred years and he'll remember this. He'll send a fleet of moonships next time."

I sighed. "With any luck the Startenders will be around to stop him again too."

"Boss, the goblin commander has been hailing us frantically," Eric said.

We had a mirror in most parts of the ship. I gave the egg to Loki to hide behind his back and pointed to the one of the wall in the airlock. "Put him on," I said. "Oh commander, are you still there? I believe you were going to tell me what you want."

"Your crewman is raising havoc on my ship."

"You can't expect him to be lowering havoc. It just isn't done," I said to an incredulous look from the goblin. "Besides you can't expect havoc to raise itself. I bet Sun would make a great father figure."

The commander ignored me and continued as if I hadn't spoken. "After you left, he chewed the hairs on his arms and spit them out, creating exact duplicates of himself." One of Sun's many powers. "These creatures proceeded to run around my ship, causing destruction. I demand that you get him, all of him, off of my ship immediately."

I smiled, crossed my arms and leaned back against the wall. "Let me see. Your propulsion and weapon systems are offline and you have one of the most powerful warriors in this galaxy or any other running amuck on your ship. You have no apparent way of stopping him. You don't even have a way to defend yourself if we decide to hold a grudge and wanted to send some more asteroids your way. I wonder how long your shields can hold out." The goblin commander become much paler after I pointed this out. "Yet, you are calling me with demands. And doing so in a rude manner and not addressing me nicely at all. I don't like your tone. Call back when you can be a little more polite." I motioned and Eric cut him off.

"Boss, he's hailing us again."

"Leave him on hold for a while," I said as we went back to the main bar room. After about a half an hour, I motioned for Eric to put him back on the mirror.

If looks could kill, the goblin commander would have slaughtered all of us. I could see even though the transmission that he was gritting his teeth. "Head Honcho Murphy, I humbly request that you retrieve your errant crew member from my ship." The goblin commander's face tightened up in a look that seemed almost akin to pain. I could see one of Sun's selves behind him, randomly ripping out bits of circuitry from the bridge. There were no less than seven goblins grabbing onto various parts of him and firing their weapons point-blank. It wasn't even slowing the Monkey King down. However, I could tell part of that was an act. Sun Wu Kong was almost invulnerable, but that doesn't mean he doesn't feel pain, and there were enough needles sticking out of him that he looked like the lovechild of a monkey and a porcupine. Those needle guns normally sliced body parts off. Sun was just putting on a good show for the goblins. "Please."

I smiled. "I might see my way clear to do that, once our requests are met."

"Requests?" the goblin commander said.

I nodded my head. "More demands really, but I'm trying to put a happy face on it. First off, we're going to insist on a non-aggression pact for this system. I know as a commander you have the power to enter into a tentative treaty of that nature."

"But for me to do that would ensure that I lose my command," the commander said. "And likely my life."

I shrugged. "Perhaps you should have thought of that before you endangered twenty-one billion lives. However, we could just wait this out. I'm sure within the day you will have a command, but you may not have a ship to return to the Empire. Which do you think your high command will look less favorably on? And we can see our way clear to put in a clause stating that all lives on board the moonship must be spared."

That confused and gave the commander relief at the same time. As Gob's military was an extension of him, he had to honor the treaties they made or lose power.

"Fine, I can see my way clear to make a five cycle non-aggression pact," he said.

I looked at Tock who corrected him. "Actually, he can do fifteen."

"Then fifteen it is, correct, commander?" I said.

I could hear the growling grumbles even through our communication system. "Fine."

"Excellent. Now for the matter of the little show you and your crew are going to put on for the Startenders."

"Show?" the commander said, sounding confused.

"The Startenders enjoy entertainment. We were thinking some comedy, maybe a little drama, followed by lots of singing and dancing," I said.

The universe has several of its own versions of YouTube. We'll record it and keep them as added leverage when we had to renegotiate the non-aggression treaty.

"Goblins do not sing and dance. I refuse to …"

"All righty, then. I guess these talks are over. Please give Sun my best and tell him to have a good time," I said. "Oh, and don't drop the soap in the asteroid shower."

At that point, Sun ripped an entire wall of instruments out of the bridge. He later told me at that same point that two of his other selves were attacking the engineering defense systems. All seven of the moonship's shields went down and the commander's crew informed him of that.

I put my finger over my mouth in a shush motion and Eric muted communications. I turned away from the screen and hit my badge. "Xen, would you mind terribly coming out of stealth mode and letting the moonship know you're here?"

"Done," Xen said.

Suddenly the goblin bridge became frantic and I nodded at

Eric to put the sound back on.

"Commander, the Nimian AI just appeared on sensors. In firing range."

"The Destroyer is here? Battle stations," the commander said.

"Sir, our shields are still down."

"Oh, have you noticed our fellow Startender Xen?" I said. Xen had a terrifying reputation, having been mistakenly blamed for the destruction of his home world and justly credited for the destruction of a starship which he stripped to upgrade his robot body. When I asked him to help rescue Tock, he had mentioned the Empire had special measures in place to watch out for him after past run-ins.

The commander turned frantically towards me. "Okay, we'll sing and dance and do whatever you want. Just no asteroids or other attacks from your ships or the Nimian AI." I motioned to Eric to cut him off.

"Okay people, we start hardcore negotiations in five minutes. I want everyone to come up with at least one ridiculous item we can ask for. Not to mention at least one useful one."

The Startenders didn't believe in killing. However, we had nothing against tormenting those that would become mass murderers, and there was nothing saying we couldn't enjoy ourselves along the way. And we owed Gob.

Yes, we were poking a tiger with a stick. But we had a lot of sticks. Another confrontation was inevitable. I was scared, but when the time came, I knew the Startenders would be ready.

Poor Gob. I wonder who he was going to pray to when he realized what he was going to be facing off against.

PATRICK THOMAS is the author of more than 30 books and 150+ short stories. Among his works is the fantasy humor Murphy's Lore series , which includes Tales From Bulfinche's Pub, Fools' Day, Through The Drinking Glass, Shadow Of The Wolf, Redemption Road, Bartender Of The Gods, Nightcaps and Empty Graves — as well as the After Hours spin offs Startenders, Constellation Prize, Fairy With A Gun, Fairy Rides The Lightning, Dead To Rites, Rites of Passage, and Lore & Dysorder. His Mystic Investigators paranormal mystery series includes Bullets & Brimstone, From The Shadows and Once More Upon A Time. Assassin's Ball is his first mystery, co-written with John French. He co-edited New Blood and Hear Them Roar and was an editor for the magazines Fantastic Stories of the Imagination and Pirate Writings. Patrick's humorous advice column Dear Cthulhu includes the collections Have A Dark Day, Good Advice For Bad People, and Cthulhu Knows Best. His short stories have been featured in over fifty anthologies and more than three dozen print magazines. A number of his books are part of the props department of the CSI television show and have been spotted on the program. His urban fantasy Fairy With A Gun was optioned for film and TV by Laurence Fishburne's Cinema Gypsy Productions. Please drop by www.patthomas.net to learn more or find out about The Patrick Thomas Show mockumentary.

Even the things that go *Bump* in the night will learn that you <u>DON'T</u> mess with...

Terrorbelle.

"Thomas certainly brings the goods to the table when it comes to writing urban fiction...I promise, you will love... Terrorbelle: Fairy With a Gun. Who doesn't love a well-stacked, ass-kicking, gun-toting, woman with bullet-proof, razor-sharp wings that investigates all manner of supernatural spookiness? I know I do, and Thomas's humor shows through in every tale. Jim Butcher and Laurell K Hamilton have nothing on Thomas." The Raven's Barrow

From The Murphy's Lore Universe Of

PATRICK THOMAS

www. padwolf.com & www. terrorbelle.com

EDWARD J. McFADDEN III

OUR DYING LAND There is a dead zone in Arizona the size of Rhode Island, and no one can figure out what caused it.

ANYWHERE BUT HERE What would you do if your son and his dog disappeared into a rip in space- time? You would follow.

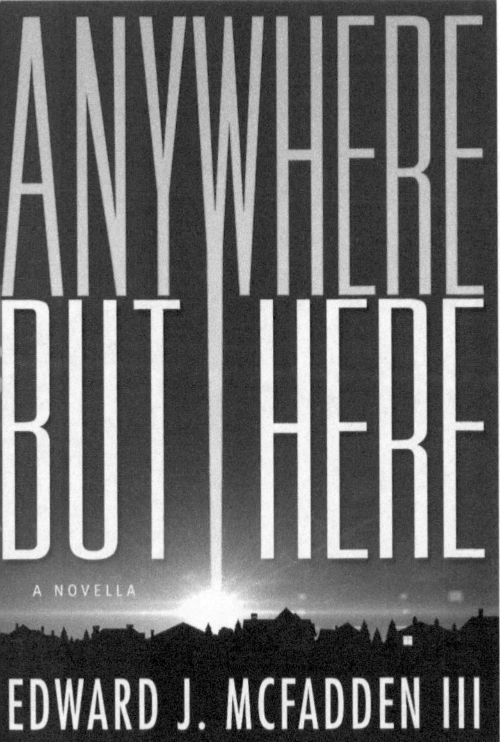

DECONSTRUCTING TOLKIEN In this collection of essays, stories, discourses, and tributes, Ed McFadden has gathered together a wide range of topics, perspectives, and outlooks on some of the most intriguing factors concerning THE LORD OF THE RINGS

More GREAT Science Fiction!

THE STARSCAPE PROJECT

As his quest begins, an artificial intelligence life form enters the galaxy and launches a series of covert attacks against the Empire. The Teconeans assume that the Federation is responsible, and galactic peace is about to unravel. As Stryker chases his nemesis into Teconean space, he finds himself thrown into the middle of the battle. Knowing that Earth will be the aliens' next target, Stryker must decide whether to let them destroy the Empire, or to join forces with his Teconean enemies against the invaders. The key to the mysterious aliens lies buried on the moon of Kennedy Prime, and it's up to Stryker to solve the puzzle before war begins. The fate of the galaxy is at stake.

ZONE OF THE TENTH DGREE

In 1912, an alien ship crash lands in the Atlantic ocean, setting up a secret colony that remains undetected for centuries, allowing them to manipulate some of the most important events in human history -- from the sinking of the Titanic to the Bermuda triangle to global warming. Now, the technology of the 26th century has discovered the aliens' distress beacon, and it's a race against time as the Navy tries to stop a terrorist armed with a nuclear weapon from destroying the colony and triggering an all-out war as the mother-ship approaches

Now available from

PADWOLF

PUBLISHING

v i s i t   p a d w o l f . c o m

"You're lucky I even allowed you to do business with me. Why, most of our everyday technology must seem like magic to you."

"No, I've seen magic. It's much more impressive." Although this world had technology much more advanced than Earth, the existence of magic was not widely accepted here. Ogra's tech was very imposing and included orbit based battle platforms that could hold off an armada. A full frontal assault on our part would have been foolhardy.

Vapella continued as if I hadn't spoken. "Let me assure you that my experts, from the greatest civilization in the galaxy, I might add, found your libations wanting."

"So you went off-world then?" I said and got a glare for my trouble. Neither my trouble nor I wanted it and I did my best not to return it.

"No, I did not."

"And who would these experts be?" I asked.

"Why me, of course." Her smile was the best money on her world could buy, complete with shiny green teeth, but the condescension in it was all natural talent. "Your baleful beverage is barely better than urine."

"So you are an expert on the taste of urine? Interesting. How many glasses a day do you have to drink to get that good? Where do you get the best urine? Do you find much work or do you have to hang around public rest rooms to practice? If it would help you perfect your craft, we'd be happy to trade some for what we need."

"I was being invective."

"You look it, but we've had our shots."

Puns never translated well and I got a blank stare. I knew I was nervous and angry from the amount of wisecracking I was doing.

"Three billion lives on Gallop hang in the balance. We agreed to trade the whiskey for the solance." Hermes was tending to the people as best he could. Assuming we got the solance, it would still take him the better part of a day to mix up the cure. For anyone else it would take a lot longer. Distributing it will take an estimated day and a half and that's figuring in everyone we have available helping. That meant we didn't have much time left to fix the issue with Lord Idiot here then get the solance to Gallop. "We approached you in good faith in order to save those people. As I understand matters, you took delivery after sampling the whiskey. Quite a lot of it."

"Exactly. By the time I took delivery, I was drunk, and simply was not of sound mind. Under Ograte trade rules that invalidates the contract. And worse, I felt quite bad the next day."

I put my hand on my forehead and tried not to yell. "You decide to get drunk, get a hangover because of that choice, and then use it as an excuse not to pay your bill. And cause billions of deaths."

"I would not have put it so crudely. It's not that I don't feel for them. Perhaps the Gallopans have something else they'd like to trade. Maybe accepting my sovereignty. I've been looking to expand my holdings and an entire world would be nice."

THE MURPHY'S LORE™ SERIES
TALES FROM BULFINCHE'S PUB
FOOLS' DAY: *A Tale From Bulfinche's Pub*
THROUGH THE DRINKING GLASS: *Tales From Bulfinche's Pub*
SHADOW OF THE WOLF: *A Tale From Bulfinche's Pub*
REDEMPTION ROAD
BARTENDER OF THE GODS: *Tales From Bulfinche's Pub*

THE MURPHY'S LORE AFTER HOURS™ UNIVERSE
NIGHTCAPS - *AFTER HOURS Vol. 1*
EMPTY GRAVES - *AFTER HOURS Vol. 2*
FAIRY WITH A GUN: *The Collected Terrorbelle™*
FAIRY RIDES THE LIGHTNING: *a Terrorbelle™ novel*
DEAD TO RITES: *The DMA Casefiles of Agent Karver™*
LORE & DYSORDER: *The Hell's Detective™ Mysteries*

MURPHY'S LORE STARTENDERS™
STARTENDERS
CONSTELLATION PRIZE

MURPHY'S LORE AFTER HOURS Books by Patrick Thomas & John L. French
RITES OF PASSAGE: *A DMA Casefile of Agent Karver and Detective Bianca Jones*
BULLETS & BRIMSTONE a Mystic Investigators™ book
featuring Hell's Detective & Bianca Jones
FROM THE SHADOWS a Mystic Investigators™ book
featuring The Nightmare, Nemesis & The Pink Reaper™

Other Mystic Investigators™ books
MYSTIC INVESTIGATORS
ONCE MORE UPON A TIME *by Patrick Thomas & Diane Raetz*

OTHER BOOKS
NEW BLOOD edited by Diane Raetz & Patrick Thomas

DEAR CTHULHU™ Series
HAVE A DARK DAY
GOOD ADVICE FOR BAD PEOPLE
CTHULHU KNOWS BEST

THE JACK GARDNER MYSTERIES
THE ASSASSAINS' BALL